The Devil & Lillian Holmes

Ciar Cullen

"I AM NOT A GOOD VAMPIRE."

She had not been a good mortal, either. Half-broken by a terrible secret, Lillian Holmes retreated into a fantasy world where the great detective Sherlock was her uncle and she could solve any mystery. Except, she had not yet found her parents. She had not yet rescued her stolen daughter. She was addicted to morphine, was still broken. And now she was bound to blood and to the caresses of the beautiful monster who sought to change for her, who had literally changed her to save her life.

But for how long had George saved her? Lillian could feel safety and sanity slipping away. Devils prowled Baltimore. Some were allies, others lustful gluttons waiting to consume every last drop of goodness. Some came from far-off lands, mercurial, unknowable, unstoppable. Others lurked closer still—in the hearts of herself and her beloved.

The Devil & Lillian Holmes

Ciar Cullen

www.BOROUGHSPUBLISHINGGROUP.com

PUBLISHER'S NOTE: This is a work of fiction. Names, characters, places and incidents either are the product of the author's imagination or are used fictitiously. Any resemblance to actual events, locales, business establishments or persons, living or dead, is coincidental. Boroughs Publishing Group does not have any control over and does not assume responsibility for author or third-party websites, blogs or critiques or their content.

THE DEVIL & LILLIAN HOLMES
Copyright © 2015 Ciar Cullen

ISBN 978-1-942886-43-3

This book is dedicated to Kathryn Hall, who helped me find my voice. And for a man I never met, who read to my editor when he was a boy. Thank you both.

6

ACKNOWLEDGMENTS

Thank you, Bruce, for always encouraging me to do whatever makes me happy. And special thanks to Chris Keeslar, for helping me push a little farther each time. You're a wonder.

CONTENTS

8

The Devil & Lillian Holmes

PROLOGUE

For the first time in months, Atil stirred.

Ursula felt the pull of her maker the moment he awoke. She stared out from her window at the shroud of dark pines, trying to pick out his form. She made the sign of the cross out of habit as she scurried down the great staircase, even though her God had abandoned her long, long ago. The irony struck her anew that the devoted worshipped her as a saint, believing she had chosen to be burned alive at Atil's hand rather than sacrificing her virginity to him. Too fearful of the unknown, her faith had failed her and she succumbed to the ruler's will. To add to her litany of sins, she'd asked Atil to protect her devout reputation. What maiden had perished in her place? *So long ago,* she thought. The guilt barely haunted her now.

Atil called her Saint Ursula whenever he was cross, which was often. He didn't like to be disturbed from his long hibernations in the forest. So what new trouble made the Elders, his sons, call him from slumber?

Ah. There. A tall silhouette barely visible against the setting sun: her twelfth child, not favored by Atil. No doubt Atil would send Vasil on another dreary journey to settle some political upheaval. Ursula thought that Vasil had kept some minute piece of humanity that only a mother might recognize. His solutions sometimes smacked of compassion, but he claimed that the Houses he ruled— young, unstable ones—required a gentler hand.

Like beetles scurrying toward a corpse they came, one by one, from the forest and the valley to the west, up over the frosty grass, toward the main gate. And finally, her maker emerged, too. She could not see the face she had once thought irresistible, but she knew the disgust and determination that would mar it.

Ursula rushed to ready the hall, where slaves already dragged heavy chairs across the floor and wiped at the table. To a man, fear made them shake and look away from her. One of them would die tonight, providing sustenance to the Elders, her children. She would plead for mercy, Atil would scowl and laugh, and she would look away.

She prayed again to the God who hated her. Please let me die. But He would not allow her to perish. Evidently she was not worthy even of Hell.

Atil burst through the door and she lowered her head.

"Ursula, you look well," he said.

"I am, my lord. What need merits this gathering? The talk of war in Germany?"

"Are you not pleased to see me and our offspring?" He pulled off his fur cape and let it drop to the floor.

Ursula didn't answer; she didn't have to. Atil had already forgotten her and turned toward the door where their boy children entered and talked in low grumbles.

I hate them all.

"Come, boys, gather around. Hurry, Vasil, this issue involves your insipid domain."

So, Ursula realized, a trivial uprising among the Houses in the Americas. Young vampires in a young land, always mucking things up.

CHAPTER ONE

A fine meal.

Baltimore, 1899

Lillian tried to run but her legs wouldn't move. She screamed, but no sound emanated from her mouth. She tried again, tears bleeding down her cheeks, turning her gown scarlet. Her hands and legs were bound to the bed, the smell of ether strong around her. Had she been drugged? Was she back in the asylum?

My baby, give me my baby!

No, not the asylum. She was in London. Had she been kidnapped?

You are dreaming. You are dreaming. Still, she couldn't make herself awaken.

A dark silhouette leaned forward, and she recognized his tall lean form. Why would Uncle Sherlock want to kill her? Ah, because she was soiled, sullied, *damned.* He hovered over her, intensity and loathing turning his sensuous mouth into a grim line, making his dark eyes blaze. The wooden stake in his hand glowed, and she turned her head away to avoid watching him plunge it into her chest.

"Anathema. Pure evil. Return from whence you came!" He lifted the stake, ready to act—

Lillian sat up, heart racing. As in her dream, scarlet tears stained her clothes.

Why did she have this dream night after night? She'd curl up next to George, struggling to keep awake, fearful that she'd find herself once again tied up and about to be vanquished by her hero, the inimitable Sherlock Holmes. The horror stayed with her through a good part of each day, frazzling her nerves and exhausting her. Wasn't it bad enough that George's enemy stalked their peace? Madame Lucifer—Marie de Bourbon was her true name—hadn't shown herself yet, but rumors were she'd put a price on George's head.

Quietly, so George wouldn't wake, Lillian crept to her dresser. She had to see for herself.

No. She sighed. There she was, disheveled but whole. Her image had not started to fade like the images of the legendary Elders who no longer had reflection or shadow. When George had talked about the Elders, about their history, that one detail had terrified her the most somehow. Despite George's promise that she would need to live a thousand years before she lost that human essence, the fear still clutched at her in weak moments.

It surprised her each time, this somewhat pleasant-looking stranger staring back at her. But her hands itched, her veins thrummed, and the cravings for a pill or liquid potion—her old "medicine"— gnawed at her. Or perhaps it was the craving for blood; at times the two addictions felt the same. At this moment, either would do.

Don't look. Don't look. But she poked into the small drawers and cubbies of her desk, unable to stop herself but also unable to find anything. One night, when George was gone, she'd crawled on all fours about the room, praying a pill might have rolled into a crack in the floorboards. But, no, they had left nothing behind. No pills, no potions. No relief.

With a deep breath she ran her hand across the satchel that held her most precious possessions: her Journal of Important Observations, the pistol she'd bought for herself on her twenty-first birthday, and a letter from her hero's creator, Mr. Arthur Conan

Doyle. At sight of the last, she gave herself a little shake. Uncle Sherlock would not stop until he had solved a case. Why had she?

Do not hate me, Uncle. In her fantasies, the ones born of reading, the ones that had sheltered her for so many years, her fictitious Uncle Sherlock was real, he loved her, he was proud of her attempts to follow in his footsteps. And wasn't she now the same woman she'd been, at least somewhere deep inside, someplace holy and untouchable by the blood of her prey and her hunger?

Perhaps not. Perhaps she did not deserve to find the daughter torn away from her arms by the girl's rapist father. How could she be a mother now? And perhaps she did not deserve to find her own. Wouldn't the woman have come looking for her years ago? What would she think upon beholding Lillian? She would turn away in horror, surely.

George. He was Lillian's only lifeline. But George had walked the earth for eons. Eventually he might find her lacking and leave, as it seemed everyone did. In only months they had lost their easy way of sparring with words, and their passion and hunger for each other had taken on a dark intensity.

I have taken on a dark intensity, she reminded herself. *George was always so.*

She regretted having told him of her recurring nightmares. He'd said, "You dream of him because you gave him up. He will not go so easily. What of your waking dream of following in his footsteps? What has happened to your investigations?"

She'd also heard what George hadn't said. *"What has happened to you?"*

George didn't say it because he knew the answer. To save her life, he'd turned her into a vampire. He'd warned her about the harsh reality she would face, but she hadn't much cared. At the time it was better than dying at the hands of her rapist. She couldn't blame George; she had made the choice herself. He was the same. But she was no longer the woman he'd fallen in love with. That headstrong, independent, human Lillian had died on her living room floor, and this Lillian, reborn in George's healing blood, was utterly lost.

In quiet times with only the ticking of the clock as company, or on solitary walks under the cover of darkness, she wondered what *had* happened to her investigations, to the burning desire to find her child and her mother. They had been replaced by the burning need to drink, to kill and feed. Although she and George took great pains to harm only criminals, those abusing others, she wondered if it was a charade. She worried that she would kill anyone should her hunger become fierce enough. At times, when she felt weak, lest she not be able to control herself, she sent away her few friends and her maid's little brothers whom she called her Musketeers. It was best that her truest friend Bess had already abandoned her. Lillian could not forgive herself for killing such a good woman.

I miss you so, my Watson.

Lillian watched George sleep for a moment and longed to turn back the clock to a time when he was the arrogant, puzzling, mesmerizing stranger who saved her more than once. She loved him more than ever, but he, too, seemed to be slipping through her fingers. Perhaps she could blame the looming threat of Marie de Bourbon. Baltimore, once a home for benign adventures and good friends, now felt like a prison. Lillian was caged with a lioness she could not see.

Marie would find them—sooner rather than later, Lillian was sure. George would want to flee before she did. At one time Lillian would have followed him anywhere. Now, her rapist and his accomplice dead at George's hand and her brain clear of opiates, she intended to locate her missing child and mother. No matter that she had given the investigation up until now. She had needed time to recover.

Or…would she bow to George's will? He deserved loyalty from her, did he not? Loyalty and devotion. He was her maker.

You go back and forth, Lil. Where will you end? You make no sense anymore. And was it their vampiric bond or her love for George that made her desperate to please him? What did it all mean, and how long would any of it last?

"Am I losing you, Lil?" he'd asked more than once.

"Don't be a silly-heart."

"You're so far away." Even a month earlier, the sadness in his eyes and desperation in his voice had tortured her. "Is it this life, catching up with you? Our ways? Please give it a bit more time."

"I am left wondering who I am."

"Who you are?"

"Yes. Everything I was, all I knew seems like a dream to me now. My child, my mother, my friends… Even my wonderful Uncle Sherlock. They are not real."

"I am real. You are real. Hold on to that, Lil."

Everything was out of her control.

Attend to your hunger first, Lillian, and then perhaps you will be able to focus.

George was still asleep. Silently Lillian picked up her boots and slipped a cloak around her shoulders. Blood or opium: either would be welcome, but only one would nourish. She shoved a few bills into her pocket, knowing that downtown a few ounces of stronger medicine than she'd ever tried could be had for a pittance.

Medicine.

No, you stopped calling it that.

She tiptoed to the end of the hallway and pushed open the window that gave access to a narrow ledge around the second floor of her home. The late fall air was cold, with a promise of coming rain in the swirl of leaves on the ground and the swaying tree limbs. While she wanted badly to ride her motorbike, to feel the uneven cobbles and dirt ruts make her sway precariously, George would hear its engine and might follow. So she held out her arms and stepped off the ledge, letting gravity tug at her for a moment before taking flight.

Flight! The dip and sudden lift lit her nerves, and she felt alive again, felt the power flowing through her veins that would help her vanquish all except for a terrifying few. Even George could not cover the distances she could without resting on a rooftop.

Immortal. She was immortal. How far could she go before she tired? She didn't know; George had always been with her, teaching her, warning her of dangers that seemed exaggerated. Mortals had little chance to harm her. A few Catholic priests and voodoo priestesses might understand that the descriptions of undeath by Bram Stoker were close—too close—to reality, but the good citizens of her town did not routinely arm themselves with ash-wood stakes or silver bullets and daggers. Still, her kind had to be circumspect, she admitted as a young couple looked up to see what streaked across the sky.

A schooner was docked near the cannery along Light Street. Resisting the urge to land on the deck and take for supper one of the burly men huddled in the cold, drinking and playing dice, she instead chose a nearby alley.

Where were the brutes tonight? The harbor hadn't yet failed her: a man pulling an unwilling woman around a corner; a young sailor who lay dying, robbed of his meager possessions and begging to God for a less painful end; a homeless vagabond, coughing up blood… Never depleted of the dead, dying, or damned, the harbor gave up meals willingly. She and George would kick the bodies into the water, and they would emerge miles away but anonymous, unrecognizable, the Chesapeake tidewaters lapping at them.

Lillian hid in a doorway, a few rats and a stray cat her only company, a far cry from her warm, richly decorated home. Her triumphant solo journey now felt foolish. Strains of music and laughter carried across the water, no doubt from the nearby brothel.

"What have we here?"

Lillian jumped and turned to a lanky man of middle years, weathered by the sun and no doubt a sailor given his clothes and knapsack. A ragged hound sat by his heels.

"Move along, sir."

"Wouldn't you like some company?"

"I will say it once more only. Move along. You will not like the consequences of attempting further acquaintance with me."

"My, my, aren't you a most excellent Miss High and Mighty! So you're waiting for a duke or prince, your majesty?"

"I told you to leave. Go shake your elbow with your fellow gamblers, or visit the brothel around the corner."

The man took a few steps toward her and looked her up and down. The man's mutt backed away, tail curled down, and growled.

"There, Abernathy, what's wrong?" The man glanced at Lillian. "You're scaring Abernathy with that silvery tongue. I'm no bad egg, lady. Not a bludger, not a lush, don't hit children nor women. So, name your price."

"I don't know what a bludger is, sir, but I presume you are telling me it is a bad trait?"

"You're a right corker, aren't you? A bludger. A man with a bludgeon."

Lillian groaned. The fellow was almost likeable, aside from being a rude oaf. Hunger tore through every bit of her at the vein that popped out now and again on his neck when he tilted his head. Who would miss him? Who would care? A wife, a daughter? Abernathy now whimpered for his master to quit the alley.

"You shouldn't be out alone like this, miss…"

She could fly away and leave the man doubting his sanity. She could take two steps and rip through his sun-weathered neck, drink enough to last for days. She suspected that alone and hungry George might take this man's life. But then, no. George had changed. She had seen to that, hadn't she?

"You are the spit and image of a girl I knew…"

Lillian didn't hear more. The pounding in her ears made her dizzy, and she clutched at the doorway. *Make your move. Lay your hand on me, so I may feel better about what I'm about to do.*

He took a last look at her and waved his hand dismissively. "No offense meant, miss, but I think Abernathy and I will take your advice and go shake an elbow. Wish me luck!"

She reached out to make her move but caught the terror in the dog's eyes as he dared cast a backward glance at her. "You have already found good luck, sir," she called.

Lillian heard him mumble "Loony" as he left, whistling for his dog to follow. "Gave you the willies, didn't she…?"

She sat on the slimy threshold and cried into her hands. What would this life be if she couldn't bear to frighten a scrawny hound, much less his innocent master? Worse, if that was even possible. But she also thought of the daughter she'd never met, how at the very least she could one day tell the girl that she had never harmed an innocent man or woman. *Your mother is no monster, my love.*

At least, not yet. Not fully.

She wiped at her tears with her cloak, wondering what the others would think if they saw her in this state: George, his brother Phillip, her own butler and governess, her friend Bess, her maid Aileen. Her Musketeers. They would not believe their eyes.

Lillian stood tall, pulled her cloak around her, took a deep breath and reached up to a windowsill where a rat scampered in the dark. She clutched it quickly, wrung its neck, and carried it with her off into the night.

CHAPTER TWO

Our heroine is attacked from all sides.

Dear Miss Holmes,

Thank you for your most recent letter. How wonderful that you have begun to follow in Mr. Holmes's footsteps! I sincerely hope that you are able to locate the relatives about whom you spoke, and I am greatly calmed that you now have a beau to assist you. Certainly you will be safer in his care, if he indeed approves of your avocation.

I fear you will not welcome the news that I am no longer writing Sherlock Holmes stories. This fact has brought some small outcry from readers in England, but certainly they will forget about him in time. My efforts are fully turned towards my studies of spiritism, a subject that engrosses me in a somewhat obsessive fashion. As a person of great intellectual passions, if I may presume to know you well enough to say it, you might understand.

You asked me about vampires in your letter. Indeed, a rather surprising question from a young lady, but you intrigued me greatly. Might you expand upon the reason for your interest? I cannot comment on a belief one way or the other about vampire souls, however fascinating the question, but, yes, I am well acquainted with Mr. Stoker; he is a friend. His interests of late involve Mesmerism, and he now loathes discussing the subject of "vampire folktales," as he calls them. He chides me regularly on my interests. In London there has been much talk of late about a supernatural connection to a recent spate of unusual murders. Most laugh at such notions, but I am not among them.

I understand your interest in me arose from my novels, and I will not presume that you desire to continue a correspondence. I am, however, quite curious about your talk of vampires. Might you humor me with a reply?

I wish you all the best in your future adventures, and of course on your forthcoming nuptials!

Cordially,

A.C. Doyle

Postscript—I will be in Baltimore within the month to speak to their chapter of the Learned Order of Psychic Scholars and will scour the newspaper for an announcement of your wedding and latest detective pursuits!

"Wedding'?" Lil murmured, folding the letter and tucking it into her desk drawer. *Wedding?*

"What's that?" George wrinkled his brow, struggling with a jeweler's tool to fix a tiny handmade spyglass she had found in her former butler's workroom. He turned to her and complained, "I can't do this, dear! You must send it to Thomas. It is his. I am a complete failure at normal male occupations. And I'm starving. I think the postman will have to do today."

"You are not so bad at *some* male occupations," she replied, thinking of the night before. He snickered, and she winked. "And please do not eat the postman. He's the most punctual I've had in ages." But Lillian's joke felt flat to her own ears and George always saw through her weak attempts to appear strong and nonchalant. She asked in truth, "You were teasing, were you not? Our bargain remains: Innocents are verboten?"

George looked away, annoyed or worse. "You have lost faith?"

"George, look at me. Have you killed anyone innocent since we made our bargain?"

"I have hunted only with you." He turned accusing eyes on her. "You, however, cannot say the same. Was that not also part of the pact?"

"I…" What to say? He was right. And he had warned her that she was unready to hunt alone, that her education had just begun. He hadn't gone as far as forbidding her to hunt without him, but that quick push at his hair told her he was angry. She thought of the chatty stranger at the dock, wondering how he had spent his night. She was glad she had not killed him.

"One mistake, Lil, one step in the wrong direction, will bring forces down on us that you cannot imagine."

"What forces? Marie, you mean? Lady Lucifer?"

"She is rogue, insane, a cannibal. The forbidden drinking of vampire blood has made her supremely strong, but there are those stronger still. I told you of them."

The Elders. She had almost thought them a legend. Hoped it, perhaps. "Yes, you told me of them. So, they are real? They are the ones that rule the Houses? You said we had no House in Baltimore."

George snorted. "The Houses are ruled by families who like to believe they have a stranglehold on a city, puffed up peacocks with an interest in wealth and position who have carried the worst of mortality into their new lives. No, the Elders are ancient. They are the ancestors of us all. And I have told you their rules. Marie breaks them regularly, and it seems you are flirting with breaking them, too. Where did you go without me?"

"I ate a rat, George! Are you satisfied? I ate a flea-riddled, scrawny rat. I was so weak I didn't even try to catch the cat who vied for the very same meal."

He stared at her for a moment. Then he stood and pulled her to her feet. "Oh, love, I'm sorry. I have had such times."

She bit back tears and forced her body to stay still as he caressed her hair. *Do not let him see you shake.* She said nothing.

"Please, Lil. I know you are a strong woman—it is one reason I love you so—but you must trust me in matters of our ways. Perhaps I've been remiss, wanting to shield you from…"

"Self-loathing?"

He didn't answer but closed his eyes and drew a deep breath. "Those first years are so hard. I remember them. It is onerous for me to see you in pain."

She verbalized her recent decision, wondering if he would want to flee Marie soon. If he would force her to choose him or her daughter. "I am in no pain. I simply want to find my child. You will still help me, will you not?"

George paused. He was worried, she saw. He was strong but practical. Where was Annaluisa Pelosi? Their friend had purportedly gone to New Orleans to lead Madam Lucifer on a merry chase but had taken too long to return. The woman claimed some knowledge of Lillian's mother also, but she had quit Baltimore before revealing her secrets.

I must find my baby, Lillian vowed.

George kissed her hand and nodded. "I want to help you find your child, dear. Just…please be careful." He indicated the desk drawer where she'd stowed her letter. "So, what does your hero write?"

"Nothing of great import."

"I know that tone." George leaned in, kissed her ear, and nibbled playfully at her neck. "What are you hiding? Let me see."

"He is my *personal* friend."

She stood to distract him with a kiss, but he pushed her back, holding her a foot away with a hand on each shoulder and staring into her eyes. "Am I to be jealous? What further secrets are there between us?"

"You should be quite jealous, for he is a great man and does not pen letters to you! Oh, you will be disappointed to hear that he no longer writes stories. I cannot bear to believe it is true."

"That is rather shocking. Why would he stop?"

"He is more interested in the study of mystical phenomena."

George laughed. "Ah, soothsayers and psychics, the scourge of every age. What a waste of talent."

Lillian fought back annoyance. "I hardly think we are in the position to laugh at a man who might believe in vampires. In any case, he will be in Baltimore soon. Might we go hear him speak?"

"Did he specifically mention vampires?" George sat and rubbed at his forehead. "Oh, Lil, did you *tell* him?"

Well, Lillian, you are a special sort of idiot, are you not?

"Of course not! He mentioned his friendship with Mr. Bram Stoker; that is all."

If she'd understood more when she'd written to him two months ago… If she'd only known how private she'd have to become! She'd lost her most beloved friend, Bess, to fear and secrecy. She'd sent her longtime companions Thomas and Addie off to the seaside and barely communicated with those servants who remained in her own home, her maid Aileen and Aileen's young male siblings. None openly questioned the constant presence of the broodsome George, but they would in time wonder why the two ventured out primarily during odd hours and no longer took meals. And why they were not engaged.

How many times had she told Bess that no husband was better than the wrong husband? George adored her, lavished her with attention, tolerated her need for adventure, her eccentricities in a way no ordinary mortal man of society would. He was her maker, her mentor. No matter her recent struggles with existence, George had captivated her, body and soul. But, *wedding?* It was laughable.

While she'd long ago given up the idea of a normal home life and family, her present state ensured nothing would be normal.

Give it a bit more time, George had said. The murder, the blood, the hollowness—it would all pass, he promised. But she'd seen the worry in his eyes. It did not pass for every one of them. No, some went insane and killed themselves. Some ate their own kind, grew very strong and flaunted the rules. Marie de Bourbon was one of those, Madame Lucifer herself.

Lillian and George had drunk from one another a few times, a dark adventure that stirred passion she hadn't imagined could exist. And yet, no one had arrived to wreak justice upon her. George had assured her it was not a sin—well, not a sin by their standards—and that they would not become cannibals unless one drained the other completely. Not like Madame Lucifer…who also went unpunished.

The Elders: the few who had lived for many millennia without insanity or cannibalism. How many were there? George hadn't been sure, although legend told of twelve brothers, all powerful, all the first generation of two damned parents. But, out of how many? Thousands and thousands of vampires through the years, likely. Many now gone. Mortals were weak but always a danger. Damn it, didn't Bram Stoker himself seem to understand what it took to kill vampires? And she had written to Mr. Doyle, his good friend…

"Please, dear, let me see the letter." George hooded his eyes, and Lil knew he suppressed the urge to force his will upon her as her maker. She admired that he never played that very special card, although she'd witnessed him press his brother Phillip that way.

What have I done? Surely Mr. Doyle is no danger?

She opened the drawer and handed the letter to George. He took a seat and read, mumbling and groaning at times. She busied herself with another project, trying to repair her riding goggles that had been run over by a trolley the night before.

"Wedding?" he murmured with a quick glance at her. Then, "I know that you adore your Sherlock and his creator, but you must now agree with me that a continued connection with the author is out of the question. You must never meet."

"Hmnnn." Lil didn't look up from her project. It was *hopeless* without Thomas around. Of course, George would not allow her to employ her former butler at the house anymore. He'd seen too much, including the corpses George had left on her living room floor.

"I would like to know something about this Learned Order of Psychic Scholars. Sounds like a ridiculous name your little Irregulars would create."

"I call the boys my Musketeers. Still, your mistake is understandable."

"The Learned Order. Aging men with time on their hands—"

Lillian knew she was being bull-headed, but she couldn't stop herself. She took a deep breath to steady her hands as she pried at a screw. A bit of medicine would be welcome now as a finger of anxiety coiled in her stomach. "Why should *you* worry about aging men with time on their hands? What can they mean to us?"

George folded the letter and tapped it against his hand as he stared out the window. He looked over his shoulder after a moment and said, "You think us invincible? Your Mr. Doyle is unlikely as simple as most in this city. Leave him be, Lil. Promise me."

Lillian thought of her fantasy Uncle Sherlock. She had so little of her former self left. "I will not give up on my investigations!"

"No, of course not. You simply must be more careful. You are not to see Mr. Doyle, ever. Am I clear?"

His tone slapped her. He'd not chastised her once since she met him, since she'd seen him leaping from her neighbor's balcony, since the moment she began to love him. But now...

"You are quite clear, *sir.*"

George was silent.

"Annaluisa should have returned by now," Lillian offered after a time. She knew George fretted about their friend. He worried about Marie de Bourbon. He worried about her. That was why he was being so strict. So…fatherly.

George turned and nodded but still looked distracted. "Yes, several weeks ago. Or at least sent word. But that is not all."

"No? What, then?"

"A feeling. Not a very pleasant one. The hairs on my neck prickle and I'm unsettled, and I'm not prone to flights of fancy like you."

Lillian eyed him balefully. "Perhaps a bottle of Mrs. Winslow's remedy to soothe you?" When he did not bite she realized he was quite serious. "George, look at me. Tell me what this dread is."

"Dread? Why, yes, I suppose it is dread. I cannot rid myself of the feeling that Marie de Bourbon is already near. Waiting."

Lillian's heart raced, though his pronouncement was unsurprising. She'd felt the same concern from time to time but associated it with being a newborn vampire unused to the myriad sensations and urges that came upon her at strange hours.

"Do you feel the presence of your vampire children?" she asked. Madame Lucifer was George's spawn as much as she was his brother's long-ago wife. "Do you know when *I'm* about?"

"No, I do not feel your presence as much as I anticipate and crave your nearness. And I released Marie's bond very long ago, to the detriment of all of us. Even so, she possesses the strength of many from her cannibalism and thus is no child." He remarked almost wryly, "I am quite shocked that our Elder has not cut her down. Perhaps he is not yet aware of her exploits."

"Our Elder? We *personally* have an Elder? I am confused. Why have you not told me everything? This talk of vampiring comes in dribs and drabs."

George arched an eyebrow and waved her letter in the air. It was a second slap, and well deserved. She sat down.

"I was not a very successful mortal," she said. "It seems I am a worse vampire."

George didn't correct her, and she hoped that he simply hadn't heard. She went to his side and rubbed his shoulders, thinking, *Please,* please, *tell me it will be fine.*

"Would that you could massage this overwrought brain of mine," he murmured instead. "While you have finally given me reason to want to survive, I'm terrified about your safety. And certainly Phillip and Kitty are at risk." George took her hand and pressed a kiss to it. "Lil, we should leave Baltimore. Annaluisa has sent no word. I know Marie will find us, and I know that she is here. We are out of time."

Lillian's heart sank. She had hoped for another month or even a few weeks before this confrontation, all time to continue her search for her baby. Now she would have to follow George or abandon him. She did not think she could abandon him.

What did she know about her child, anyway? The Hebrew Orphan Asylum had once cradled her but had little interest in helping Lillian find the girl again. The stern director had looked over her spectacles at Lillian and done the arithmetic quickly.

"Seven years old? I'm afraid no girl here is that age. Are you quite sure?"

"I was sixteen," Lil had murmured, clenching her bag lest her hands shake. *You don't dare look at me like that! Blame the scoundrel who took me against my will. Blame the physician who was complicit in the cover-up. Blame the world for wanting to lock me away and for stealing my baby.*

"Sixteen? I see. How unfortunate. I wish I could be of assistance, but these matters are treated delicately, and we rarely learn the true surname of a child. Are you sure she was left with us?"

Was she sure? Perhaps her governess and butler had been wrong about that as well. Lillian wasn't sure of anything. Someone should have tortured the truth from the Jackal and Dr. Schneider before George killed them.

"My baby," she whispered.

George brushed her cheek. "We will return when it is safe. Your child is no longer a baby and could live anywhere. I promised I would help, and help you I will."

"Where would we go? Might I have a few days just to try again to find her?" Lillian found herself asking against logic. "If only Bess could help. She is quite smart and would be willing...if she didn't loathe me. I wonder how she fares."

"Bess would never loathe you," George said. "She is hurt at your secrecy. Give it time, Lil."

At her look, he ran his hand through his hair and blew out a breath. "I know, I know, I've said that too often lately. I did my best to prepare you for the isolation. It is not something words can adequately convey."

"Indeed," she acknowledged. "But, then, I am used to being alone."

What had she done with her time before spending day and night with George, learning the basics of "vampiring," a term she'd coined to amuse George? Most of her new life came seamlessly, innately, if she found herself questioning it later. She hungered and fed on the scum of the city, creatures who were monstrous in their own right. She grew tired in the sun and sought shelter. She slept less and moved about the city less, not knowing when or if someone might recognize her nature or ask a too-probing question. And still, while the police had accepted their explanation for the deaths of the Jackal and Schneider, deaths overall had risen in the city.

Risen by perhaps a third, Lil reasoned. Phillip, George, and now she were adding to the toll. And of course there might be others in this city that had no ruling House, no allegiances or long history. The city detectives must be wearing through a lot of shoe leather.

"I do miss my reading, George; there's so little time without Addie and Thomas's help about the place. How trivial that must sound to you! And yet, my books have been my solace for so many years..."

All my escapes are gone. Just one pill, she wondered, what would one little pill do?

"Not at all, dear," George said. "The things that made you special are never trivial. Do not insult me that way. I value your odd ways and...I understand your desire to find your daughter. Let me discuss these matters with my brother. Phillip has a fairly clear head at all times."

Lillian jumped. Her little charges had burst through the front door, her maid Aileen O'Shaunessy and Aileen's beau Officer Johnnie Moran hurrying behind. Lillian smiled at the boys. These were her Irregulars who called themselves the Musketeers. She smiled also at the flush on Aileen's cheeks. Had the maid's beau finally proposed?

She rushed to the girl's side and reached for her hand, hoping to congratulate her, but Aileen pulled quickly away.

"No, miss!" the maid whispered and drew Lillian to the side. "Ah, you have done your own hair again! What a mess!" she called loudly over her shoulder as she pretended to straighten Lillian's tresses. Then she leaned in and whispered, "What is he waiting for? Perhaps he doesn't love me?"

Lillian turned and pressed a kiss to her cheek. "Nonsense. I will have a chat with him presently. Perhaps he does not have money for a ring. George can fix that immediately—"

"No! Oh, miss, he would die before taking charity. Johnnie is so proud—"

"I say, Lil, can you finish that at another time?"

Lillian turned to see George looking uncharacteristically sheepish. Paddy Moran—Officer Moran's brother and the youngest of the boys—had taken hold of his hand, and Lil smiled at his shocked expression. George was so unused to this happy company of mortals, so unused to being liked by a youngster.

"There's been a *murder*, Miss Holmes," Darby O'Shaunessy squealed, his mop of red curls shaking as he wiggled in excitement.

"A very bad murder," Darby's older brother Billy said. Then Billy straightened his suspenders and stood ramrod straight, trying to appear as adult as possible.

"Indeed, Billy, I've never heard of a good murder." Lillian looked to Johnnie Moran for confirmation, him being a policeman, but they were all distracted by the stumbling entrance of the Musketeers' giant mutt, Mr. Abraham Lincoln.

"What on earth have you done to poor Mr. Lincoln?" George asked with a laugh. The boys had wrapped little burlap booties on the feet of the unfortunate hound sliding haphazardly across the wood floor.

"So he can come in the house," Darby explained. "Miss Holmes said all of us has to wear shoes inside and outside."

"Mr. Lincoln may not come in the house no matter the footwear," Lillian said. "I do, however, applaud your attempt at following my instructions. Now, to more pressing matters?"

Johnnie Moran pulled off his police cap and brushed it against his trousers. He cast a sideways glance at George, and Lillian knew George had been right: Everyone suspected something was amiss with them but hadn't quite hit on the truth. How could they, though? Sensible Johnnie would be the last person on Earth to believe in vampires.

"Never seen the likes of it, miss. On the roof of the Rennard, she was."

"Who, Johnnie?"

"We don't know. Not sure we'll ever know, unless someone files a report that she's gone. Hard to tell even how old she was."

"Boys, why don't you and Aileen go tell Cook that it's time for a sweet? Perhaps there are crullers left from yesterday."

"We want to hear about the dead lady," Billy whined.

"Yes, I'm sure you do. To the kitchen, now!" Lillian then sent a stern plea to Aileen to manage the boys, who hustled them out of the room.

George and Lillian sat across from Johnnie, who remained standing.

"And how did she die?" George's tone was disinterested, but Lillian could practically taste his intensity.

"She'd been there quite a while, so it's a bit hard to say, you see. The heat up there…well, it was about the worst sight I've seen. Not bloated, like you'd assume, but shriveled, like an Egyptian."

"You mean, mummified?"

"Yes, like a mummy, shriveled. Thing that has us puzzled is where all the blood went. Morgue reports not a drop of the stuff in her body. Never seen the likes of it. You see, once someone dies, the blood stops flowing, as the heart no longer pumps—"

"Indeed, we understand that," Lillian said.

"Right. We didn't find any blood on the roof to speak of. Well, what with the rains…" Johnnie shook his head.

"Puzzling," George murmured and lit his pipe. "Wounds?"

Johnnie winced and glanced at Lillian. "Perhaps Miss Holmes would prefer…"

"Oh, now, Johnnie, you know I'm hardly squeamish. Tell us."

"She looked to be attacked by some devil of a creature. If she weren't on a roof I'd say a bear had escaped from the circus or a wolf wandered into the city! Neck and chest all shredded to bits."

Lillian put her hand on George's. *Please do not let it be Annaluisa!* "Her clothing? What manner of lady was she?"

"That was just as odd. All dressed up like some kind of gypsy woman. Scarves and exotic things about her wrists and waist."

"A hapless drifter, perhaps," Lil managed. No one spoke for many moments, and the mantel clock seemed to take on an impossible volume.

George bolted to the window, pulling on his pipe and lost in his own world—a world of grief, Lil knew, for hadn't he and Annaluisa been friends for years? No, for *centuries*. Lil felt a stab of grief, herself, for the woman had claimed knowledge of the identity of her mother. If Annaluisa was gone, wasn't that knowledge gone with her forever? It seemed Lillian would always be an orphan with an orphaned child. But the worst for them all was that Madam Lucifer, the vampire who ate vampires, was in Baltimore and no doubt now took direct aim at them.

In truth, it wasn't clear to Lillian why the woman stalked George. He'd been her maker, true, and many fledglings went through phases of misery and anger more powerful than that of Lillian's own, but so many decades had passed since. Could Marie de Bourbon have harbored such intense hatred for all this time? Had she hated George all while becoming the intensely feared and loathed "Madame Lucifer"?

No, it will not happen. She will not destroy him or us.

"Johnnie," she said, "I'm horrified to hear of these details and wish you the best in solving this mystery."

"But…but Miss Holmes. I thought you'd want to learn more. To maybe assist…?"

Lillian tamped down regret for her lost identity. "I fear that George has business out of town, and I am likely to join him. Now, will you please go help Aileen with your brothers? It sounds as if Mr. Lincoln is sliding around on the kitchen floor and creating quite the racket."

Johnnie glanced again at George, still frozen in position, still staring outside. "Yes, miss."

"And, Johnnie, please tell Aileen that I will not need her tonight, and perhaps not tomorrow. You should feel free to take her out on the town. If you need any assistance in planning a nice evening for her, please do consult with me. Any assistance at all."

Johnnie tilted his head and joined Aileen and the boys in the kitchen.

"That was not subtle, Lillian," George chided.

"I cannot bear to see Aileen sad. What is he waiting for?"

"Likely an ultimatum."

An ultimatum? Lillian bit back a sharp retort. Certainly he referred to Johnnie and not himself? She had not pressured George to propose marriage!

"I am sorry about Annaluisa," she said, cutting off her anger. "Surely it is her."

George remained quiet, staring at the street. When he turned, Lillian started at the fury in his eyes, black as night and rimmed in red.

"Annaluisa was harmless. A gossip, perhaps, but harmless. It was a strike at me. A message *to me.*"

"Yes, I know."

"Marie's hatred for me is extraordinary. One can often come to despise their maker, but after all this time... Why has she elevated her hatred to an art form?"

The very questions Lillian had been asking. "There must be something more, George. You will never be rid of her until you learn what that thing is."

"We will find your mother," he said suddenly, a vehement promise. "I know that weighs heavily on your mind, too, like your daughter. I regret that I didn't press Annaluisa further on the topic, but at the appropriate time I didn't know you, didn't know what you would come to mean to me. Someone else has the clue we need, though. It did not go to the grave with her."

Lillian nodded, knowing the last was a lie to calm her.

"For now, I care only about keeping you safe from Marie." George shook his head, musing, "She will surely hate the one I love. I do not know if you are safer out of my presence or where I can watch over you."

"It does not matter," Lillian said, "and you know why."

She stood on tiptoe and pressed her lips to his. He breathed in deeply and returned her kiss.

"I don't want to be parted either, Lil. But you have a target on your back like me. God, it seems I am paying for all my sins. And there are many."

"Don't I have some say in this? You are all I have in the world, George. If you leave… No! I simply won't have it. She will have to kill us both, or we must find a way to stop her."

"Did you not just hear about Annaluisa? That cannot be your fate. Yes, we must act, and quickly. I'm simply weighing whether I should lead Marie away from you or be selfish and take you with me." He pulled her close and pressed his lips to her hair. "I love you, Lil. You are everything. I cannot lose you."

Although she hated the desperation in his voice, his words wrapped her in the first warmth she'd felt in days. A warmth that was almost human. "I love you too, George."

"Let us keep up our strength. I need a meal. No doubt someone is to be clubbed over the head at the docks tonight, and we can offer relief. After, I want to speak with Phillip. He must hear about Annaluisa, and I must warn him about Marie. Then we will decide what is to be done and where we—or I—should go."

* * *

Indeed, someone *was* being clubbed over the head at the docks, as George predicted. The Baltimore police department did their best, Lillian supposed, but they didn't seem to concentrate their foot patrols on the areas where most of the crime was. The wealthy citizens wanted their mansions protected and cared not a whit about the immigrant flotsam and jetsam packed like canned oysters in flophouses near the harbor.

Lil cared. In fact, shame washed over her whenever she thought of her mortal days of highbrow isolation from those suffering just a few miles away from her home. She had wealth enough to help at least some of the orphans and poor but had never done a thing. Well, taking in Aileen and Johnnie's siblings perhaps counted, but that wasn't enough. And now one of the poverty-stricken young men she should have helped was barefoot, nearly in rags, and about to die.

"Which will it be? As if I need to ask," George joked.

"I would prefer the aggressor, yes. You *will* let the poor chap on the ground go if he has life in him, George?"

"Do I have a choice? I would hear about it forever."

George descended from the roof of the warehouse upon which they stood onto the back of the attacker, a giant of a man wielding a huge plank of wood like it were a baseball bat. Lillian hurried after and also hit the man, who was shocked and on his knees, with a solid right hook. She noticed offhandedly that they were only yards from the place of her encounter with the sailor the night before.

"You do love to punch men," George said. "It gives me pause sometimes, Lil. Perhaps we should put you in the ring like your Uncle Sherlock?"

"Please attend to the victim! Is he alive?" The ruffian under her stirred a bit, so Lillian punched him again. Then she punched him a third time for brutalizing a young man for what was likely nothing more than a drunken argument.

"No, I'm afraid that board crushed his skull. Little chap, practically a boy. Can't imagine what he could have done."

"Let's find out, shall we?" Lillian slapped her captive to consciousness, but he passed out again when he saw her teeth and blood-red eyes. No doubt the sight of George over her shoulder was equally shocking.

"There's so little mystery in this," she muttered. "I long for a real battle with a criminal of wit and cunning."

George sighed. "Be careful what you ask for, Lil. Now, drink before he dies. I would have a sip as well."

CHAPTER THREE

The Orleans brothers formulate a plan.

"She's *your* ex-wife!"

Phillip cursed and looked up at him. "You're the one who turned her! Oh, see, why do you draw me into this ridiculous debate again and again?"

"Why do you fall so easily into the same argument?" George laughed despite the horror they faced. Phillip was so easily goaded, and he never grew tired of the game.

He's such a good man, and all my destruction hasn't changed that. Phillip, turned by George eons ago, had become his confessor, his voice of reason, his compass when there were no stars in the sky to guide him—which had been often before Lil.

"I lay this at your feet," Phillip snapped. "What in God's name did you do to her to have Marie declare this war on us? I told you before, you underestimated her affection for you, made more potent by you being her maker. Poor Annaluisa. Killed indirectly by the Orleans brothers."

"Madam Lucifer does not seem to need a reason to hate, and I barely remember our tryst," George said. "Perhaps she is insane. How many of her own kind has she killed now? Poor Annaluisa, indeed. She was torn to shreds according to that Moran fellow."

"Don't tell Kitty. I don't want to frighten her again. I'll find a way to explain at a better time."

Phillip paced the length of the room, footsteps in time with the mantel clock. It drove George insane, this habit of his brother's.

Why couldn't he even *walk* without keeping beat? He'd been that way from boyhood, the sheriff of the household, ensuring the needs of servants were met, however petty, and taking care of every stray creature—and there were many—that breached the palace walls. And George had ruined it all for him in one moment of intense hunger and rage at the woman who had borne them. Phillip had known similar moments, though, especially in the early days, when his hunger was uncontrolled and his good looks and wealth drew unsuspecting women his way. Many had never returned home. George had shown him how to sneak bodies from the castle, had helped him bury the evidence of his gluttony.

"How did you do it, Phillip?" he asked, thinking suddenly of Kitty. "How did you make a mortal woman look past it all?"

"I have a lot of common sense and some knack for nuance that you lack. Lillian loved you before you turned her, didn't she?" Phillip shook his head and looked mournful. "Look, George, Kitty does nothing but plan this wedding. I cannot imagine how I'll ask her to leave town again. We're weeks away, damn it!"

As if such could compete with the likelihood of certain death.

George grunted and said, "I am tired of hearing of weddings. Where will you go?"

"I'm half tempted not to tell you, brother. Marie is on your heels, not mine, and not Kitty's."

George tilted his head to the side and smirked at Phillip's attempted independence. His brother stopped pacing and threw his hands out in surrender. "Oh, for the love of God, don't look at me like that! Of course I'll tell you."

"No, don't. Actually, I'm not sure Marie couldn't torture it out of me. Just go, go quickly, and take care of Kitty. And, Phillip?"

"Hmnn?"

"I know I have failed you. I truly tried to leave you alone so you could find peace with your beloved mortal. This time I will do better. But please be careful."

"Yes, yes, I love you as well, damn you," Phillip snapped. "But what of Lillian? Surely she is next if Marie wants to hurt you?"

"Lillian won't abandon me, and she won't let me send her off to be safe. I don't know what to do about it. She wants to find..." George growled. He still wrestled with anger at the men who had nearly destroyed Lillian, who had abused and tortured her into a darker beginning than he could ever imagine. Even though he had killed them, it wasn't enough. They should have suffered as she was suffering now.

"Lil had a child, Phillip," he said. "That monster solicitor of hers raped her when she was a girl, and she bore a daughter. She won't leave Baltimore until she finds the girl, or unless I force my will upon her."

Phillip grimaced. "You may be her maker, George, but wielding that power over her will put a chasm between you."

As it has between us, brother? You should let him go, George. Why can't you let him go?

"Why are you marrying Kitty, Phillip?" George found himself asking. "It's simply...not done. Not necessary."

"She's mortal. She's a normal woman with normal needs and expectations." Phillip paused. "I imagine when she finally dies, since she will not let me turn her, I will not marry again."

George sighed. "A normal woman with normal needs and expectations. Not so, my Lillian." He eyed his brother surprisingly ruefully. "Of course, we have not been lovers for long. I suppose we are an aberration in Baltimore society, not engaged and living in—"

Phillip burst into laughter.

"What? Stop that!"

"You have the Devil herself after you and you're concerned about Baltimore society? This is not my brother speaking!"

"Oh, shut up. Gather your Kitty and off with you."

Phillip closed the distance in three strides and pulled George in for a quick hug. "Go. Leave," he begged. "Marie's minions have not extended west as far as Annaluisa could tell a month or so ago. California is splendid, I hear. We can go together if you like."

"You would go with me? You and Kitty, me and Lil." How lovely that sounded right now. What a wonderful dream. He really *had* changed.

"Yes," Phillip said. "I would take a different route, that is certain, to ensure I keep Kitty safe. Of course, there will be a lot of convincing to do. Kitty has her heart set on this wedding at Christmas."

"And Lil on finding her child." George sighed and flopped into his favorite chair near the window, looking out onto the serene neighborhood he'd grown to tolerate in this home he and his brother had shared for five years. "There was a time, not so long ago, when we could have gone anywhere together without consulting headstrong women. We could still, I suppose…?"

Phillip sneered. "Ah, yes, the life that led you to become a brooding idiot and me a nervous wreck. What fun we had. Don't be stupid. I haven't seen you so full of life since you were…well, alive."

Life. Yes. Thus his conundrum. He *cared*. "Damn it. I don't know what to do! Ask her to abandon her search for her child? Leave without her?"

"Or…"

George arched a brow and sniffed out a tired laugh. "Stay and fight? Stay and be destroyed."

"Perhaps not. Perhaps it's time you stop running. I sense you'd like to stop. I know you cannot bear to leave me, as you seem unable to do so for more than a fortnight."

George glared at him, even though he knew his brother was only joking. "You greatly flatter yourself. I am only looking out for you. In any case, I cannot defeat Marie alone."

"No, I don't suppose you can." Phillip sat next to him and rubbed his chin. "In truth, I'm a bit tired of running as well. But what do we have? We're feeble compared to Marie. Just the two of us…"

"And Lillian, if I let her stay."

"A newborn. A strong newborn, I'll give her that."

George shrugged. "What else?"

"Let's think this through. Does anyone in the New York House tolerate you enough to fight Madam Lucifer?"

"No, they detest me as well."

"Do they detest Marie more?"

"Of course they do. I think so." George looked at Phillip again, surprised anew. Was it possible? Phillip would stay, would try to help? No, too many innocents would be put at risk. *But, George, when did you care so about innocents?* Not before Lil.

They sat in silence for minutes, mulling over the absurd notion that Marie de Bourbon could be defeated.

"Anyone in Philadelphia?" Phillip muttered.

"Lone wolves like us. Hoodlums."

"Beggars can't be choosers, George. A few hoodlums would come in quite handy right now, if we could give them some incentive. I wonder how many of us it would take."

"Too many. Where is our Elder when you need him?"

"For the love of God, don't even think about him, George. We're lucky enough that he ignores us."

"You haven't broken any rules, nor have I. What do we have to fear in Vasil? Isn't he supposed to take care of renegades like Madam Lucifer? In fact, why hasn't he already destroyed her?"

Phillip shrugged. "Perhaps the stories are true, that he is derelict in his duties to annoy his father. Annaluisa told of rumors of his incredible palace of earthly pleasures somewhere in the Caribbean. Perhaps he doesn't even exist; perhaps none of the Elders do. What if they are merely stories designed to keep the Houses powerful? 'Be good and listen to us or the Bogey Man will get you.' But I'm not going to get on a ship bound for the islands to knock on Vasil's door in any case."

George sighed. Phillip sighed as well and turned their conversation in another direction.

"Do you know anyone in New York besides *him?*"

"No one, really."

After a moment of silence, they spoke at once: "Sullivan is a devil himself."

"Sullivan is an interesting notion," Phillip added.

Chauncey Sullivan. He was rarely heard from these days, so ashamed of what he'd become was the rumor. A quiet man, black as coal and hard as diamond, he'd feasted on his own kind for nearly a century and amassed great strength. He had only bowed to the New York House because he couldn't tolerate vampire politics. He'd been born into the life without guidance, with no one to tame him, to warn him that insanity and suicide typically followed cannibalism. In that way, he had become like his maker...Marie de Bourbon herself. She'd not only broken the rule of cannibalism but broken the rule of abandoning her newborns. Why *hadn't* Vasil or one the other Elders taken her down?

"This can't be a good idea, Phillip. Sullivan doesn't like to fight. The last time I saw him he was feeding birds. I mean that literally. He sat on a bench with a bag of breadcrumbs, *in the daytime,* throwing them out onto the snow. He is as kind now, it seems, as he was once evil. I imagine he seeks to redeem himself, but who knows?"

"This would be an excellent path to redemption—at least in his mind, don't you think? Kill Madam Lucifer herself?"

"Kill his maker? Break another commandment? He'd never do it, even if he were capable. Her control over him—"

"What if he thought we could help him redeem himself? What could be more appealing to a repentant cannibal than the destruction of the strongest of his kind, the one who made him what he is? To stop her reign of terror. If he truly has turned his back on all she made him, couldn't that break the bond?"

"I don't know... It's been years since I've seen him."

They fell into silence again. George felt the wheels grinding in Phillip's brain, and a thrill shot through him. All talk of fleeing Baltimore had fallen away.

"How would we keep the women safe while we go look for allies?" Phillip asked.

"Don't ask Lillian that. You'll have your head served to you."

"Kitty...yes, Kitty would be more fearful, but I could hide her away somewhere, I think." Then: "What are we doing, George? Is it suicide?"

"Probably."

CHAPTER FOUR

An evening in Central Park.

Chauncey Sullivan kicked the lifeless woman off the dirt path winding up from the side of the Croton Reservoir and watched her roll into a ravine. New York wouldn't miss another prostitute. Why she'd roamed so far away from the center of the things, he couldn't imagine; another half mile and the city dwindled to shacks, stables, and pig pens. He knew the area well, for in life he'd dwelled in one of those shacks, tended to those pigs and horses for his wealthy employer.

General Atherton had been his first kill. The pompous bloated miser never got the chance to serve in the revolution he so desperately wanted. Chauncey hadn't been in his right mind, but if he had been, he thought, he might have beaten the man before killing him. Chauncey's physical scars had faded since Madam Lucifer turned him, but his memories had not diminished.

Too long ago, Chauncey. This bitterness was your ruination. Trust in God and move toward good deeds.

He'd promised Phoebe to try to let go of the past. She hadn't been able to tell him how to do that, how to forgive and forget his sins, but she read scripture to him nightly to soften his anguish. *You are forgiven*, he'd repeat ten times, as she had instructed him.

"But I don't have a soul," he'd argue. She'd cry and wring her hands whenever he lost faith, so he'd try his best to humor her although he knew her delusional.

"We all have souls, and if you don't give it to the Devil, then you are in God's hands."

He'd smile and nod, unwilling to remind her that she likely didn't have a soul either. So simple, so lovely, his Phoebe. Given another chance, would he have given mercy to the woman who had just found freedom from slavery in the North? Let her live out a normal if harsh existence as a pig slop or washerwoman? Yes, given the chance to do it over, he would not have turned her. But now she waited for him at home, and after five decades together, it still thrilled him to be making his way to her.

He walked up the dirt path toward Fifth Avenue when a streetlamp flickered. That alone did not alarm him, but a rustling of animals in the brush made him spin around. A half-dozen squirrels and a few hares scampered across the path, all fleeing some hunter. Then, as one, dozens of birds stirred from their slumber and took off together, circling up from a pine and winging away as if blown by a hurricane. But the air didn't stir.

What kind of creature hunted small mammals at night? Chauncey stopped, listening for sounds of stray dogs. The air was so still that he could hear his own cold breath.

"Who is there?" he called.

"Who indeed?"

Chauncey spun around but saw no one. A branch moved, and the gravel crunched on its own as if a person walked toward him. Ice flowed through his veins, colder even than his own tainted blood. He picked up a handful of dirt and cast it in the direction of the voice and movement.

"Clever fellow." The voice was low and clipped, laced with a foreign accent Chauncey didn't recognize. Then, from thin air, a silver shimmer like mercury flowed up from the ground until a form gradually took shape. A tall, fair, handsome man with long hair smiled and waved his fingers as would a flirtatious woman.

Chauncey's legs grew watery as legends rushed through his mind. *"They are from the North and are fair both in complexion and countenance. They love to laugh and to enchant with their beauty and wit. They can move without being seen, speak without being heard, kill with a glance. The children of Atil and Ursula are invincible, and it is best to not discuss them. Obey their commandments but do not dwell on them lest they hear your thoughts. Do not speak of them often lest they come to learn your intentions."* Chauncey fell to one knee and prayed that the end would be fast. *Poor Phoebe.*

"Not tonight, *lieber Freund.* Rise, and walk with me."

Chauncey looked up at the ancient one but winced at an icy blue stare made intolerably intense by the red circles surrounding the pupils. "The legends are true, then?"

"Get up, Chauncey Sullivan!" The ancient reached down and pulled him up by the arm, practically throwing him into the air with the one easy movement. *Yes, true.* No human or ordinary vampire was that strong, had ever been that strong. "Now, do me the honor of walking with me for a while."

The ancient linked his arm through Chauncey's as if they were lovers out for a late-night stroll. "Some legends are true, yes," he said. "Some are not. You and I, we care not about legends. We care only about our own hides, our own pleasures, our own days and nights. It is true of all men and most women, I find. Do you agree?"

Chauncey couldn't find words. His arm burned from the creature's icy touch, yet he dared not pull away. His limbs felt numb, but he moved as if in a dream, with no control. They strolled, and more small animals scampered away, and birds again rose from their slumber to fill the chilly sky. So, his sins had finally caught up with him. This Elder would exact justice.

But not tonight, he had said. What did that mean?

"I'm sorry. I didn't know, I didn't know. And by the time I understood—"

"Pish-posh!"

"I don't understand."

"No, of course you don't. If I cared about our children eating one another, I would have stopped it, yes? One goes insane or one doesn't. You didn't. Is very much a...how do you say...self-correcting behavior, yes?"

"It is one of the commandments."

"*Vater* is fond of his commandments, it is true." The ancient stopped and faced Chauncey, who tried to take a step back but couldn't.

Father. Atil. Which son was this?

"Vasili. Vasil. Basel. Your choice."

Vasil, as Chauncey had heard him called for decades, smiled, his pale cheeks flushing. Except for his build, with his waist-length pale golden hair and flawless fine features he looked nearly like a beautiful woman. He cocked his head to the side for a moment, and Chauncey squirmed under his scrutiny and at the unfamiliar pull the creature had. It felt for all the world like falling in love. He wanted desperately for the Elder to leave, and at the same time he never wanted to be parted from him.

"And now we sit," Vasil said and motioned to a low stone retaining wall. He moved close to Chauncey and took his arm, made the burning come alive again. Then he chuckled and said, "What we will do for the love of a beautiful woman! I should say, what *you* will do. I am not so drawn to beautiful women."

"Please don't harm Phoebe! She is no cannibal!"

"You will stop speaking now, yes?" Vasil scratched his overlong nails on his trousers, making a noise that sounded like trolley wheels squealing loudly only inches away. Chauncey covered his ears and tried to ask Vasil to stop, but he couldn't make a sound.

"Good. Just so, you already suspect that I will destroy your Phoebe, and not in a kind fashion, should you refuse my order. Of course, your life is at risk as well. And for good measure I will add everyone you ever turned. You are a guilt-ridden man, so that should make your decision so much easier. I am generous, am I not?"

Vasil rubbed the backs of his fingers lightly along Chauncey's jaw, setting that side of his face afire. Chauncey nodded, wondering what he could do for Vasil that Vasil could not do for himself.

"The first commandment is…?"

Again, Chauncey could only nod. *Do not breed.*

"Correct. Offspring, in the extremely unlikely event they survive, can tear the curtain between our world and the next. We would not like that, now would we? We survive forever here, but what awaits us on the other side of that curtain?" Vasil shuddered dramatically and pulled his cloak tighter around him. "At least, *Vater* does not wish to perish in Hell just yet. Perhaps someday. So, that brings me to you!" He patted Chauncey's arms happily. "Just so!"

"What the hell does this have to do with me?" Chauncey realized he'd been allowed to speak, and he wished he had chosen different phrasing. Chatting with Vasil felt like dancing through a field of sharp-toothed animal traps.

"Yes, so you will take care of a little problem for me. You will kill Madam Lucifer."

"My maker? That is also forbidden! How would I do that?"

Vasil waved away Chauncey's objections. "She flaunts her broken commandments, yes? She is one of the cannibals who has neither gone *completely* insane nor become at all penitent. So you will kill her. And so, Phoebe lives on happily, as do you, and I may go home."

"You could kill her with a glance! I cannot harm her." *I would like to,* he realized. *With all my being, I would like to.*

"And, moreover," Vasil continued, ignoring him, "you will kill everyone who is dear to her, who is near to her. Her maker, her children...anyone you can find."

"I thought you didn't care about cannibals?"

"Madam Lucifer claims to have bred. Whether she did or not, it would be good to kill her, no? Pleasurable for you, no?"

"How? I'm no match for her! You could—"

"Tsk, tsk. Manners, please. It is not a request. I choose not to approach a torn curtain."

"I still do not know how," Chauncey said. *I will fail, and Phoebe will die.*

"Silence! Your chattering annoys me." His girlish smile gone, Vasil's blue eyes flashed black until he closed them and blew out a deep, freezing breath. He withdrew a small gold vial on a chain from his cloak and let it swing in the air, which rippled and shimmered along that arc. "A few drops, that is all. Marie will want it, crave it, which will make your task easy!"

Chauncey recoiled. The vial seemed to have life, to stretch and breathe on its own.

"Take it. It will not bite." Vasil laughed loudly, sending more birds aloft.

Chauncey extended his hand, eyes closed. Vasil clucked and leaned forward, put the chain around his neck.

The cold hit his chest but gradually abated. "What is it?"

"Elder blood." Vasil shrugged. "Mine. Not the most potent, but it will easily do. Use it wisely."

"Won't it make her stronger? Elder blood makes one invincible!"

"As we said, some legends are true, some are not. Some are...less black and white."

Chauncey nodded, anxious now for Vasil to leave him alone. "Where will I find her?"

Vasil waved his hand again, and Chauncey looked away lest he annoy the ancient further.

"We will likely not meet again, my handsome friend." Then Vasil kissed him on each cheek and disappeared. The void he left cut through Chauncey like the worst grief ever felt. Why wasn't he relieved instead?

Chauncey rose and tucked the vial under his coat. It reminded him that he hadn't been dreaming.

CHAPTER FIVE

A Scotsman arrives in town.

Arthur looked at his pocket watch for the third time and let out a sigh, bringing on a cough that made his chest rumble. The voyage had not been restful, and he didn't feel himself. His lectures in New York were well attended, but except for a very few spectators he knew they wanted to hear about his stories and not about his serious studies. America had not caught up to the notion that he'd put aside fancy for the fantastical.

Perhaps this leg of his journey would differ. Hopefully the Learned Order attracted more serious investigators into spiritism. At the moment, he wasn't terribly impressed with the city or his host. While Americans didn't seem to be able to keep their trains to a schedule, he wasn't so late that Donnelly should have given up.

He bought a paper on the platform and took the stairway to the general reception area, a sorry place imitating a much grander relative in New York. It smelled, however, like every rail station he'd visited—of coal, soot, hot metal, and the faint aromas of burnt coffee and stale tobacco. Taking a seat on a centrally located bench lest someone try to pick his pocket, he scanned the crowd for his contact, taking in the slightly different mix of people Baltimore seemed to offer. Some familiar characters: the shoeblack, the newsie, a shabby man with a telltale bulbous nose brought on by overindulgence, a few confused-looking immigrants, some Italian, some Irish… Those were the same at nearly every station.

Standing among them, as still and erect as a statue, a beautiful young woman stared at the station's great clock, which was as big as an elephant, and compared it to her own small pocket watch. Arthur fixed on her, wondering why she intrigued him so much aside from her lovely face. Her deep green dress, matching feathered hat, and raven hair brought out a very pale complexion, but as much as he tried he couldn't characterize her further except for being from wealth.

At another time in his life he might have constructed a great mystery around her person, to have it unravel before his readers with painstaking care. She reminded him of no one he'd ever known, although he'd penned such exemplary figures into his stories. He thought briefly of his wife, once nearly as lovely as this mysterious female. She'd languished for years with tuberculosis and a premature dementia, both illnesses that seemed unwilling to take her, unwilling to let her go. Drink had nursed him through the first awful months after Louisa stopped recognizing him, but good friends had convinced him to put that down and face the bleak truth. Yet from the misery of grieving her before she was dead Arthur dearly needed this break.

The young lady looked worried and glanced at the clock again. She scanned the crowd as well and tapped her gloves on her palm as the conductor held up the placard that announced the imminent departure of a train to Chicago and points west.

"There you are!" she cried at the sight of an elderly pair shuffling toward her, a porter following quickly with a trunk in tow. Arthur folded his paper and stood, feigning interest in the placard so he could get a bit closer. The woman didn't notice him.

"You must hurry! What took so long? Oh, never mind. Here, Addie, let me take that."

The elderly woman and man exchanged a quick embrace with her. *Parents?* No, too old. Some other relation perhaps.

"I told Thomas we should have left sooner, as one never knows—"

"Don't worry about that now, Addie! Go on, I will follow behind."

Addie and the porter moved toward the tunnel to the platform, and Arthur moved another few steps to listen.

"Hurry, Thomas, please do catch up to Addie!"

But the elderly man would not be brushed off easily. He was bent and used a cane, but Arthur could picture a time when the tall lean man stood proud. A veteran of the War Between the States, he surmised. He'd seen many in New York, most of them drifters and homeless, and so many with cut-off limbs. A crueler war he'd never heard of. Arthur silently asked the young woman to treat this crippled friend or relative with respect and tenderness.

"Now, Lillian, tell me that you will be careful while we're in Chicago. That young man is looking after you, isn't he?"

"Of course, Thomas. Trust me! With the Jackal gone from this world, I am in no danger."

Thomas scowled. "Aye, your young man killed him. We know, and we are grateful."

The young woman named Lillian grimaced. "I suspected you knew the entire sequence of events. Yes, George rescued me—and would let no further harm come to me, so you needn't worry about a thing!"

"You don't look yourself, Lil." The woman named Addie seemed concerned but forced herself to shake the feeling off. "Well, Constable Moran is around all the time now, isn't he? He'll also help if you need it. We miss you, dear."

The young woman's face softened, and she stood on tiptoes to place a sweet kiss on the man's cheek that made Arthur sigh in approval. "Take care of that leg," she said, "and take care of Addie. Enjoy your stay with your cousin! Now, hurry! And do write to me!"

The conductor waved the placard and gave the final call. The young woman's shoulders dropped, from tension falling away or sadness weighing her down, Arthur couldn't tell, as the conductor helped the older man with his bag.

Just another ordinary scene, Arthur decided: a woman seeing off relations on a journey of no consequence. Except that they had discussed the murder of someone called the Jackal. Most extraordinary! Why he'd felt the need to spy...

Well, old habits died hard, certainly. *But you are only a simple doctor,* he thought, *with not even the bravery of John Watson, much less his great friend.* This matter was for American police. Still, Arthur gave himself high marks for curiosity, although his wife's urgings to live only vicariously through his fiction had grated on their marriage. He barely knew how much of his current character was formed of natural cowardice and how much Luisa's constant nagging to stay close to home.

Arthur broke from his ruminations when the young woman turned and caught his stare. She froze. Her assessment grew curious, and he feared that he'd been caught eavesdropping. Was this Lillian dangerous? A murderess herself? His blood ran cold.

But you are in a public place, and she is a slender female. Arthur looked over his shoulder to ensure the police officer patrolling the station was still present.

The young woman tilted her head, raised a quizzical brow, and turned toward the grand entrance. It was if she might have recognized him, but that would be ever so unlikely. Whatever small fame he'd garnered in America, he knew only three people in Baltimore, and none of them well.

Oh, and he'd corresponded with that woman whose letters were certainly not typical of the dozens of inquiries he received monthly. He made a mental note to inquire about her before leaving town, but he truly doubted she shared company with his companions, a group of stern scholars, eccentric psychics, and fellow writers. What was her first name? Miss Holmes, he recalled, but he should have brought her letter with him, which also would have contained her address.

A pity he'd left it at home.

CHAPTER SIX

A troubling pest returns.

Lillian hid behind an ornamental column of the Union Station building, watching for the emergence of the Staring Man. How could she have been so stupid, letting Thomas speak openly of a murder in such a setting?

Once sure she hadn't been followed, she waited for the stranger to appear. The October sun should be less strong, she grumbled to herself. While she didn't mind the daytime as much as George, it *did* have some effect on her, turning her mood a bit dourer, draining her energy. But so essential was it to get her former governess and butler out of Baltimore, she'd arranged for a grand trip for the brother and sister. They would stay in Chicago with their cousin for several weeks and then see some of the Western wonders that intrigued Thomas so much. A shame, the great White City was long gone from Chicago. Even Lillian would have liked to see its spectacular offerings.

Lillian leaned in an unladylike fashion against the building, not caring much what anyone thought, exhausted by so many threads that needed mending, required her attention. She couldn't put everyone in Baltimore on a train. What of Aileen and the boys? What would Phillip do about Kitty? And she thought of Bess with a pang of hurt that was never far away. Bess had perhaps come upon the truth of Lillian's existence but had evidently not shared her knowledge with anyone else. That proof of her love frustrated Lillian even more.

"I would have my Watson back," she whispered. But, no. Bess was now out of harm's way. She wouldn't suffer Annaluisa's fate.

Lil shuddered and pulled herself out of her dreary thoughts as the Staring Man exited the building, joined by a porter and a companion about his age and social standing, chatting amiably with him.

"No, that was *The Murders in the Rue Morgue!* Ah, had he lived, so I might pay the homage due to him. I would see his grave before leaving Baltimore," the Staring Man said.

His companion sighed in agreement. "Well, his second cousin twice removed, I think it is, bears the same name and is in our group. I'm unsure whether it is a boon or curse to bear that name, but it did him no harm, as he was graduated from Princeton and has done quite well for himself, as you will see."

"Indeed? Is he a poet?"

"A lawyer."

"He's more reputable and much less interesting than his cousin, I would imagine."

"He is my dearest friend; you must give him a chance," the other man chided lightly.

So, Lil thought, *a quite learned gent,* for rarely did one hear praise of Edgar Allan Poe these days. And he was a Scottish gentleman with a pleasant expressive voice. Perhaps a man of forty or so years …

She suppressed a squeal of delight.

"I was terribly sorry to hear about Louisa's state," the Scotsman's American companion said. The Scotsman simply inclined his head. The two were standing in line for a hansom, and the next driver urged his horse to move up and accept passengers, so Lillian could hear no more of their conversation as they embarked. But she hurried to the following driver and motioned him down.

The man's horse fretted at her nearness and whinnied and tapped at the cobbles. Lillian hated that animals sensed her true nature and now reacted negatively to her. Even Mr. Lincoln gave her a wider berth these days.

"Now, Sophie, quiet with you!" The driver pulled a bit of apple from his pocket and offered it to the horse, who wouldn't be calmed. Lillian stepped back a yard and motioned for the driver to join her.

"Where to, miss?"

"I will pay you double your fare—no, *quadruple* your fare—if you would follow that carriage in front of us and then report to me the final destination of the taller of the two passengers. An extra reward for your total secrecy."

The driver grinned and tipped his hat. "Not the first time, not the last, miss. But you must hurry before he turns down Howard. Traffic is fierce this time of day! How do I find you?"

Lillian reached into her satchel and tore a corner off of an envelope she thought to mail to Bess. It is a sign, she thought. *Leave Bess be.* "Here is the address. If I am not about, my maid will take the information. Here is one note for you, another upon the completion of the task."

The driver's grin turned to awe, and Lillian realized how truly naïve he must think her. No matter, Mr. Conan Doyle meant the world to her. She intended to learn why he stared at her, and if he'd heard her discussion. Why, how wonderful and terrible to meet her hero in such a fashion! She couldn't wait to tell George. Of course, she would leave out the part where he stared at her, lest George scold her about needing to be more circumspect. Or worse.

She decided to walk home, lighter of spirit for having seen her hero in person, regardless of his opinion of her. Lost in thoughts of George, Mr. Doyle, and a gnawing hunger to feed within a few hours, she walked up Charles Street, the sun casting long shadows as it began descending behind the towering five-story buildings of the city.

"I am here for you, waiting."

Lil froze and swung around in a circle, scanning for the speaker. Everyone went on normally; no one was close. The *clip-clop* and clang of the tinker driving next to her made the most pronounced noise.

"Don't forget me. Come back tonight and ride. I'll show you the way!"

She stopped, feeling a vertigo that hadn't plagued her since George helped cure her addiction. *God help me, not again!*

The voices grew louder, and she covered her ears—with no result.

"Forget about George, forget about everything but riding, riding fast. Come see the dark treasures I have waiting for you!"

"No! Stop it! Be gone!"

A man turned to see what was amiss and started to approach her, but she held out her hand in warning. *God help me, God help me.* The city spoke to her again, words only she heard. How could it be? It had been the morphine before. How could she hear such things now, so pure her blood, so immortal her body? The Jackal and Dr. Schneider were long dead; no one poisoned her mind or her blood; there was no one to lock her in an asylum again. Was that where she truly belonged? This she couldn't share with George. Her hands shook as they hadn't in weeks.

She stumbled toward home, and a woman practically collided with her, a mere silhouette in the blinding setting sunlight. A lilac *eau de toilette* had been applied so profusely that it created a sickly sweet curtain around the woman, who, rather than offering an apology, chuckled.

Lillian's head ached so that she didn't turn to see who had been so rude.

"You can't ignore me forever, my dear!"

But had the woman spoken, or was it the city again?

CHAPTER SEVEN

A honeymoon is over before it starts.

"I thought you'd be happier." George tried to keep the frustration out of his voice. Lillian had been through enough in the last months to last an average mortal a lifetime. Still, why didn't she seem remotely pleased about the plan Phillip and he had constructed over three hours of debate?

She would stay with him in Baltimore and be free to search for her child. Kitty, albeit a very angry woman, would be spirited away by Phillip to New York, where Phillip would recruit Sullivan and any of the New York House he could convince to help fight Marie. On the way back he would rustle up some of the "ruffians" of Philadelphia if he could, hoping to appeal to their mercenary instincts. Whether any of it would work George had grave doubts, but he was certainly willing to try, as the alternatives were running, perhaps forever, or dying a gruesome death at Marie's hand.

"I'm not feeling well, George. Just a bit of a headache." Lillian rustled through her satchel, banging her pistol on her desk.

"I've not seen you so careless, Lil. That isn't loaded, is it?"

She didn't answer but continued to fumble through her bag.

"What are you looking for?" he asked. But he knew and his heart sank. What desperation she must be feeling to search for a pill so openly. "How did it go with the Adencourts? Off safely? We must discuss your household, for surely Marie will target those living in—"

"I said I'm not feeling well! Cannot I have a moment's peace?"

George sat, stunned. In the few months he'd known her, Lillian had not once spoken so sharply. She'd already gone through the initial anger and shock that came with the change, and he'd found intense relief that she hadn't come to loathe her maker—at least, not yet. At least, he had thought that the case. His heart ached at the possibility his unexpected fortune—no, his unexpected salvation—might be at an end. Perhaps she didn't love him.

But, such a change in the space of a day? Why, just last night they'd shared a bed, shared secret thoughts and desires, expressed love and devotion. No, this was an aberration.

"Come on, let's dine. Down to the docks for your favorite menu—"

"I'll eat a rat or a cat, as that's all I seem to manage on my own!" She looked up at him, eyes rimmed in red and hair falling from its chignon.

"Lil?"

"May I not have this night alone? I have been so worried of late about Marie and about your safety, about finding my child…I must recoup my strength a bit. I must have some quiet. Do you understand?"

She might as well have taken a knife and plunged it into his chest. Why didn't she want to share her troubles with him? He was her *maker*. And her *lover*.

"Of course." He would not argue, so George stood and gathered up his coat and hat, wondering how such simple acts could feel so unfamiliar and awkward. He felt frozen in time, as if each motion were captured by an artist. Was it the end? If so, he would remember this moment forever. She had loved him despite his evil, loved him for his peculiarities. He had loved her for hers.

She turned toward her desk and he resisted going to her and planting a kiss on her head before leaving.

"I will see you tomorrow, George."

"Lil?"

She didn't turn. He craved to stroke her raven hair, to thread his fingers through it and nibble on her neck, to hold her so she could never get away.

"Marie is in town," he reminded her, just to be cautious. "You understand how tenuous things are, do you not?"

"Yes. I will be careful."

"There is no amount of care that can be taken to guard against her. At least, not with our current numbers. You are unsafe out of my sight."

"Unsafe with or without you, so what does it matter?"

Another knife thrust. They were hounded by a devil, and Lillian might be giving up on everything.

As he left her house, George prayed for perhaps the second time in a century.

* * *

Lillian flattened out a page of her journal, intending to write about seeing Mr. Conan Doyle. She also listened for any commotion at the door that might be the hansom driver with information on the author's whereabouts.

Not telling George had been difficult. Very difficult. And yet, it hadn't seemed the time or place to point out the presence of a man who had expressed an interest in vampires. She was still embarrassed about her mistake. God, how angry would George be if he learned she'd discussed a murder before one of the greatest investigative minds ever? And Doyle was a physician, she remembered, who might recognize more quickly the peculiarities of her person.

Peculiarities. Her hand shook too much to write. Not all of her peculiarities were related to vampirism. Why had the voices returned? What would George think of her, should she tell him that the old delusions had resurfaced and were not related to her medicine? Would he believe her that she hadn't yet taken a pill? He hadn't hated her for it before, but he'd gone to great lengths to help her recover.

Perhaps I am truly insane, she thought. *And if I am insane, I am not worthy of George. I will certainly put him and his brother and all they care about at more risk than I already have. Mr. Doyle. I cannot even remember what I said to him!*

When feeling her best, she had been reckless in her letter to Mr. Doyle. What would she do to endanger George's secrets if she were hearing voices, running down the streets of Baltimore, pushing past strangers and talking to herself? What choice would George have but to lock her away? God, how could she have imagined herself fit to be a mother?

Perhaps…perhaps it was simply the stress of things, the constant worry, the recent changes in her body and mind. Not being able to speak honestly to her friends, not being able to do anything normal… It thrilled her to catch criminals in the act and dispose of them before they could do mortal harm, but sometimes, sometimes she chastised herself. Weren't those criminals still human? Did she enjoy being judge and executioner a bit too much? Where was her former strict adherence to law and order? Was "justice" simply an excuse to tear into a neck and suck a body dry, to feel the life throb in her veins and strength stir in her limbs? It came close to the ecstasy she shared with George in their bed, and at times even exceeded it. Had her metamorphosis left her with any sanity, any humanity?

Do you truly want me to find you, my child? She had already assigned a name to her missing girl: Jane. Lovely Jane—with long dark hair, no doubt. Lillian refused to believe the child had inherited any of her rapist father's looks or temperament. *But are you any better than he, Lillian? You're a devil yourself.*

Where is she? Why can't I find a clue? And there were no good choices about the future.

Too much, too much. Lillian laid her head on her desk and wept until she had no strength to even change her clothes. She closed her journal and opened her desk drawer to return the book to its proper place. As she did, one tiny pill rolled forward. Her medicine. Lillian stared at it and wondered, for the thousandth time, if Jane would want to be found. If her own mother would want to be found. And what they would think of her should she be successful in her search.

She should not have sent George away. But she would make it right tomorrow, she swore, and she put the journal back and picked up the pill.

CHAPTER EIGHT

An unlikely friendship develops.

Johnnie Moran tapped lightly on his commander's door, his stomach turning with worry. Lieutenant Worthington rarely had good tidings to deliver in person, so this likely meant trouble. How would he support his brother if he lost this post? What had he done? What hadn't he done? Damn it all, he'd been preparing to propose to Aileen, to take her two young brothers into his household—

A grunt of acknowledgment and the sound of a chair sliding on the wood floor made him pull his thoughts together. He'd take misfortune like a man and do whatever needed doing. Hadn't that been the case since he was a boy?

He entered his commander's room and took off his cap.

"Moran, have a seat," Worthington directed. The Walrus, named for his enormous whiskers, had company much to Johnnie's surprise—a stranger, a well-dressed man who seemed to take him in with one quick glance.

The Lieutenant made introductions and returned to his seat behind a cluttered desk. "Johnnie here will be able to tell you a bit more about the Rennard murder. It's one of a half-dozen over the last year that come to mind. Despicable. We aren't prone to such violence, I assure you, Mr. Doyle. These anomalies *may* be the work of a single man. A regular Henry Holmes he seems to be, although his targets are not only women and children."

"Ah, I'm only vaguely familiar with your famous Henry Holmes. Sensational cases, I understand."

"You didn't name your Mr. Sherlock Holmes after America's serial killer, did you?" the Lieutenant asked with wry humor.

"Ah! Indeed, I did not! It's a most unfortunate coincidence."

"Fortunately—and I mean that speaking as a native of this city—most of his horror was perpetrated in Chicago during the World's Fair in 'Ninety-three, although he managed to collect victims on the eastern seaboard as well. Many of them children. Some estimates put the number of victims as high as two hundred."

"Dear Lord, he makes our Ripper seem a choirboy in comparison."

"Well, his execution brought some note of satisfaction."

Doyle nodded. "If I had written his story, I would have been accused of creating a profoundly unbelievable villain."

Johnnie sat up straighter, fascination overcoming his nerves. "Why, *Sherlock Holmes the detective?* You are the writer? Oh, I have a friend who would like very much to make your acquaintance straightaway!"

Worthington cleared his throat and shook his head slightly, an annoyed frown quickly masked as he turned to Doyle. Johnnie's flush crept down to his collar. Why couldn't he hold his tongue? As if this gentleman would socialize with a friend of his. He desperately wanted to add that it was a lady of society, but Worthington would have his head.

But, Miss Holmes would also never forgive him if he didn't do his best to put them together. So he would find a way to tell Miss Holmes that didn't jeopardize his position.

Doyle made some mild noise of interest without answering. He leaned forward and, hands tented on his lap, stared at Johnnie with anticipation. But the next words he spoke were not about his fictional creation. "This may strike you as a bit strange, Officer Moran, but I am quite interested in unusual phenomena, including psychic connections with the spirit world and other evidence of a plain of existence we cannot see with our eyes."

What?

Worthington cast a quick warning glance at Johnnie, who managed to remain focused on the guest.

"I see," Johnnie said.

"I read in your newspaper about the murder of the gypsy woman on the roof."

"Yes…" Johnnie resisted squirming a bit in his seat, wondering again where the devil this was leading. *Had* he done something wrong? Perhaps he shouldn't have discussed the case so openly with his friends.

"Tell me what you saw, if you would," Doyle said.

"Well, not a real gypsy, sir. A gypsy woman would have darker skin, at least by the few I've seen. Of course, it might have been the sun and the shriveling… Hard to tell what she looked like."

"Scarves, colorful scarves, and many layers of chains and wrist ornaments, the newspaper report said."

"Oh, yes, she looked dressed for the circus. Like one of those fortune-tellers. That is what I meant by gypsy."

"Precisely, my good man!" Doyle turned to Worthington and added, "I wish you hadn't already buried her. Perhaps I could have been more certain."

"There wasn't much of the body to see, sir. Shriveled, like a mummy. Otherwise I would try to get an order for exhumation. It wouldn't help."

Doyle frowned. "If that is my acquaintance, her body should not have deteriorated so in such a short time. Why, I corresponded with her only last week! But it does sound like her. A terrible tragedy. She seemed to truly have the gift."

"And what was her name again, Mr. Doyle?" Worthington took up his pen.

"I knew her as Madam Annaluisa Pelosi, although I am unsure if that was her given name. In truth, I heard her once claim to be French and on another occasion to be from New Orleans, which is where I corresponded with her. She toured through England and Scotland, as well as France, giving extraordinary exhibitions of her talents. She was to entertain at the meeting last evening I discussed with you. My lecture fell somewhat flat without her performance to enhance it. We were sorely disappointed she did not keep her appointment. Had we known…" He let out a sigh and seemed genuinely troubled by her apparent loss.

Johnnie rubbed at his chin. *Madam Annaluisa Pelosi.* Why was that name familiar? He'd not met any fortune-teller, yet… Wait! Hadn't Aileen said that Miss Holmes and Miss Wheeler saw a fortune-teller at a dinner party? "I—"

Worthington coughed to interrupt him.

"But—"

Another cough and a quick hand gesture of dismissal. "Thank you, Johnnie."

The Scottish gentleman stood and offered his hand, a generous gesture Johnnie felt. Evidently *he* didn't think Johnnie lower than the oyster-shuckers and shoeblacks. "Thank you, officer," the man said, "for your help."

"I didn't get a chance—"

Worthington stood with a look that said the next word would bring serious consequences.

Johnnie left. Shutting the door behind him, he muttered, "Pompous fellow. He should learn something from Mr. Doyle."

Straightening his coat and hat, he quit the station at a fast pace to begin his shift. At least he had harbor patrol tonight, which would put him in a neighborhood where cursing on the street was not only common but an essential part of keeping the peace. He had plenty of curses on the tip of his tongue of late.

Johnnie had taken but a few steps when a tap on his shoulder made him spin around. *Doyle.* And the man had a smile for him.

A friendly poke of a walking stick to his chest and a twinkle in the man's eye put Johnnie at ease. "Forgive me, Officer," the Scotsman said, "as I do not wish to put you at odds with your commander, but may I walk with you for a moment? I have the feeling we left something unsaid."

"I don't think the Walrus would be happy to see me talking with you," Johnnie warned.

Doyle chuckled and brushed at his own mustache. "The Walrus, is it? Don't fear, Officer Moran. I asked for an escort back to my hotel. Can't be too careful in a foreign city."

"It's not *that* dangerous in daylight here, sir. Not every visitor is murdered on the roof of their lodgings."

Doyle remained silent, and Johnnie regretted coming terribly close to calling the great man a coward. Doyle didn't know the city, perhaps didn't even know his way back to his hotel.

"At least you'll be safe from pickpockets in my company, sir!"

Doyle laughed. "Capital. Do call me Arthur."

Johnnie straightened, suddenly hoping the pompous Walrus was watching. *Won't Aileen be proud when I tell her this great man asked me to call him Arthur!*

CHAPTER NINE

Driving the snakes from America.

Phillip put his finger to Kitty's mouth to silence her gasps at the magnificence of the cathedral. He reminded himself that while he'd lived in a castle and seen the natural and manmade treasures the world had to offer, Kitty's life had started on a small farm in Ireland. Since she was a girl, she'd spent nearly all her time as a cleaning woman for a bakery, a jewelry shop, and two spinster sisters in Baltimore. Her artistic talent had brought her some modest success recently and she could now live in comfort without his fortune, but even her love for a vampire hadn't purged her totally of naivety. She was devoted to her Catholic God, and now she was in His house.

Phillip shrugged, having seen far grander cathedrals, but he didn't mention that to Kitty, who rushed to put a penny in the box and to light a candle. He knelt next to her and whispered, "Do not move from this spot, Kitty. I will try to make this quick."

She stared up at him, her beautiful blue eyes sad. "Does it hurt you to be in a church?"

"Oh, love, no, it does not at all!"

But he lied. It hurt just a bit. He could dip his hand in blessed water and make the sign of the cross without consequence, but an irrational fear that some great holy man might divine his true nature always nagged at him. No matter, though. How many truly holy men resided in New York?

He sniffed out a laugh and rubbed at Kitty's shoulder. "Whether he is here or not, I'll be but a moment. At least, that is my hope."

Phillip had found Chauncey Sullivan's home easily enough, but not the man. He didn't expect to find the giant in church despite the wife's assurances; no doubt Chauncey had made excuses to her to cover other escapades. But, as Phillip strode quietly along the aisle, he saw his quarry midway up the nave, sitting in a central pew.

So, Sullivan's yearning for redemption was this deep? This boded well for his mission.

Phillip slid into the pew next to Chauncey and moved close.

The vampire didn't even turn, just threaded his fingers together as if to calm himself. He said, "How long has it been, Phillip?"

"You don't seem surprised to see me."

"Somehow, I'm not. Phoebe is a trusting sort, isn't she?"

"She's lovely. I'm happy for you."

"Yes, she is. She frets for me, wanting me to pray but worrying for me when I come here to do it."

"You don't strike me as superstitious, Chauncey. The holy water and crucifix won't hurt you."

Sullivan turned to Phillip with a smirk. "The good fathers would drag me out for being a Negro, Phillip. It is why I come only at night. That's a bit ironic, wouldn't you say?"

Phillip groaned, and they sat in silence for a minute, taking in the gilt and glowing candles that threw shadows on the altar and statues. Then Phillip suggested, "You could go anywhere, live as a king in another land."

"You *were* a king, as I recall. Or was that your brother? Did it bring much happiness?"

"You're really as miserable as I recall. Isn't it time you put all that in the past?"

Chauncey turned, an inscrutable expression on his face. "I sense you are going to tell me exactly what I should do to obtain a bit of peace. I also sense that you came to New York to find me for a very particular purpose." He stared harder at Phillip. "I'm feeling a bit peckish, so get on with it."

Phillip rubbed his hands together, fully aware that Chauncey could kill him in an instant. "Your Marie de Bourbon is hounding us, Chauncey. She's killed Annaluisa Pelosi and takes direct aim at George. We don't know why, but there's a rumor she's put a price on his head. Perhaps she's taken this long to want to destroy her maker."

Chauncey's expression did not change. "Always liked you, Phillip. Never much liked your brother."

"He liked you, though. After all, you are as a grandchild to him. George is a tough one to—"

"Of course I'll help you."

What? Just like that, Chauncey was willing to go up against his maker? No protests, no conditions? Phillip had been ready to offer Chauncey leadership of a Baltimore House with allegiance from the Orleans brothers; a small prize, but something. Now he blew out a deep breath and kept silent.

"Just keep Georgy at a distance. He gets under my skin."

Why? Why would you do this? But aloud: "Of course. We'll talk more about it…when you come to Baltimore."

Chauncey reached into his coat and clutched something close to his chest. For a moment, Phillip thought the vampire might pull out a dagger, so he slid away a few feet and stood. "Right. Wonderful, then! My home is—"

"I wondered where she was, and how I'd hear about it." Chauncey shook his head. "I'll find you. Say nothing of this to Phoebe. She doesn't know about Marie. About *us.* "

"What doesn't she know? That she is your maker?"

Chauncey glared and arched a brow. "Phoebe might give up on rescuing my soul if she knew who turned me."

Phillip shuddered. "Oh. No, of course I'll say nothing." He paused. "Well, then, I'll be on my way and leave you to your prayers."

"Prayers?" Chauncey chuckled. "I simply like the stained glass. The images. They help me think. To plan."

Phillip nodded, wondering if the man had evaded insanity after all.

He rushed to the back of the church and grabbed Kitty by the hand. She protested, "I'm not finished praying."

"You can pray on the train home, dear."

"Whatever is wrong? Did you find your man? You look like you saw a ghost!"

Phillip nodded. "I feel like I saw a ghost."

CHAPTER TEN

Miss Holmes's nighttime rendezvous.

George lit his pipe, knowing that neither the smell nor flicker of the match would be seen or smelled from two stories below.

He'd sat like a gargoyle throughout the night, feet hanging over the edge of Lillian's roof, watching for activity below. A cab had pulled in front of her house and the driver spoke briefly with the maid, Aileen, but then left whistling happily. That was curious, but surely not the work of Marie de Bourbon. No one had died, at least not as far as George could tell.

Hunger gnawed at him, but he wouldn't leave Lillian alone with that she-devil running loose in the city. As Lil had noted, rather coldly, there might not be much he could do to protect her, but she was a target because of her love for him and he wouldn't abandon her. At least, not until she ordered him to.

He'd relived the scene over and over: how dismissive she'd sounded, how willing to be without him. They'd not been apart since the night he saved her mortal life and gave her his own blood as sustenance. Well, except for a few nights before, when he'd felt her slip out of bed and heard her tiptoe out of the room. He'd thought to let her hunt alone for the first time, to give her the gift of confidence. Surely she hadn't gone to another man?

He couldn't imagine being apart from her ever again, but evidently she could. He had been a fool, so used to women falling at his feet—literally and figuratively—that he'd assumed Lil would feel the same.

Phillip had chided him earlier in the night when he returned home, tail between his legs. "You speak as if you've never known a woman's temper, George. I know damn well you've angered legions of them. Perhaps Lillian is simply tired. It happens. Not every acerbic tone means the end of things. You'd last five minutes with Kitty. Now, speaking of angry women, I have to gather up mine and sweep her off to New York. If I don't come back, you'll know it didn't go well with Sullivan."

"You were always well-liked, Phillip," George had promised. "He'll hear you out at least. I know he'd slam the door in my face. Seems that everyone feels that way these days."

"Oh, blazes, George. You're picking a sorry time for one of your fits of self-pity. Let it go, and visit Lillian in the morning. You forget what it is to be newborn, to wrestle with all those annoying deep thoughts that inevitably arise. And buy her something pretty. Women like pretty things in my experience."

"Buy her something? She lacks for nothing."

"Oh, if we get through this horrid adventure you'll need a long talk with my Kitty. Your courtship manners are sorely lacking."

"I'm not courting her," George had snapped. "I'm her maker."

"That may be the problem. Take it from another of your children. Now leave me to my packing."

"Release her?" George had guessed at his brother's meaning. "Release her from our bond? She's not ready! She wasn't even making sense today. Phillip, I think she may be taking her medicines again. I pray not, but…"

Phillip looked up. "When *will* she be ready? When is anyone? Is she the one who is not ready, or do you wish to hold her close no matter the consequences? You have power over an obstinate, eccentric woman that a normal man wouldn't. Surely you see that. The sooner you can release that bond, the better."

She is not ready, George knew. But Phillip was. How many times had he come close to releasing his brother's bond only to pull back in fear that they'd never speak again? How many tests would Phillip have to pass before being granted the dignity he so assuredly deserved?

He does not even fight me over it, George thought. *He thinks me afraid.* How could his brother be so generous? How could George himself be such a coward?

Sitting on Lillian's roof, George wondered what pretty thing she might like and tried to put his brother out of his mind. *Buy her something? A new pistol? Another book on poisons? She needs new goggles.* But Phillip had said something pretty, and he had no idea what that meant to Lillian.

He'd done his best nonetheless. He already had something to give to her.

"Feckless idiot," he murmured aloud in the tone his mother had so often used to say the same. Then he quieted when he heard a rustling in the yard.

He crept to the back edge of the property to see his Lil, dressed like a boy, mounting a contraption and walking it toward the street. He knew he should call out to her, be honest with her about his presence, but curiosity won. Did she go to meet another? Is that what the driver had been about, arranging a tryst? His blood boiled at the thought. And she was putting herself at risk, going out alone at night!

Stupid George, she's a vampire. Only another vampire can harm her. And if it's Marie de Bourbon, what will you do but join Lil and die?

She was probably just hungry. But she liked flying so very much and was so much better at it than him. Why would she ride that motorcycle?

George wondered what else he didn't know about Lillian—a million things, probably—as he trailed her from above. He wanted to know all those things, but would he ever get the chance to learn? How arrogant it had been to take her for granted, how perfectly like him. He'd made her, and in truth owned her. That's how he thought. But this was not a woman to be owned, cajoled, guided, or bribed. Everyone in her life had robbed her of power, and he had been doing the same. No wonder her resentment built.

Lillian rode north, away from the harbor, at a dizzying speed. What was so urgent? And why hadn't she confided in him? He leapt from building to building until rooftops became so sparse that he was forced into the true flights he could maintain for only minutes at a time. This would exhaust him in due course, but not before she would run out of fuel—he hoped. She'd torn off her cap, and her long hair whipped wildly about her face as she approached Druid Hill Park.

Where in God's name is she going?

They were approaching the city limits when she slowed a bit and turned down a barely lit lane. This far away from the center of things, the stars shone brightly and George could see her in the moonlight. She cut the engine and leaned her bike against a lamppost, and he landed on a roof and watched her. She pulled a paper from her pocket and looked east toward the great mansion at the end of the lane. George presumed it was her final destination.

"Mansion" was a bit of an understatement. Someone in Baltimore had constructed a gothic monstrosity on the edge of a modern city, no doubt many decades earlier. If a public work, the architect should be promptly sued and the building razed. If it was a private residence, and it seemed to be, the owner had the poorest taste. George had not seen such a building in America. It combined, rather uncomfortably, sprawling porches on three sides and castle-like turrets on two of its corners.

As she made her way forward, Lillian ducked behind trees and bushes. So, she was unlikely an invited guest to the mansion, which soothed George's ire. His Lil was being a detective. But, was he not to share in those adventures with her? Had she indeed ceased to trust him? He followed at a distance, wondering if she felt that he kept her under lock and key. She needed so much nurturing, so much instruction. Perhaps he'd underestimated her desire to sleuth about.

When she reached the property, she scurried along the porch and leaned her back against the house, listening at a great bay window open to the night air. George approached with care, keeping his eyes on her should she need help. Then, to his very great amazement, she waved her hand in his direction, motioning for him to get down.

Impossible! He looked around, wondering if someone else was about, but no, he was alone.

With a great leap, he landed noiselessly at her side. She cautioned him to further silence with a finger to her lips, and he winked in answer, thrilled to be included. Had she known he was following her the entire time?

No one seemed to be inside the great room, but Lil waited and George stood close behind her, letting the scent of her hair fill him, letting the pull of her pale neck send lightning through his veins. As if she read his thoughts or perhaps just felt the same, she leaned back against him and rubbed her hand along his thigh.

He bent in and kissed her ear, her neck, and pressed his hand over her mouth lest she make a noise. Then he spun her around and pushed her against the stone. Her dilated pupils and fast heart rate confirmed his fears. She'd taken her drugs.

"Why are you here, Lil?" George asked as he fondled her and pressed kisses on her cheeks, unable to help himself.

"Why are *you* here?" she whispered back, arching into his caress.

"I'm ashamed to say I dislike any distance between us. I don't want to give you a moment's peace. You will have to fight me for solitude or send me away."

"Then I will fight, for I do need occasional solitude." But clearly she hadn't lost her taste for him completely. She wrapped her fingers in his hair and pulled him down for a deep kiss with one hand.

When he let out a moan, she smothered it with another kiss. "Quiet! Mr. Conan Doyle is within!"

"What?" He spoke louder than intended.

"Quiet, you idiot!"

"'Idiot'? What are we doing here? And how the blazes did you know I followed you? And more importantly, what is this about Conan Doyle?"

"I believe this is where Mr. Doyle's society meets. I saw him today at the station. How did you enjoy the evening on my roof?"

"It was splendid. If you knew I was there, you could have at least invited me in. Now, what do we care about this society? Lil, we must concentrate on Marie. This pastime isn't the best use of your—"

"Pastime, is it?" She blew out a breath, and he waited for her ire. But: "I suppose it is. I would rather consider it a profession, as spinster heiress isn't very impressive."

"God, I didn't mean... Look, this isn't the time for this discussion." *Spinster heiress? Is this the cause of her petulance?* He shook his head. "All right, we'll do it your way. Tell me what you hope to accomplish here and I'll assist you."

"It is a long story, but the crux is that Doyle knew Annaluisa."

"Where did you hear this?"

"From Aileen. Johnnie Moran met the man today, and they conversed for a good while. It seems Annaluisa was to perform a séance for this society last night. That is what this group is all about: psychics and spiritual goings-on. The appearance was scheduled a few months ago, before she became embroiled in this Marie de Bourbon debacle."

"God, what did Johnnie tell Doyle? Do you think he knows about us, that she was a vampire?"

"I don't think so, but I came to find out what Mr. Doyle believes. He does know Annaluisa was drained of life on the roof of the Rennard, and now the police have a strong lead on the identity of the victim. If they were friends, perhaps Doyle knows something mo—"

George motioned for quiet as a light was flicked on inside and friendly chatter filled the great room. A man in black, likely a butler, opened the window, and George and Lillian hung back in the dark.

"I thought we agreed you would not speak with the man," he whispered in her ear. George hardly thought Annaluisa would have mentioned Lil's mother to Mr. Conan Doyle, but Lil would evidently leave no stone unturned. "You have not learned to be circumspect at all."

"I believe you agreed with yourself."

George groaned. He had few choices. He could force her to leave with his maker's will, but she would be furious. Or he could risk revealing too much to this silly society.

The event seemed to be convening, as all the attendees became quiet except for one. This one said, "I call this meeting to order. Last night's lecture was a wonderful start to Mr. Doyle's visit, but tonight we have the chance to speak more openly without the larger audience present, as we are all brothers in arms. Excuse me, Miss Langhan, brothers *and a sister.*"

"Etta Langhan!" Lillian mouthed to George, and he rolled his eyes. So, now there were two people who knew them inside: Etta and Mr. Doyle. That busybody Langhan woman would be the death of him. An intimate friend and patron of Kitty and her artwork, Etta appeared at the most inopportune times.

"For the record, Miss Langhan, would you kindly record the presence of our members in addition to yourself? Guest member Arthur Conan Doyle, the honorable Charles Coyle, Henry Holt, Edgar Poe, George Frederick, and yours truly, Henry Grattan Donnelly." There was a pause before, "Would anyone like anything else to drink…? That is all, James."

George wanted to scream. These men might have some foolish notions, but they were men of stature. A congressman, an influential publisher, a lawyer, a writer of some small note, and a writer of great note. Oh, and that Frederick fellow, Baltimore's premiere architect. How had Etta Langhan burrowed her way into the mix? Well, George supposed it was the woman's forte.

He exchanged a glance with Lillian, hoping tonight's meeting was not on the subject of vampire-banishing and that the death of Annaluisa wouldn't even come up, but Doyle dashed his hopes within moments, after some foolish protocols of the society.

"I have rather grim news to report this evening. The psychic who was to be my partner last evening has been dead these few days. You may have read about the murder on the roof of the Rennard. Her name was Annaluisa Pelosi. I had the pleasure of knowing the woman, albeit not as much as I would have liked. She was a great proficient."

Damnation, George thought.

The murmurs of the group were topped by a squeal of horror from Miss Langhan. "Why, I knew the woman. She *was* a great proficient, as you say. This is terrible news. She was often a guest at a friend's house."

A friend? This time, Lillian groaned. Etta would not shut up, of that they were both certain.

"See why we must be here, George?" Lillian asked.

Inside, the discussion continued. "Are you able to name the friend, Miss Langhan, or is the situation sensitive?"

"Oh, of course. Two brothers, Phillip and George Orleans. They own the great shipyard, so perhaps you have heard of them? They are not out in society much, but I am patron to artist Kitty Twamley who is to marry Phillip Orleans at Christmas. Kitty must be crushed by this news." Etta paused. "I assume the brothers are believers, as they were friends of Madam Pelosi, although they seemed to regard the séance at their house as entertainment. They are queer fellows, indeed, keeping mostly to themselves."

"How so?" asked Doyle after a moment.

"When Phillip began courting Kitty, she said some odd things about the man which she has since denied." Etta laughed as if embarrassed. "I suppose because of my interest in the spirit realm I may have misunderstood her. George spends his time now in the company of a very well-to-do lady of society, Miss Lillian Holmes. I suspect a wedding sometime next year."

"Lillian Holmes! How extraordinary!"

Doyle's distinctive Scottish brogue boomed through the night, sounding a terrible alarm it seemed to George. *What a mess.* He cast a look at Lillian, wondering what she thought of the mention of a wedding. She fished through her sack for something, but he knew she hadn't missed a word.

One of the other men spoke. "Do you know this woman, Arthur?"

"I've corresponded with her. She wrote initially as a reader of my stories, but her letters have been out of the ordinary to say the least. Miss Holmes seems to believe she has met vampires in Baltimore!"

This brought chuckles and a joke from one of the men inside, which pleased George; he did not want them taking the matter seriously. "She must have attended the legal convention in town last year!"

"I say!" another voice protested, but with a good-natured tone.

Then Etta Langhan hammered the last nail in the coffin. "Why, that is what Kitty Twamley thought of her beau at first!"

There came silence, and George almost groaned. Doyle wouldn't pass off *everything* as a coincidence or the ramblings of a busybody. He would likely have to be handled now.

Another man spoke, albeit quietly. "You don't think this murder of Mr. Doyle's friend is related to the deaths of our former members last month, do you?"

Last month? George shuddered. God help them, but did this man mean the Jackal and Dr. Schneider? He glanced at Lillian, who obviously wondered the same. She looked frightened for the first time that night.

He pulled Lillian close and whispered into her ear. "Heard enough?"

"We must learn what they intend to do about it!"

George tightened his grip on her arm. "Trust me for once. We must not be discovered here. It is time to leave. Unless you would like to murder them all and be done with it? They *must* be talking about your Pemberton and Schneider. It's all piling up too quickly."

Lillian turned her head away, and so much frustration was etched on her face he thought she might be winding up to punch him. Then she glanced out into the night and he let his gaze be led.

When he glanced back at her, she swallowed, hard. Given the look on her face, she may as well have punched him. Had her life become so unbearable that only drugs would dull the ache? Or was she simply that severely addicted, so consumed that the fast he'd helped her live through would have to be repeated again and again?

He couldn't understand how she could ingest opiates, why her vampire body didn't reject them. She did have a few other unusual qualities, too. She shared a fair tolerance of sunshine with his brother Phillip. Her reaction to the change had been especially mild, and she tolerated modest amounts of tea and liquor.

Regardless, she could be totally addicted again and he would not know. She had chosen not to share it with him.

It was time, he thought with some asperity, to leave the premises.

CHAPTER ELEVEN

A failed proposal.

As Lillian watched George sleep, she brushed a lock of his black hair out of his eyes. Slumber had eluded her, although she was exhausted and drowsy from her medicine. At least the voices had stopped, and she hadn't dreamt horrible nightmares these last two nights. She would thank Mrs. Winslow's remedy for that.

This is not logical, Lillian. You blame the medicine for the voices, and now you praise it for stopping them? Which is it? Reason above all else—you are not immune from the rule.

She could not discuss the matter with George or with anyone. He would not want to stay with a lunatic. He had worked so hard to heal her. Well, perhaps he would stay and she was making excuses. The horror of swearing off her medicine had been almost worse than the change from mortal woman to vampire. She would have to go through it again.

Just not yet.

"Would I could sleep now," she muttered. "Forever."

She watched George's steady breathing, his coal-black lashes against pale skin. How beautiful he was, her love. Did he think her as beautiful? He said it rarely, but surely his insistence of being by her side constantly meant something. Upon their return he'd been an attentive lover and fallen asleep from his efforts shortly thereafter. Of course, he was her maker and took the raising of his favorite newborn, as he called her, quite seriously.

Lillian rolled onto her back and stared at the ceiling, listened for the first birdcalls of dawn, the first carriage wheels on the street below. They would not be long now.

"What a fucking mess!" George had cursed as they left the mansion. She'd created a good deal of that mess by corresponding with Mr. Doyle at all, and now they had to find a way to thwart the society's membership before their probing added to an already trying time. And if somehow it came out that George had killed two of their members…

It made no sense, no sense at all. Lillian's head reeled. Too many coincidences, all surrounding her with their threats, closing in on her, whispering that her life would always be such.

No doubt George badly wanted to leave Baltimore now, but with Phillip off rallying the troops he'd feel stuck. Lil's own optimism toward asking Mr. Doyle to help her find her child and mother was dashed. Although she had not given up all hope, she almost longed for a time when the truth was hidden beneath her fantasies, when dear Bess chattered on about silly things, when the worst that would happen in a day was that Musketeers would get into a scrape and she would have to rescue them. She understood, just a little, some of the brooding despair she'd first encountered in George. This was not an easy life. There *was* no easy life.

No, it will not do to brood. Lillian got up and stood before her dresser, silently promising her daughter Jane that she was not forgotten. She reached into the drawer for her bottle of medicine— and slammed it quickly shut at the rustling of the covers behind her.

"Penny for your thoughts," George said. He was propped on one elbow and motioned her back to bed with a finger. She prayed that he was not about to lecture her, but his dawning smirk seemed to counter any such intention.

"You, sir," she said, taken again by the beauty of those dark brown eyes, "should be dressed and ready to take on the challenges of the day. Hear the birds? We've much to plan."

"You, madam, should remove that ridiculous gown and come walking quite slowly, quite provocatively, toward me."

"You, sir, are insatiable."

"I suggest you not throw stones. I have not met a wilder creature in several hundred—"

"George!"

She rushed toward him and beat him about the head with a pillow, but he just laughed and pulled her in for a kiss. "I knew I could get you over here."

She leaned into his arms and wondered what would become of them.

"I have something for you, Lil," he said, releasing her and rising to retrieve a tiny oval box from his coat pocket. "I bought it before perching on your roof to watch over you. Shame on you for letting me sit out in the damned fresh air all evening."

She laughed. "I do not feel sorry for you at all. You didn't trust me." She gave him a sideways glance. "Oh, don't look at me like that. Yes, with good reason, I suppose, but I was certain you would follow me and didn't mind very much."

He held out the velvet box but said nothing.

Her heart thrummed offbeat. *Don't be silly, Lillian!* She tried to sound lighthearted but felt anything else as she said, "It is not my birthday."

"I was present at your new birthday, so consider it a late gift."

Lillian pulled the scarlet ribbon from the box and opened it. Inside lay a stunning ruby ring, with pearls, set in gold.

"I thought the color would be good for you. Not quite blood-red... I didn't want to be cliché."

"It's lovely, George. I'm not sure what to say."

"That will do. Aren't you going to wear it?"

Lillian hesitated, wondering what it meant to give a woman a ring when you hadn't proposed marriage. Bess would come in very handy at this moment to counsel her on the protocol.

She placed it on her right ring finger and stretched out her hand. "It's stunning."

George nodded, eyes hooded, and smiled. "I'm glad you like it."

Then her languid lover vanished. He popped out of bed and pulled on his trousers, his back to her. Dressing quickly he said, "You are right, we have much planning to do. I dearly wish Phillip were back to help, but we'll have to deal with this blasted Society business sooner rather than later."

Ah, yes. "And I must take advantage of this time to look for Jane. Who knows how many days we have left in Baltimore."

"Jane? Oh, I see." George walked back and cupped her cheek with his hand. "Yes, we will discuss what to do about Jane as well. I must go home for a bit, but I'll return this afternoon and we'll chart out a plan. Yes?"

"Of course."

George left in such a hurry that Lillian didn't have time to thank him again for the ring. She rushed to her drawer and took a deep swig of her medicine, to calm the confusion, and then sat on her bed and stared at the gift. What exactly did it mean? What exactly did any of it mean?

After only moments, George broke back through her door, face grim, motioning for her to come downstairs. "I'm so sorry, love. There is terrible news."

"Tell me!" Lillian commanded.

"It's Aileen. Constable Moran is downstairs. It seems…it seems the Devil has struck again."

"What?" Lillian could barely hear through the sudden buzzing in her ears. "What are you saying about Aileen?"

"I'm so sorry, Lil." He pulled her close, and her legs felt as if they would give out.

In a fog, she let George lead her down the stairs to the parlor where Johnnie Moran cradled the lifeless body of her friend and maid of five years. Aileen O'Shaunessy's normally rosy cheeks were white, and her hair hung limply over a bloodied dress. Lillian rushed to Aileen's side to feel for a pulse, hoping that she could offer the girl the same chance she herself had been given when at death's door. Circumspection be damned, she would—

"No, I checked," George whispered.

Lillian hugged Johnnie and wept with him, wiping quickly at her tears so that he could not see that she cried blood. He was not processing much, however, and seemed in severe shock. She could not even get from him where the body had been found.

George pulled her to her feet and held her closely. "We must find the boys. They cannot see this."

"Oh God, what will become of them!" Lillian turned to Johnnie. "Where are the children, Johnnie?"

He still looked as if he didn't recognize her. "They took Abraham outside."

"I'll see to them, Lil." George had to shake her shoulder to get her to look up. "I'll take them to my home for the nonce, until we can figure out the best way to break it to them. Will you be all right here until I return? Will you?"

"Who did this?" Johnnie wailed. "A demon did this! My Aileen, my Aileen!" He rocked her limp form in his arms and stared at Lillian. "Who did this, Miss Holmes? The person who killed the gypsy—it is the same person. I will kill him myself, I swear!"

"I will help you," George said before leaving the house.

"Where did you find her?" Lillian asked again.

"In your rose garden. I saw her last night...alive...so beautiful. I was going to ask her to marry me, but I could not for some reason. I wanted the perfect time, the perfect words. I waited. I waited! If I would have acted we might have spent the night in one another's arms and she would be safe. I came early today, hoping to take her for a nice breakfast. I shouldn't have left her!"

Lillian wanted to ride far away and curl up with her medicine, hide in the park and be alone. "It is not your fault, Johnnie! Do *not* do this to yourself. But we must call for the police and the undertaker."

"I am the police, miss. I didn't protect her. God help me—"

"The children must not see or hear of this just yet. Do you understand? You must be strong. Your brother, her two brothers— we must break it to them gently, but we must also handle it with care and speed."

He nodded, but Lillian was sure he understood nothing of what she'd said. "'It'? My Aileen is nothing but a thing now."

She turned to find someone to help her, but Addie and Thomas were in Chicago. Aileen normally would be the one to send a note through the boys, but now... Lillian began to weep again. Her home would become a morgue if Marie de Bourbon wasn't stopped.

She wiped her tears for a second time and stood, staring at the awful, unreal scene. Guilt and resolution melded within her. *She* had brought this devil into her home, through her love for George, and *she* would exterminate the witch. She would learn all she could from George and Phillip, learn how to build an army to fight this abomination. And she would not fail. Just as she would not fail in finding her daughter.

Rushing to the door to find help, Lillian had the fleeting and contrary intuition that Mr. Conan Doyle might be useful somehow. That was, if he weren't already dead from having a fleeting acquaintance with her.

CHAPTER TWELVE

A sad goodbye and tender hello.

The short religious service over, the mourners, especially the children, flocked to Lillian's side as if she would have some solace to offer. Johnnie Moran stayed kneeling at the graveside, praying and talking to his beloved as the priest left. The gravedigger leaned impatiently on his shovel.

If Lillian thought George inhuman at times, that feeling dissipated when her lover went back to the heartbroken constable and knelt with him, a comforting arm around his shoulders, waiting for the man to finish his goodbyes. Of course, George had seen—and caused—enough death in his lifetime for a thousand men. How would Lil herself ever get used to it? How many people would she outlive? The children clutching at her skirts, Kitty Twamley, who now leaned on Phillip's shoulder... How did Phillip remain so pleasant, so gay, knowing his beloved would wither before him?

Lillian leaned over to ruffle Paddy Moran's hair and wiped the boy's tearstained cheeks. He sucked his thumb, a habit she'd typically scold him for, but what other comfort could she give these children who'd now lost sister and mother, as Aileen had been to all three, even Johnnie's brothers? Well, *she* would have to become their mother, and they would all stay in her home, and she would offer the same to Johnnie, who needed the care of a mother now as well. Phillip and Kitty had wanted to help, too, and for once Lillian would take them up on an offer. And her house was now guarded by someone who had perhaps a slim chance against Marie de Bourbon.

George had described Chauncey Sullivan perfectly: a giant man with arms like tree trunks, a frightening countenance, and a bewilderingly mild personality; once a cannibal, now a sworn foe of those he considered evil, at the top of which list was Marie de Bourbon. He would fight to the death to defend innocents from her. At least, that was what he had promised George and Phillip.

Along with Sullivan, Phillip had secured only one more combatant, Chauncey's lover Phoebe, a slim Negress who was evidently steadfast in her devotion. While the couple now resided with the Orleans brothers, they would appear at odd times during the day, strolling down the street or alley near Lillian's home, but they were eyes everywhere, watching, guarding.

"Shouldn't they be more circumspect?" Lillian had asked George and Phillip.

Phillip shrugged. "I am almost sorry I brought them here. I cannot shake the feeling that Chauncey knew I was coming to retrieve him and has his own motives."

"What do we care, Phil?" George said. "As long as he targets Marie, his motives hardly matter."

Lillian hadn't added that she felt a chill whenever Sullivan was near, but she'd pointed out, "They say so little." George had watched her very carefully these past few days, and she didn't want to give him reason to examine her every move. A deep shame mixed with panic swept through her. *He will take my pills away.*

They had all been interviewed in depth by a Lieutenant Worthington, who, with Johnnie Moran, saw the unmistakable link to Annaluisa's murder. That a pattern had formed, they were sure; exactly what had happened to the women they seemed to have no clue. Johnnie wanted revenge, badly. In the lucid moments he had between fits of overwhelming grief, he spoke of nothing but finding the perpetrator.

At least they were all on the same side, Lillian thought, although the mortals could not share the full complexities of the story.

Kitty gathered Darby into her arms and took Billy by the hand, and Lillian picked up Paddy, and the two women led the boys to the carriage and away from the gentle slope that now swallowed the remains of Aileen. George pulled Johnnie to his feet and encouraged him to follow after. Lillian watched them approach, silhouettes against the sun that climbed higher in the morning sky. Then she saw a figure in the distance.

"My God!" she said, her nerves on fire, wiping away a new round of tears to make sure she wasn't imagining that the woman shaded under a wide nearby oak was her friend.

No, it was true. There was the awkward stance Bess used to hide her disfigurement, the frilly bonnet, the full figure. She had come. For Aileen, no doubt, but she had come. No one else save the vampires, the boys, Kitty and the priest had cared enough to attend. Of course, Bess and Aileen had been friends. Although separated by circumstance, they had chatted on about frocks and men, teased Lillian about her appearance.

That was so long ago, Lil thought. Or so it seemed. Had it only been weeks past that Bess had rejected their friendship, angry at the loss of trust?

She glanced at George, unsure what to do. They were better off alone, he'd said more than once. Even if Bess wanted to renew their friendship, Lillian would be putting her at risk. She would also be putting the secrecy of all vampires at risk.

George followed her glance and straightened in surprise. When he came to her side, he leaned in and whispered, "I know how you have missed her, but that is part of our life. Still, it is your choice. You know the dangers. If she will have you as a friend, you have much to consider."

"Are you saying this to test me?" Lillian asked. "I cannot ignore her. I cannot. Will you command me to walk away?"

"I have never commanded you, Lillian," he whispered.

"No? I suppose not. So I will see her, George."

George smiled sadly and placed a gentle kiss on her forehead. "I know. That is one of the things I admire in you. That loyalty is one of the things that made me…come to care for you."

Out of habit, Lillian straightened her bonnet before approaching Bess lest she be chastised. She swept quickly up the grassy hill, knowing that Bess might flee, but that she had to approach decisively or lose nerve.

When she was several feet away, she saw Bess's tears. Lillian took a few more steps, but her friend held out a warning hand.

"It was so good of you to come, Miss Wheeler," Lillian said. She was horrified that her voice shook, and she wanted to reach into her bag for medicine to calm herself. This matter needed steadiness.

"Aileen was a friend, Miss Holmes."

Bess's chin quivered, and Lillian thought she'd scream if things were to stay so formal. But she did not say so. "Indeed. She loved you well."

"How did she die, Lil? I could find nothing in the paper that I believed. She was as healthy as…healthier than us both."

"A terrible accident."

"Do you know that your left brow arches when you lie? In all of these years I never told you, as it gave me one small advantage where otherwise I would have none."

"Did I lie much?"

Bess sniffed out a tired laugh. "No, no, I cannot say you did. Only when you thanked me for my opinion in clothing." She sighed. "I see you and George are still…connected. I suppose I shall leave, then."

"George?" Lillian repeated. "Is that why you severed our friendship? I have room in my heart for you both!"

"Partly," Bess agreed. "But what is the point of a friendship in which truth is a stranger?"

Lillian felt heat rise to her cheeks, though she knew she appeared as pale as ever to her old friend. She had no answer for Bess, either, for the truth must remain hidden. Secrets, secrets, always secrets.

"I suppose you have not found your child yet?" Bess wiped at her tears and shifted her weight off of her bad foot.

"No. And I would have your help if you could find a way to forgive me. I would have you back, Bess. I would do anything. You can't know how I love you."

"You would do anything?" Bess asked.

"Nearly anything. Anything within my power! You saved my life by running to George for help. You were my Watson. You were...*are*...a wonderful woman. I never deserved such a friendship. I suppose I do not deserve it now."

Bess straightened and stared proudly into Lillian's eyes. "You look unwell, Lil. This new life does not so much agree with you, I think." Then she turned and made her way carefully down the hill toward the path to the entrance of the cemetery.

A voice whispered through Lillian, so faint she might have not heard it for the surrounding stillness. *Always keep secrets. Stay safe, and ride at night so others cannot see you. They want your destruction, they mean you harm. Stay quiet, be still.*

"Stop!" she cried aloud, to silence the voices. But Bess stopped as well, and turned, nearly tripping as her bad foot gave her issue in the damp uneven grass.

Lillian closed the gap and pulled her old friend into an embrace. When she heard the beating of Bess's heart, the rush of blood through her veins, she pushed down the pull it had on her.

"I trust my left brow will remain even now, Bess. You will hate me, and you will flee, but you will have the truth even if you don't believe it."

Bess pushed her away in order to see her face. "You are like George, like Phillip. You are not like me now."

"I am still a woman. I am still full of flaws and all the horrid habits you came to overlook. I..." Lillian could not finish the sentence. She could not quite bring herself to betray George's trust.

She did not need to.

"You are a vampire, or something like it."

"Yes."

"And you will drink my blood or kill me, or offer me as some kind of sacrifice? Or will I, too, become a vampire? Is that how it happens?"

"No!" She stared into her friend's eyes. "I swear that I could not harm you should my own life depend upon it!"

"Your beau might not be so generous. These are rare circles you run in now, Lillian."

"George only hurts those who deserve it. Criminals. *Heinous* criminals."

"I cannot believe we are having this conversation, but I see your brow is level." Bess blew out a deep breath. "I knew it, somehow. It is why you survived the battle with the Jackal."

"Correct."

Bess nodded. "Thank you for the honesty."

Lillian paused. "You could destroy me—*us*—with this knowledge."

"If you do no evil, why would I destroy you?"

"There are days I would destroy myself." Lillian looked away. "It was the only way. I was dying. George gave me a choice. I chose to live."

"Because you love him. And because you want to find your daughter and mother."

"I named her Jane."

"I always thought that a lovely name."

"Yes, I know. That is why I chose it," Lillian admitted. "I do not think much about whether names are lovely—or hats, or anything. I need you for that."

Bess brushed away new tears. "Where are Addie and Thomas?"

"I sent them away on an extended vacation to keep them safe. There is a horrid, devilish woman after us, Bess. That is why I avoided you. I would not have you share Aileen's fate. Annaluisa's fate."

"So, *that* is what happened to Aileen." Bess looked sad. "And Madam Pelosi, too? Why, I rather liked her, although she was…well, one of you, is that not so?"

Lillian nodded.

"And what of Kitty Twamley? Do not tell me that a normal woman is going to marry one of the Orleans brothers!"

"Your feisty Irish friend is almost as courageous as you. She is mortal and will stay that way."

"Mortal? Does that make you immortal?" Bess fretted with her bag and gloves and grew pale. "I cannot understand any of this."

"Dear Bess, this is enough for one day. I can barely take it in myself. Please do not worry. Your life shall go on as normal."

"That is my fear! My life is abysmally boring, and I have you to blame. You take me on exciting adventures and train me to stand on my own two feet—albeit one of them hideously deformed—and then you tell me to reenter my normal life? Now you tell me things I can barely believe and advise me not to worry. You are not changed at all, Lillian. You may be some sort of…creature…but you are still very much self-absorbed."

"I suppose that is true," Lillian agreed. "But I will make it up to you. Come to my house, for there are more tears to be shed for Aileen, and we will talk more. And perhaps we can venture out together somewhere. Shopping, or strolling through the park."

"I doubt very much that shopping has made it onto your schedule. Do you still keep that ridiculous life list of things that need doing? You were to find me a husband; you put me on the top of your list once."

Bess nearly smiled, and Lillian's ramrod posture crumbled at the lovely dimples that surfaced. She broke down and hugged her friend again. "I am so lost, Bess. Please. Let us be friends again. Help me find my daughter before it is too late. I will find you a husband."

Bess looked nervous. "I prefer he not be…a creature, if you don't mind."

Lillian laughed and brushed at her tears. "I am not at all offended. We will find you a kind, handsome, human male. Now, will you come with us?"

Bess glanced at George, who stood with his brother in the distance, watching. When he tipped his hat she admitted, "I am afraid of your beau a little."

"I believe," Lillian said, "he may be more afraid of you. Oh! And I must tell you the most extraordinary thing!"

"I believe you have told me extraordinary things enough to last my life," Bess replied as Lillian linked their arms and pulled her down the hill before she could change her mind.

"I saw Mr. Conan Doyle! The creator of Sherlock Holmes! He is in town, and part of the most unusual mix of society's brightest, including the tiresome Etta Langhan."

"Is this a fantasy again, Lillian?" Bess asked, staring up at her in surprise.

Lillian laughed and felt a bit lighter of spirit. Then the crying boys ran over and she remembered this was no time for mirth. Perhaps someday.

CHAPTER THIRTEEN

Mr. Doyle spies on his companions.

Arthur paced the length of his room at the Altamont, tortured at what to do. He'd missed one lecture in New York and would soon miss one in Boston if he didn't board the train today. And yet, now did not seem the time to leave.

He lit a cigarette, only to realize one burned in the tray on the desk. Nerves frayed, tired from the chest cold that hadn't lessened, he finally sat to read the telegram from his booking agent, waiting for his arrival in Boston. *Yes,* as he'd thought. He scanned the few lines and saw what he expected. BREACH OF CONTRACT and REPUTATION PUT AT RISK.

What kind of city was this? The alleys of Whitechapel couldn't claim to be more threatening and mysterious than the streets of upper-class Baltimore. Four deaths in the last month, and two of note in the month before that, including Baltimore's mayor? He imagined that a bit more digging would unearth additional crimes. Lieutenant Worthington had not greeted him as openly this last visit, as evidently Baltimore's law enforcement was taking criticism that even the better neighborhoods weren't safe, that they couldn't catch a brazen murderer and didn't know where to begin.

And now this, the demise of Officer Johnnie Moran's lady friend.

The news had shaken Doyle, as he liked the young man who was more intelligent than his simple demeanor might indicate, and honest and straightforward. Until two days ago, he'd seemed a fairly happy man, but his happiness was taken by the same hand that killed the psychic Annaluisa Pelosi, it seemed.

Drained, Johnnie had said. Drained of life, of blood, of dignity.

He'd had no details on the deaths of two members of the Learned Order of Psychic Scholars, men of whom Arthur knew very little, a Doctor Schneider and a solicitor named Pemberton. But subtle inquiries had put them at the house of one Lillian Holmes, his devoted Sherlock Holmes fan and a friend to Johnnie Moran himself.

He stood again and paced. *Confounding!* The woman at the train station had to have been her; there could not be two Lillian Holmes of that standing and description. And she had mentioned the murder in her home of a character called the Jackal, which was perhaps her name for Schneider or Pemberton. Then there was this astounding vampire business. Etta Langhan's stories weren't to be trusted fully, that much he knew by the woman's displayed taste for gossip, but the topic matched what Miss Holmes had written in her letter.

Arthur shook his head and released a great sigh. Why, it was easier to create complex mysteries in his head than to unravel this real one under his feet. And much safer! What would Sherlock Holmes do, he wondered. Not likely take the next train to Boston to give a lecture to half-believers and skeptics.

How I wish I had the man's courage, intellect, and loyal companion.

Here seemingly was a tale of spiritism under his nose—unless these Baltimoreans were all insane. Perhaps he should knock on Miss Holmes's door or visit the "odd" Orleans brothers. But, no, Johnnie Moran was the safe point of entry into this mystery.

But the poor man is grief-stricken.

Damn, how he wished Bram shared his interest in the spiritism studies! A man with a full knowledge of vampire folklore would come in quite handy at the moment, either to cast it all aside as nonsense or point him in the right direction. But Bram did not share his interest and thus Arthur was left to make his own decision: Get on the train, or stay and try to see what evidence of other realms this city had to offer.

Do the sensible thing, Arthur. The booking agent would have his hide otherwise.

But hadn't he done the sensible thing his whole life? He'd become a physician rather than an explorer, a writer rather than a hero, a second-rate husband and perhaps a poorer father. And he wanted a chance to visit with the Society again. A few of the members, notably Congressman Coyle and Donnelly, the writer, were part of a more elite club, as he'd heard them speaking privately in a room of the congressman's mansion.

"Where is the child?" Donnelly asked. "Dr. Schneider was to take care of all that. This is impossible! All our work gone to hell because of Pemberton's heavy-handedness."

"She is not a stupid woman," Coyle answered. "And she has friends, it seems. Powerful friends."

"Aye, but she has a very powerful enemy. Still, tell me where the child is."

Then Arthur had been interrupted from his eavesdropping by a squealing Miss Langhan blathering on about his novels and the wonderful lecture. Had the men been speaking of Miss Lillian Holmes? Did the woman have a child? Was that the reason Schneider and Pemberton were murdered, to keep some sordid affair quiet? Sherlock would know what to do next; why didn't his creator?

Pulled from his thoughts by a knock on the door, Arthur answered it to see a young, rail-thin man in a cheap suit of clothes.

"Yes?"

"Sorry to interrupt, sir, but I am a reporter for the *Morning Herald*, and I wondered if you would be willing to discuss your stories with me."

"Absolutely not, young man. I have put that work aside for a more profound calling."

The reporter looked crushed, and then angry. "I see, and you wouldn't be willing to discuss anything?"

"You would discuss anything?" Arthur snapped. "The weather, my dinner last night?"

"I write on commission, Mr. Doyle. I do what I have to do. If you have an opinion on Baltimore's weather or your meal, I'll dutifully record it."

He needs a hot meal and employment. How old is he, even past twenty years? Arthur combed his hand through his hair and let out a breath. "Sorry, my good man. I'm usually not so disagreeable, I hope. Come in, and let's see if we can work something out. That's a difficult calling you've chosen."

The young man smiled and extended his hand. "Journalism? I find it incredibly easy. Just tell the public what they should think. Once inked, an opinion becomes truth—at least until the next morning's edition comes out."

"I say! Then I should be careful about what opinions I express to you."

"Don't worry; I'll likely change your words to suit the public's expectations."

"How old are you, young man?"

"Younger than most, Mr. Doyle. My name is Mencken. My friends call me H. L."

"Well, H. L., my friends call me Doyle or Arthur, so you can take your pick. What do you think of the recent murders besieging your fair city? Isn't that a better topic than what some novelist thinks about Baltimore?"

"I know nothing of the murders, sir, except what I read in the paper I'm trying to work for. I assume none of what I've seen is true."

"So, now we do have something of interest to discuss. Come, sit, and I'll order some dinner for us while we chat. Perhaps I can point you in some very interesting directions. And if you unravel this story, you *will* get that post at the paper."

Mencken sat. "I imagine Mr. Holmes would solve a mystery far more quickly than I could."

"Ah, true. I do not, however, possess Mr. Holmes's skills. And in any case, he is dead."

"By your hand," the reporter accused. "Did you grow bored of him?"

"A little. Perhaps a little jealous."

Mencken nodded. "I understand."

Arthur examined the youth carefully. Perceptive, quick, and no doubt educated at the school of hard knocks. He'd had trouble in his life, and jealousy no doubt as well. "Yes, I think perhaps you do. How did you get to be such a cynic at so young an age, H. L.?"

"A cynic? I prefer to think of myself as a realist."

"My boy, you are then likely never disappointed in your fellow man, as you expect so little."

"I have said that very thing myself!"

And with that, Arthur's decision was made. He'd made a new friend, and Baltimore felt a trifle safer already.

I never liked Boston, so this is no great shame.

CHAPTER FOURTEEN

A message in blood.

Lillian imagined that her home had never been so busy, as she hadn't properly entertained in it, ever. Entertained? She hadn't even run her own household until she shipped Thomas and Addie to the seaside, and now to Chicago. She loathed gatherings and parties but wanted to give Aileen's mourners a proper repast, so she had hired the grocer Eisner's wife to drape the mirrors and prepare a banquet. She herself could barely make a proper cup of tea. No responsibilities had made her soft, she reflected, and prone to ineptitude at every normal female undertaking.

She had made a few concessions to what she considered morose traditions but put her foot down at others she considered downright barbaric: No portrait of Aileen's corpse was allowed. Of course, in its horrid state, even Johnnie would not have wanted that. Lillian had instructed Mrs. Eisner to ensure the boys' room remained bright and cheery, with no black bunting, and even allowed Mr. Lincoln in the house. Their lot was gloomy enough. If she were married she might look into how to adopt the boys, or at least Aileen's brother, though that was likely not necessary. In truth she could call all the children her own and no one would care. No official would come calling; a judge would consider her plea a waste of time. The boys were disposable, and legions like them roamed the city, filled jails, and worked as little better than slaves in the factories and canneries.

Her boys would go to school for once in their lives, she vowed; they would be literate and have adventures and gay times along with their sister Jane. But at the moment just the thought of raising three children let alone four felt beyond her ability.

She would need help but could hire it. She did not have much to offer the world, but money was in plentiful supply.

Addie, why am I rich? Can't someone please tell me at least that much?

Her new solicitor, Bess's cousin, couldn't. He had bolted upright in his chair when he opened the folder of documents secured from the Jackal's law firm. "I know you believe Mr. Pemberton could have been stealing from you, Miss Holmes," he'd said, "but if he did, he also invested your money wisely and you are none the worse for whatever he took."

Yes, I will hire a lot of help, Lillian decided. What else would the money be good for?

She surveyed the parlor, where Bess made uncomfortable small talk with Kitty as if she clung to the one person she was sure wasn't a "creature." She'd given Sullivan and Phoebe a wide berth, as well as George and Phillip. Poor Bess, how long would she be able to sustain her composure? Still, how wonderful to enjoy her presence again!

Johnnie Moran sat quietly, politely accepting occasional attempts at conversation but without true interest. The man was numb, in shock. Lillian thought she might be as well, but that numbness was a bit better than feeling grief. George had tried to encourage her true feelings to surface, as he knew her long habit of burying her troubles. He'd held her tightly and whispered that it was quite fine to cry. But the tears had stopped coming. Lillian only felt fury and knew not how to express that.

Her medicine had helped calm her a bit, and the voices had once again subsided. Yet, George had barely left her side for a moment, which made her anxious. She knew he watched her carefully, no doubt afraid she'd create more of a mess. Every hour brought more bad news, more worry, and the desire for more medicine. At least Addie and Thomas were safe. A telegram had announced their happy arrival in Illinois.

Lillian gathered up the boys and a plate of cookies and ushered them up the stairs to Aileen's room, now theirs. George and Phillip had replaced the boys' simple pallets with real beds, and even created a spot for Abraham on the floor with an old blanket. Lillian had quickly made other changes, removing feminine accoutrements with blinding speed so Aileen's personal effects wouldn't chisel away at this charade of normalcy she'd struggled to maintain. Except for the lingering lavender of Aileen's ghostly presence, she'd made the boys a home of their own.

Billy O'Shaunessy, the oldest, pulled at her skirt and she stopped on the staircase. "Yes?"

"Mr. Lincoln must go out, Miss Holmes. Just for a little bit, if you take my meaning."

"Yes, Billy, I take your meaning. Don't be long."

"Can't we go out and play for a little?" Billy's brother Darby asked.

Lillian was taken aback. Play? His sister was dead and he wanted to play? Was this normal?

"Do you want to play as well, Paddy Moran?"

Paddy shook his head, but slowly, as if he weren't sure of the proper answer, and when she looked back Lillian saw in Billy's eyes a child far wiser than his twelve years, far wiser than she'd been at his age.

"Well, it won't do for the neighbors to see you having a merry time today. You must keep to the yard and not roll a hoop or kick a ball in the alleyway, is that clear?"

Billy squeezed her hand, which squeezed her heart. "Thank you, miss. I think it's for the best."

"I suppose it is, Billy. You are in charge of keeping things quiet."

The boys were off in a flash.

Good, Lillian thought. She now had a chance for a last inspection of the room, to ensure there was nothing left to cause anguish to the boys.

She carried the plate of cookies inside Aileen's old chamber, but she must have dropped them, as she heard the plate break on the floor. It sounded miles away. On the mirror over the chest of drawers, scrawled in blood so fresh that she could smell it—and to her horror, it smelled appealing—were the words I HAVE YOUR CHILD.

CHAPTER FIFTEEN

Bonds between brothers.

George believed the truth of the note in blood. He lied to Lillian, told her it was part and parcel of Madam Lucifer's cruel tactics and likely false, but he knew she didn't believe him.

He'd done his maker's duty in the first weeks after her transformation, teaching her Atil's commandments, which forbade breeding. She'd questioned the obvious error in logic. "If vampires bear no children, why must reproduction be forbidden?"

"Vampire and mortal unions. Tales of such abound, although I never met a child of such parentage. In divine retribution for the mating of Atil and Ursula, whose children are our Elders, the offspring of such unions are said to be caught between this world and the next, doomed to insanity. Merely folktales to scare young vampires, I imagine."

George had never considered trying to father a child on a mortal. The paternal gene had not seemed to lurk within him, and why would he create something so frail and helpless? Oddly, though, he had recently been taken unawares by strange longings, imagined raising a mortal child with Lillian, imagined finally being a father, however unworthy. Lillian's daughter had seemed the perfect opportunity, perhaps to carve a bit of normalcy from the insanity their lives had become. But Madam Lucifer had taken that dream as well. If they found little Jane, she was likely frozen in childhood and monstrous, having lived a tortured existence with the Devil herself.

He wondered if Lillian had ever considered the possibility. Her child might no longer be an apple-cheeked angel.

It did not matter, though. Not with the larger problems at play. So George now sat with Sullivan and his brother in Lillian's parlor, wracking his brain for a path of action.

"But *how*, George? How could Marie have known about Lillian's child?"

"It's on the edge of my brain, brother. I simply *feel* it to be true. Something about that lawyer and doctor of hers. And do you recall that Annaluisa claimed to know something of Lil's mother? Perhaps Marie tortured it out of her. Perhaps Annaluisa knew something of the child as well."

"I am not smart enough to put it together," Phillip said, giving up. "What is your plan?"

"Plan? Do I look like I have a plan?"

Chauncey rose and looked out the window. He kept his back to them. "Is this how it is with you two now? Chattering fools?"

George was relieved he had moved away; the man made his skin crawl whenever he was physically close. "Yes, Sullivan, we are chattering fools. What would you have us do?"

"Find Marie. She is not so far. I feel it."

"You feel it? Because of your bond?"

Chauncey turned and shot him an annoyed look. "Does she seem the sort of woman who would release me, *Grandpapa?*"

"Is that why you dislike me so, because I turned her? How could I know what she would become?"

Chauncey laughed, a low rumble. "No, George. It was your arrogance and self-absorption that put me off. Many years ago."

"He's changed a good deal, Chauncey," Phillip remarked. "You'd be amazed."

"I'll believe that when he releases *your* bond. Now, I'm taking Phoebe out for a nice meal. Stop your childishness and find Marie if you will not send me to her alone. Then we'll deal with her. I'd like to quit this city."

Chauncey left, and George let out a deep breath. He also noticed Phillip relax.

"Sullivan may have stopped eating his own kind, but I don't like being around him. Not at all," George's brother whispered, as if the dark-skinned vampire could still hear them. "If only we could trust him to destroy Marie alone."

George nodded in agreement, uncomfortable that Chauncey had mentioned his and Phillip's bond. But generous Phillip, he knew, would not bring the topic up.

"So, how is Lillian taking this?"

"How do you suppose? She's ingesting that poison again, and I have no idea how her body doesn't reject it. Bad enough when she was mortal, but when I took a sip from her one night long ago…" *Not so long ago, Georgy. Not really.* "It nearly made me pass out. I can handle a bit of liquor at times—as you can, as she can—but these opiates…"

I must go through that again with her? he asked himself tiredly. *Convince her to give it up? Yes, I must. Anything and everything for her. She would do as much for me.*

And he deserved much less.

To Phillip he said, "It is not the greatest problem, and I'm loath to distance her further over it. It is the nature of such indulgences, as you witnessed with me. There are no guarantees that any time will be the last."

"Mother sucked that lust for drink out of you." Phillip shook his head. "So we sit and watch Lillian pine away, and we wait for Marie to attack us."

"I am not pining away." Lillian stood in the doorway, in her boy's clothing, her pistol holstered on her hip.

"You are not going out to ride *tonight, Lil?*"

George stood and held out his hand to silence his brother.

"I am, Phillip. I would like George to join me. You may come also if you like, but I'm afraid there is only room for one other on my transport, so you will have to fly."

"Go back to bed, Lil," George said.

He regretted the words as soon as he uttered them. Lillian narrowed her eyes and crossed her arms and looked for all the world like the woman who intrigued him so much the night they met. If she were the petulant sort, she'd be stomping her foot or throwing a vase at him. He'd ducked many such missiles in his lifetime, and he'd deserved every one.

He quickly rescinded the command. "I didn't mean to tell you what to do. I care about you, Lil."

"You have wanted to tell me what to do many times and have shown great restraint to this point. You are forgiven, as I care about you as well. Will you come with me, or must I search alone? I would have your help, but only if it is given willingly."

"I will come with you. Where are we going?"

"We are paying a visit to Mr. Conan Doyle. And when we are finished speaking with him, we will visit each member of that damned Learned Order of Scoundrels to which the Jackal belonged. Someone knows where Jane is, and I will wring the truth from their throats."

George stared into Lillian's eyes and saw danger there, a danger he had tasted many times but repented, one sweet peril of immortal strength and power. "Be careful, Lillian, or you may not be much better than your foe. Don't take innocents down with the guilty. I could live with that. You could not. At least, not yet. In time, perhaps. But I would bet you become like my brother: a lifelong do-gooder."

"Damn, George, be easy on the woman. These are hard times for her," Phillip said.

"He is easy on me, Phillip." Lillian furrowed her brow, seeming to consider. Then: "I care not about anything but finding Jane."

Phillip stood. "I'm going home. Where are the boys?"

"With Johnnie."

He sighed. "Safe enough, I suppose. As safe as any of us."

George held out a hand. "A meal before we visit Mr. Doyle, Lil?" He hoped some of her aggression might be spent on a victim. He knew this fury, unchecked, would bring disaster. Lil could not live with herself if she corrupted innocents, and for the nonce she seemed prone to act first and question later.

Her eyes flared. "I'm sure one of these fools will do." She stared at him. "Are you coming or not, George?"

He sighed. "I will be honest, I am coming to keep an eye on you. You are nearly frothing at the mouth."

"That is wise. Thank you for your honesty."

She walked over and kissed him then. It was on the cheek, but this was a rare display of affection before company. He stared into her eyes to see if her medicine was to blame, but no, her pupils were not dilated; neither did he hear her heart race. What a confusing woman. But she was his. Murderess-to-be or not, he was glad he had her for eternity.

Perhaps she had taken seriously his warnings about indiscretion; it indeed seemed they would be taking her motorcycle. As they walked outside to her shed, she called over her shoulder, "I heard what you said to Phillip. I have failed you, haven't I? With my medicine."

God, she how she hated this life. He could hear it in her voice. Yet, how could it be otherwise?

George swung her around. "No! No, Lil, you have not failed me. *I* am nearly ready to ask for some of your pills."

"I am not a good vampire. I wasn't a very good normal woman either."

"I'm not a very good maker, Lillian. So perhaps we are meant to struggle together."

"I am tired, George," she said. "So tired."

She stood straighter, fighting tears he could tell. "Then I will carry you, feed you, hold you until you gain strength."

"Is that what a maker does?"

"That, in my very limited experience, is love."

She looked up at him, something inscrutable in her eyes. "At times I think: How has he survived centuries of this? What has he seen and done, what sins accumulated, what guilt burning in his gut, what losses? I fear at those times you will give up on me, and I will be alone with my burdens."

Heart ready to burst, ready to comfort her, he pulled her close but she did not cry. He found himself admitting, "I am also without a compass. I have never been in love with one of my newborns. Perhaps I have never been in love before you."

"I could not have asked for kinder words right now," she whispered, brushing a lock of his hair away. But part of her remained reserved.

He leaned in and kissed her. She broke away and held him tight, and they stood in the dim cloudy night for minutes until their hearts beat to the same rhythm.

"Do you think she is alive, George?"

No, no I don't. So he said the only truthful thing he could. "I believe we must find out."

CHAPTER SIXTEEN

Dear Mr. Doyle…

Fortunately, Mr. Doyle had not kept it a secret that he stayed at the Altamont hotel. Though, why would he? He was famous to some, inconsequential to most, a harm to no one. The *Morning Herald* always reported visits of foreign notables to Baltimore, including sightings of them with local celebrities, so it had taken Lillian only a few inquiries to locate him.

That was the easy part, she thought. Facing the man who had changed her life—for better or worse—would be more difficult. Only George and Bess understood how Mr. Doyle had given her an instrument of escape, a way to disappear into fantasy, a way to survive her former life. How many times had she imagined this meeting? But she had been a great detective then, at least in her mind. Now she was a tired, broken creature with nothing to offer.

She expected to be brushed away at the desk, but the clerk came back breathless. "Mr. Doyle would like to see you right away, Miss Holmes and Mr. Orleans. Follow me."

Her case of nerves intensified, and she took a swig of Mrs. Winslow's Remedy in clear sight of George, who groaned but looked away. This wasn't time for shame. She would meet her hero and find out if he was also her foe.

The clerk had barely a chance to knock on his door before Doyle opened it to an expansive suite. The man looked as he had at the train station, dressed in tweed with a pipe in his hand.

But for a curious glance at her attire, he seemed to recognize her. He shook hands with George and invited them in. "I am happy to have this chance to meet you in person," he said. "And this would be the young man I heard about in your last letter?"

Lillian searched the air for something to say that would not sound trite. But: "Indeed, we are both great admirers of your writing."

George offered a similar pleasantry, but Lillian barely heard the exchange. She knew Doyle would be astute, and that it would be easy for him to throw her off balance if he so desired, if he were involved with her enemies. She was trying to think of a way around that.

"We have already met, in a way, Mr. Doyle," she began.

"Through our letters, of course. May I offer you a sherry, or ring for tea?"

"At the train depot. You watched me, and I followed you."

"Indeed?" The man sat back in his chair, hands tented on his lap, staring as intently as he had in the terminal. Then he said, "Good. That is what a fine detective would do. Did you know my identity?"

This was a bit like her fantasy meeting, she had to admit. *Be brave, Lillian. Be the inquisitor you were once sworn to be.*

"It took a moment or two. Your conversation about literary matters with your friend, your accent and bearing… In the end it was not difficult to identify the Staring Man," she offered with a small smile. Perhaps that would throw *him* off balance.

"Ah. You bettered me then, Miss Holmes, as I did not know your identity while I stared. I only noted your loveliness." He inclined his head as if he paid her a great compliment, but he used the gesture to cast a nervous glance at George and Lillian knew that he was quite curious about them both. Did he know the truth, or at least part of the truth? Could he have taken the ramblings of that busybody Etta

Langham seriously? If so, why didn't he greet them with an ash stake or holy water?

After a short silence, Doyle turned to George. "An acquaintance of mine said that you are the owner of Baltimore's largest shipyard, Mr. Orleans."

Damn Etta Langhan, Lillian thought.

George shrugged. "My brother has the head for business. What acquaintance do we have in common?"

"I've forgotten the name. Someone I met at my lecture. I cannot remember how the topic arose, but... Hmnn."

Lillian almost laughed. *Well, he may be a brilliant writer, but a fine actor he is not.* Yet, why hadn't she talked this through with George beforehand? What was the approach that would elicit the most information without them having to reveal themselves as part of the bargain?

George crossed his legs and folded his arms. It was a casual gesture which Lillian knew. He was readying for battle, preparing for a game of verbal chess. But, this was already the endgame. Many pieces had been already taken off the board.

Let him help, Lillian. He has been on this earth far longer than you, hidden his nature for far longer. He also has a stake in the answers.

As if sensing her approval, George spoke. "Tea. I think I might quite fancy a cup now that you mention it, sir. If it's not too much trouble."

"None at all."

Their host stood and walked to the bell pull. As he did George said, "I understand that our late friend, Miss Annaluisa Pelosi, was to perform at your lecture. Perhaps that is the person we had in common?"

Doyle swung around. "Perhaps. I am extremely distressed by her death."

"We were close friends. And perhaps you have heard of another great loss of ours. Lillian's maid, Aileen O'Shaunessy. She was in Lil's service for years, and betrothed to another friend of ours. The deaths seem quite similar to me."

"And to me!" Doyle raced back to his seat. "My good man, I was just speaking about these awful crimes to a young reporter. He needed a story to secure a full-time post as a journalist, and I pointed him in just that direction."

"Oh, I know a few journalists," George said. "What is his name?"

"Mencken. Odd young chap, quick and cutting. He should do well."

Wonderful. One more snoop in the mix. Lillian knew that George was cursing inwardly as much as she, but would he visit this Mencken fellow tonight and make a meal of him?

Her beloved kept his composure, asking, "Did he come to interview you about your novels, or about your interest in matters of a spiritual nature? Perhaps he was curious about the Learned Order of... I cannot quite recall the name of the organization."

"He—"

"I myself am curious about all of these things," George continued, cutting the great author off. "I hope you might consider dining at my home during your stay so we can enjoy hearing your thoughts. Lillian has been your most devoted fan—isn't that right, dear?—and would love nothing more."

"Nothing more, indeed!" Lillian agreed. It would be easier to deal with the man in one of their own homes regardless of the method of resolution.

"I'm afraid I'm not here that long, Mr. Orleans. But I am very sorry for both of your losses and would like to understand more about Johnnie's fiancée. If you would enlighten me."

"Johnnie? Oh, Officer Moran. Do you know everyone in the city, Mr. Doyle?" Lillian asked.

"Do call me Arthur. And it would seem this city is very small indeed, based on these coincidences."

"Smaller still if you add to the number members of your own Society, the late Francis Pemberton, esquire, and Dr. Schneider," George said. "They, too, died within the last month or so. It seems that everyone we have in common...well, *had* in common... When did you arrive in America, Mr. Doyle?" Here George cast a slightly startled look at Lillian, and she was so taken aback by his acting that she had to bite her lip to stop from speaking. Was he trying to make Doyle believe himself suspected of murder?

The ploy seemed to have worked, for the author was terribly fidgety and had started to perspire. This was no Holmes, nor even a Watson, Lillian realized as beads of sweat rolled down his forehead. He was just an ordinary fellow. A brilliant, kind, ordinary fellow.

Doyle seemed relieved by the knock on the door, and when the butler finished laying out tea, Lillian poured.

Doyle tried to get back control of the conversation.

"As you know, Mr. Orleans," he said, "I am no detective. Merely a man with a pen and some fanciful ideas. I'll leave the investigative work to Miss Holmes." He smiled kindly at her, and Lillian returned the expression, wishing that this meeting could have taken place a year earlier.

"Still," George pressed, "your curiosity must be piqued! As must be the curiosity of the members of your group! There are too many entwined threads for these deaths to be unrelated, wouldn't you think?"

"I cannot say."

A very bad actor indeed. So, bring the topic closer to my Jane, George! He is ready to end this game!

"Such a pity, about Annaluisa," said Lillian's beloved. "Well-liked, although a complete charlatan."

"Charlatan! You could not be more wrong, Mr. Orleans! The woman was a proficient. I saw it with my own eyes on many occasions. Why, I grieve for the loss of her gift—"

"Truly?" Lillian interjected, unable to wait but working hard to keep her tone level. "You saw her proficiency? As I think I wrote to you in my first letter, I am an orphan. Miss Pelosi seemed to know something of the whereabouts of my mother, but we never had a chance to discuss the particulars. I don't suppose she would have brought up such a thing to you...."

"Alas, no." Doyle seemed genuinely distressed. "She did not discuss her friends with me."

Of course she hadn't. Lillian nodded. But the conversation was frustrating, and that fueled her fury. Her hero couldn't help her at all, had no interest in her, and evidently he didn't care about solving the mysterious deaths of Baltimore. Where was Jane? She needed to leave this place and—

"Might I ask you something, Miss Holmes?"

Ah, the worst part. He had come to it. *This* she had prepared for. "Of course."

Doyle cast a quick look at George and then said, "In your letters, you mentioned something of a peculiar nature. You mentioned my friend Mr. Stoker."

"I did? I do not recall. Perhaps you have me confused with another?"

George glanced at her, his eyes dark.

"I'm quite sure it was you," Doyle said. "And the topic fascinated me. You mentioned vampires."

"Vampires?" Lillian laughed, and George joined in. She hoped they did not sound hysterical.

"Indeed. Because I am interested in paranormal events and phenomena, I took special note."

"Perhaps it was someone from your Society," Lillian suggested, praying he did not have her letter with him. "I assure you, the paranormal is not a topic of interest to me."

"No?" Doyle sat back and stared at her, and then at George. "You're sure?"

"Quite. Unless someone forged a letter from my person to you…"

"Why would anyone do such a thing?"

"Why would I write such a letter and then forget about it?" Lillian challenged.

"Unfortunately I do not have the letter with me."

"A shame," George said, "as it would clear things up."

"Yes," said Doyle, clearly frustrated. He seemed none the less friendly, however.

"Well," George announced, "we have likely taken too much of your time. You've been incredibly gracious, Mr. Doyle, and let's hope the murderer of Miss Pelosi and Miss O'Shaunessy is quickly caught—as quickly as if your Mr. Holmes himself were on the case." He rose. "I do hope you'll reconsider dining with us?"

"What? Oh, yes. I mean, no, I'm so sorry. My schedule will not permit."

Lillian's heart pounded. She'd lied to her wonderful Mr. Doyle, who seemed unable to help her in any way, and who seemed remarkably uninterested in the curious crimes surrounding his acquaintances, instead focusing on the bizarre and paranormal. This was not at all what she'd expected. How her fantasies had formed her expectations! *So stupid,* she chastised herself. But at least Doyle did not seem to be laying any crimes at their doorstep.

George extended his hand and helped her up. The trio exchanged goodbyes, and Lillian and her beloved were just ready to step across the threshold when Doyle stopped them.

"May I ask one more thing, Miss Holmes?"

"Of course."

"Who is the Jackal?"

Her heart began to pound again. "'Jackal'? I had a pet dog named Jack, but I know of no Jackal."

Doyle ran his fingers across his mustache, and Lillian could not fathom his expression as he said, "I hope you will pardon my candor, but I believe you came here seeking something you have not gained. I am sincerely sorry for that. I am no detective, as I said. But I wish you great fortune in finding your mother."

"Thank you," Lillian replied, seeing real kindness in his eyes. Then, "In truth, I am looking also for a girl."

She was not sure why she'd said that, but Doyle let out a breath and stood statue-still. "A child?"

"Yes, a child." Lillian watched her hero, hope rising in her breast. "Annaluisa never mentioned a child, did she?"

"No, she didn't. I am sorry."

Lillian's hope fell flat. At least, hope of peaceably getting what she wanted.

They repeated their goodbyes, and George and Lillian descended the hotel stairway. As they did, George whispered, "That was incredibly pointless and disheartening, as well as awkward."

"Yes," Lillian agreed. "We spoke in circles. But, George…did you see his eyes when I mentioned a child?"

"No. But I heard his pulse."

"As did I. We could go back and torture it out of him…." Her blood was burning, and she was fighting back the instinct to do just that. Whomever would stand between her and her daughter would die. Painfully.

George eyed her with surprise. "If you wish, we can—"

"No." She had mastered her emotion and realized just how foolish she sounded. And, there was no reason to suspect Doyle of wrongdoing. *Yet.* "I was joking. You know how I feel about him. And, although he is not at all what I expected, I like him."

"As do I," said George.

She took a deep breath. "I am discouraged that he overheard me discussing the Jackal with Thomas in the train station."

George sighed and shrugged. "I don't think you need worry about that. The Baltimore police have their hands full with more recent crimes and seemed to fully accept our explanation of those deaths. And while Mr. Doyle did not seem willing to tell all he knows, he does not seem overly afraid of us, which he would likely be if he knew the truth."

Lillian's blood began to burn once again. "Do you think he heard talk of a child amongst his Society members?"

George sighed again. "It's a place to start. My love, I do believe the game is afoot."

"What of Marie?" Lillian asked. "Dare you come with me to inquire of Mr. Doyle's compatriots? I fear for the children, George. And Bess, and Johnnie. The list is endless. She got into my *home.*"

"Strength in numbers, Lillian. It's our only hope." George put his hand on her shoulder, and she drew comfort from it, but that comfort was sapped by his next words. "Madame Lucifer watches and plans. At times I wish she would simply take me and be done with it, let the rest of you alone. But I doubt that something so simple would satisfy. She aims to end us all."

"I am next," Lillian whispered. "I feel it."

"You will *not* be," George swore.

"If it would satisfy her," Lillian realized, "I would perish to save the rest of you. If you promised to find my daughter and—"

"We both prefer a happier outcome. Let's give it a try, Lil. We have Sullivan on our side."

"Is he truly on our side? I cannot read the man."

George linked her arm through his and led her down Charles Street without answering.

CHAPTER SEVENTEEN

Women's talk.

During daylight, George was less insistent that everyone remain inside. According to Annaluisa's confidences, he said, Marie de Bourbon was terribly affected by the sun. She had also evolved so completely as to have lost her reflection. What humanity she'd once possessed seemed lost forever to her darker nature.

Lillian and Bess sat on a bench in the park, watching the boys and Mr. Lincoln frolic as they had done before their world shifted on its axis. Johnnie Moran had returned to work, even though grief had him in a tight grip.

Bess kept eyeing the duo on a neighboring bench. "Truly, Lil, must they follow us everywhere? It's disturbing."

"It would be more disturbing to have a 'creature,' as you so delicately call us, rip your throat out."

Bess reached toward her throat and nodded. "I do not mind Sullivan and Phoebe much, I guess. They are quiet, and she is actually quite charming. Although, the neighborhood will think it odd that a Negro couple is always in our company."

"Sullivan and Phoebe care even less than I do about the attitudes of our neighbors. See? The boys have taken to him. He's kicking a ball about now."

"They must be very bored, sitting around your house or Phillip's, running out at odd hours to do whatever it is that vampires do. Eat, and such."

"We're trying desperately to develop a plan of attack, so I doubt they will be bored much longer."

They sat in silence for a moment before Bess took a deep breath and said, "Speaking of vampire men..."

"Must we?"

"Lil, listen to me! I risk a great deal being friends with... Oh, you know what I mean. I tire of calling you a creature. You are more than a creature to me. Please, how do we talk about these things?"

"I'm still me, Bess. The same confused, selfish woman who has cared about you for years."

"In any case, I am curious."

"About George? Yes, I rather thought you would be. What is it you would like to know?"

"Did he buy you that enormous ruby?"

Lillian frowned. Truth be told, the ring had brought more confusion than delight. "Yes, indeed he did. A simple gift."

Bess snorted. "A simple gift that, should it be sold at auction, would likely pull my family out of their present financial woes. Take care lest I steal it from you."

"If you would let me, *I* would pull your family out of debt. I may do so behind your back. There is no reason for needless suffering and worry."

"Is it an engagement ring?"

"What?"

"Well, I thought, perhaps among your kind...you might choose them differently."

"Oh, I see," Lillian said. "Blood-red rings instead of diamonds? Oh, Bess, we don't drink out of human skulls or cackle over bubbling cauldrons, you know."

"No, I don't know! How in blazes would I? Now, answer my question. Are you engaged?"

"I don't think so. At least... No, I don't think so."

"You would know, my dear."

But she didn't know anything. Bess had been the one to tell her such things.

"Then I am not," she said.

"But you spend all of your time together. And by that, I mean *all of your time.*"

"I take your meaning," Lillian said, sensing her friend's distaste. "Yes, we are intimate."

"Lil," Bess commanded, "you must marry the man. It's simply not done. Has he explained why he has not proposed? I know that you both are 'creatures,' but surely you haven't given up on everything! What will you say to Jane about him? Is he to be as a father to her? What do you want?"

Lillian choked back a lump in her throat. How she'd missed Bess, who could see through any fog to the truth of the matter. Bess's questions were good ones, yet she prevaricated, "Not all social conventions must be followed."

"I am asking what you *want.* Do you love him?"

"I do," she admitted. "Although...I have nothing to compare this feeling to. It is more complicated. Our relationship is muddled by some...'creature' issues."

Yes, Bess, I am in love with my maker. But would I love him if he didn't hold my bond? Would he still love me?

It bothered her sometimes that their relationship had progressed so fast. In her twenty-four years, when had she truly been in control of herself and her emotions? She had desired George, yes, and had been intrigued by him. Then she was in love with him, and then she was one with him. He had "made" her, forced by circumstance. They were both trapped by circumstance. So were the feelings *real?*

Who could she ask? Kitty would not understand, and Lillian certainly did not know Phoebe well enough to speak of such intimate matters. Nor, she thought sadly, was there another woman to ask.

Phillip might have the answer, but he would surely tell George if she shared any doubts.

"What sort of creature issues?" Bess asked. "He does not mistreat you, does he?"

"Of course not!"

"Then the man must marry you. I shall speak with him on the topic. He won't chew on me, will he?"

"Only if he wants to answer to me. But…you must remember that to speak of his nature to anyone… Promise me, Bess. Promise me that you will not." She squeezed Bess's hand. "I have given my assurance more than once."

Lillian nodded, knowing as much was true. So, "Bess, he is happy for us, that we are reunited. He will not chew on you if you keep your promise. Still, it's not the time to worry about such mundane things as marriage. We must find Marie and Jane. After Aileen, the danger is all the more apparent. She is clearly set on destroying all he cares about."

"I don't understand how Marie could hate him this much."

"He is the one who created her, Bess."

Lillian's friend looked equally confused and aghast. "Your ways are confounding to me."

And to Lillian, too. How could she ever explain this existence?

"Many come to loathe their fathers and mothers, both mortals and…'creatures,' but especially creatures. Because this life is very hard, and they wished they could have remained mortal."

"But it would be patricide, in a way. Do you feel that way about George? Angry?"

"At first, and for a brief time. It is very confusing, to resent the one who saved me, who gave me back life." She paused. "To be honest, I think I resent the two who gave me my first life much more than George."

Bess nodded. Then, after a moment she said, "Lil, may I ask you something? It is out of curiosity and nothing more, though. I am not asking to be chewed on. But if I were to become a creature, would I be able to walk properly?"

"No. I'm afraid not."

Bess's quiet sigh tore at Lillian's heart—as had her lie. In fact, Lillian thought there was a chance Bess could be made whole, as George had explained that frailties and injuries often faded with time. But she said, "Now, Watson, I think we should bring the boys home, as we have a long night ahead of us."

"We? *I'm* to do something?"

"Didn't I tell you? We are going to the Spring Grove Asylum to see if there is any record of a birth there when I was sixteen. Well, *you* are to go. Addie and Thomas said the child was given to the Hebrew Orphan Asylum, but there was no record of Jane there when I asked." Lillian looked down at the ground and then up again. "The woman was awful, Bess. You should have seen how she stared at me."

Bess held her hand, and Lillian found comfort in its warm pulse. "How will we get the information?"

"George has a lovely plan. You two are going alone there. They might recognize me."

"Oh, Lil, are you serious?"

"Quite. You said you wanted to help."

With a great sigh, Bess stood and straightened her skirts. "Lead on, then, Miss Holmes."

CHAPTER EIGHTEEN

George and Bess follow the scent.

"Mr. Orleans, you *must* slow down. I am not a creature and cannot move at your pace."

"Creature? Is Lillian also a creature, or do you reserve that endearment for me?"

Bess fiddled with her bag and George reminded himself what a brave mortal she was, how she had helped saved Lillian, and in so doing how she had helped to redeem him.

"Miss Wheeler, might we call one another George and Bess?"

"We might. But not today."

Surprised again at her pluckiness, George stopped and turned. *I can hear your quickened heartbeat, my dear.*

Indeed, Lillian's friend was flushed with nerves and exertion as she gasped, "I say, don't look at me like that! I know it is not lust in your eyes."

George laughed and bowed his head, deciding to ignore her previous incivility. "I am simply anxious to get there and back to the house before sundown. Perhaps Lillian explained—"

"Yes, of course. The devil woman comes out at night."

"Indeed." He motioned for the carriage driver again to wait, and linked his arm in Bess's, drawing her up the path to the asylum. "Now, do you have the story straight?"

"You are very bossy," the young woman said. "Do you know that? I don't know how Lil can love you so, aside from your handsome face. Of course, you did save her life...."

George half smiled. "Did she tell you she loves me?" He fully smiled. "Oh, Lord, did I actually just ask you that?"

"She did. Not that you deserve her attentions." Bess put her hands on her hips and caught her breath. "Why have you not made her a proper offer of marriage? Her reputation, what is left of it, will be in ruins soon."

My God, George thought. *So she does want marriage!* It was ridiculous, but these things were entirely foreign to him. He had gone so long not caring what anyone wanted but himself, it was difficult to suddenly change his perspective. "Did Lil want you to ask me that?"

"I am asking, not she. She claims there is nothing more important than finding Jane and destroying your she-devil. But in the meantime, sir, you are doing her a great disservice."

"So she does *not* want to marry?"

"Is that relevant? You should offer her the choice!" Bess gave a snort of disdain. "Oh, you are both quite simple in the head. Let's finish this horrid chore. I have never been in an asylum, although you two may drive me to one."

"We will try to avoid that," George said.

She flinched under his grasp when he took her arm again, prompting him to add, "Please, relax. I only want to warn you about Spring Grove Asylum. You may see people here, hear noises here, that you'll find disturbing. The staff will be used to most any reaction you have, so that's no worry, but do not let anything break your story. Clear?"

Bess pulled away and huffed as she straightened her hat. "Quite clear."

She tilted her head and examined him for a moment. George, annoyed at her scrutiny, forcibly quashed a slight instinct to remove her from the equation. Bess was on their side and could be trusted. Lillian had promised.

"I asked Lillian a question," Bess announced, "and, as her left brow arched, I know her answer was a lie. I would have the truth from you."

"Her left brow arches when she lies? That is a handy piece of information." George smiled to clear the air between them. "You are my now my best friend for life."

Bess snorted again. "Oh, honestly. Buy me a ruby ring like the one Lil wears and I'll be satisfied. My question, sir, is this. If a person is turned into a creature such as yourself, what happens to them exactly?"

"This isn't the time—"

"As you do need me to carry out this plan, I would say it's the perfect time, as I am asking the question."

"What *exactly* would you like to hear about, Miss Wheeler?" George asked with some asperity. "The blood or the rebirth? The soul, the hunger, the strength…or perhaps how to kill us?"

She flinched a bit at his words. "All of those are of interest, but for now can you tell me if a person carries their infirmities into their new life?"

Oh, no wonder Lillian had told a lie. George grimaced. "I am immune to illnesses, and injuries typically heal quite quickly."

Bess glared at him. "You to know to what I am referring, Mr. Orleans. I am lame, and I would have the truth. If I were to become a creature, would I remain disfigured?"

"Dear Bess, is it so horrible? You are really a very pretty, likeable woman. I can assure you that you are much happier as you are than after accepting such a bargain."

"How can you know about my happiness?" Bess snapped. "Give me an answer, won't you?"

"I'm afraid I cannot. Not a certain one. While you would cease to age, at least in appearance, there is no guarantee that physical infirmities such as yours would be repaired. I have seen it happen, but I have also seen it not work. I believe it depends on the bloodline of your maker. Others say a positive result is merely chance."

"I see." Lillian's friend looked down at her misshapen shoe and toed the soil as if she might unearth an answer there, but after a moment she breathed in new air and stood erect, looped her arm through his, and announced that she was ready to do battle. "Let's find Jane."

"Yes, let's find Jane," George agreed. "We can talk more later if you like."

Bess nodded. After about four steps, however, she added, "Truth be told, I think you are a fine match for Lillian. Please do mind what I said about making things right with her, however. She could use a bit of normalcy in her life, if that is remotely possible."

If only it were.

They entered Spring Grove and were politely ushered by a receptionist to the central office. The rail-thin, middle-aged director, Dr. Arnold Epstein, had deep grey circles under his eyes and a pallor George had come to recognize signaled poor health, especially of the heart. But the man was generous and mannerly, and he bid the "newlyweds" sit and be comfortable.

"How can I help you, Mrs. and Mr. Johnson?"

"It is a delicate topic, Doctor. How long have you been at Spring Grove, if I might ask?"

"Oh, I may be trusted, sir. The identities and circumstances of all of our patients are treated with the utmost discretion. But I have been here for only three weeks."

"Three weeks! Oh, then perhaps you will not be able to help us. It concerns a former patient. What happened to the previous director, a Doctor…?"

"Schneider? Ah, that is a very horrible story. You did not read of his…death in the paper? Ah, well, we are doing our best to carry on the high standards he established. In fact, security is much tighter, I assure you."

A loud moan sounded from the hallway, startling them and belying the doctor's proud assurance. George spoke to spare Epstein more embarrassment, as a scuffle outside the door seemed to be taking place.

"Indeed? My wife Clara had a dear sister who was hospitalized twice here. Once not so long ago, isn't that right, Clara?"

"Yes, within two months." Bess pulled a kerchief from her bag and sniveled into it, obviously in deep distress. "She succumbed to death by her own hand only two weeks ago."

Epstein looked aghast and genuinely moved. "Oh, how terrible. Perhaps she should not have been released? Of course she should not have!"

"She actually escaped. It seems she must have had help, but we never learned from whom. I don't suppose anyone on your staff currently?"

She'd managed just a hint of accusation, enough to make the doctor prickle a bit. *Good show, Bess.*

"Absolutely not! Our staff is now top-notch! But I am very sorry for your loss."

Bess sniffed into her kerchief and nodded. "You see, this was not the first time she was here, as we said. I am afraid that I know the road to Catonsville all too well."

"It was the *first* time, Clara, wasn't it?" George prompted. "When it happened? How old was she then?"

"Yes, I was only fourteen, but I remember it clearly. My governess tried to keep the truth from me, but I knew. My sister had a child, Doctor. While at Spring Grove. She was only sixteen, so you can understand…" She turned to George and wept so well that he wondered if she were actually grieving.

"There, there, dear," he said to her. "Doctor Epstein, we have not been able to locate Clara's sister's child. We were told she was taken to the Hebrew Orphan Asylum, but they have no knowledge of such a child. We were hoping…well, Clara and I would dearly love to bring her into the family, give her the love and life in society she so deserves. It would complete our lives and be such a tribute to Clara's sister's memory."

"Indeed, I understand," said the doctor. "Though I cannot guarantee that I will have the information you seek. Some families do not allow us to keep such records, as you might imagine."

"Of course."

Epstein stood and walked to a large credenza full of folders and notebooks. "I will need the name of your sister, Mrs. Johnson, and the approximate year."

"Holmes. The name is Holmes, and it would have been in the fall of 1881."

Epstein flipped through his leather-bound files, and George winked at Bess. The doctor finally pulled down a book and ran his finger along the entries. "Holmes, you said? Lillian Holmes?"

"Yes!"

He read silently for a bit and finally peered over his spectacles. "I wish she had been my patient. This strikes me as a very common case for a female of that age and in her circumstances. But let us skip those details and find what you are—"

"No! Please, I would like very much to know what happened," Bess said. "We owe her that much, don't you think?"

"Keep in mind that treatment has evolved a great deal in the last seven years."

"Of course," George agreed. But, *God,* what torture had his Lil gone through?

"Female, heavy with child. Age sixteen. Depressive, suicidal, delusional. References to an enemy. Poorly nourished. Given medications… Ah, they did no shock therapy, as she was with child. *That* is good news. Restraints were necessary. And…yes, it records the birth of a healthy child."

"Does it say where the child was taken?"

"Released into the care of Doctor Schneider under orders from your sister's solicitor, Francis Pemberton. To be taken to the Hebrew Orphan Asylum. Just as you were told."

George's heart sank. Here was nothing they didn't already know. But his beloved had been restrained and drugged while pregnant? He wanted to leap across the room and tear out Epstein's heart for being one of the misguided ghouls who tortured those who couldn't defend themselves. He hadn't expected much, but Lillian had thought this worth a try. If only he could give her something, anything…

"No one else is mentioned? No other family members or our parents?" Bess asked.

"I'm afraid not, but that is not unusual. Quite often families leave these matters to their physicians."

Bess stood and wiped at her tears, which seemed quite real to George now. "Thank you for your help, Dr. Epstein. I would have dearly loved to have found Jane."

"Jane?"

"Oh, the name we thought to give the little girl should we find her."

"I think you are confused, Mrs. Johnson. Jane wouldn't suit for a boy child." The doctor smiled ruefully, obviously sincere in his desire to help.

"Are you quite sure? A boy?" George grabbed Bess's arm. Could Lil have been wrong about such a basic fact?

"The record seems quite clear. Male, six and a half pounds, healthy."

"Thank you, then, we'll be off." George hurried Bess toward the door. In a moment of gratitude he turned back and stared at the confused director, saying, "Dr. Epstein, might I recommend that you let one of your colleagues listen to your heart—and suggest that you rest a bit more?"

"What on earth…?"

George didn't hear any more. He pulled Bess quickly outside and put her into their carriage.

"A boy!" Lillian's friend squealed. "I don't know what to think! Is that good news or bad?"

"I do not know," George said. "But Lil told me that the caretaker at the orphanage said they had no girl child of that age, so I know our next stop. Are you game, Bess?"

"I am, George!"

His heart was pounding. What would Lillian say if it was true, if her boy was at the orphanage and Madam Lucifer was toying with them? He wanted it to be so, wanted it desperately for her sake, wanted above all things for her to have this one happiness. And there was only one way to find out.

The carriage ride back to the city center seemed to take forever. Across from George, Bess wiggled her foot anxiously. "Do we keep the same charade?" she asked. "Or do we approach more directly?"

"I think the same. But follow my lead, will you, Miss Watson?"

"What else."

The orphanage was only slightly less foreboding than the asylum, an ornate grey monstrosity that more resembled a prison. While the generous souls who had financed a home for unfortunate children were to be commended, George was certain that life in the building was akin to prison. How many Lillians wondered where their children were? How many had abandoned them on purpose? How many parents had died and left a child behind? But for Lillian's money, she might have grown into young adulthood in this very place.

Put this melancholy aside and concentrate on finding the boy, George reminded himself.

Bess straightened her dress and hat as they took the short staircase to the front door. It was locked, so George knocked.

"Unusual," he said. "It is not even twilight."

"I imagine they must guard the children from the outside," suggested Bess, "as well as keep them in."

"True." He knocked again, but still no one answered.

Bess found a bell and rang it several times. She peered through a side window and said, "I believe someone is coming."

A rough-looking man opened the door a foot and peered out. "Didn't have to knock to wake the dead."

"It seems we did," George retorted. He had expected a kindly old lady, not a man who looked as if he'd just come up from the docks. He carried the unmistakable odor of liquor on his breath, too. "We have business with the director of the orphanage."

"Do you now? If you're looking to donate or adopt one of these ruffians, she'll be happy to see you. If it's anything else, good luck to you."

George bit back several curses and wanted to bash past the man. The sun was losing warmth, he had been in the light too long and was losing strength and patience, and soon Marie would be free to move about the city. "Happily, it is one of the former matters."

"And, we are in a great hurry," said Bess.

"All right, all right. I'll tell her. No guarantees she can see you today… Depends on her mood, the new director."

Bess whispered behind George, "Have all the establishments hired new directors?"

They followed the orphanage employee down a dimly lit hallway to a door that was open wide. Without introducing them or going inside, the man pointed and strode up a staircase, leaving them alone. The office beyond seemed large enough to double as a ballroom, but in a corner a plump matron in a garish gold and scarlet striped dress rested in an oversized chair. It made her look like a grotesque doll abandoned in the corner of an empty doll house.

"I don't like this, George," Bess whispered.

George took in a deep breath, and the particular smell of old blood in the air and a vibration of power filled him with foreboding. "No, I would think not."

The woman stood at the sight of George, or perhaps the smell of him, and dropped the papers she'd been reading.

"Stay here, Bess. Better yet, why don't you go outside?"

"I don't think—"

"Go outside. Now."

He heard Bess leave but kept his gaze attached to his unfamiliar foe. He crossed the room in several strides and faced her square on. She feared him, and she should. They both knew instantly that he was older and much stronger.

"I'm surprised Madam left such a youngster to guard this place of castaways."

"I have no idea what you are talking about, sir. I am Miss Defarge, the director of the orphanage."

"Defarge?" He laughed and heard the woman's pulse quicken. "That was the first name that came to mind? My, you must be more prepared in the future. If you have a future."

She lifted her chin and stared at him defiantly. "What do you want here?"

"I know why the wolf guards the henhouse. Now I would like to know what Marie has done or plans to do to these children, although I have my suspicions. And I would have the whereabouts of one boy in particular."

"I am not Marie's servant," the woman said, forgoing at least that much pretense. "Of course I know of her. We all do. I am here for my own purposes."

"You imprison children so Marie can feast on them at will? I have heard many things in my day, madam, but that is one of the most repulsive."

He took another step but she didn't back up. She tried to appear defiant, but her chin quivered in fear. "It is not against the commandments."

"The boy. Don't make me ask again."

Her eyes now red-rimmed and dark, her skin pale and veined, she prepared for battle. "Fool. I am not alone here. You cannot defeat us."

"You *are* alone. My senses are not impaired in any way. You are one of many pawns that Marie cares not a whit for, and unless you tell me where the boy is you will soon be vanquished. You have a choice. Give me what I want, and I will shelter you."

A flash of anguish in her eyes made George realize how welcome his offered sounded. But, "You offer nothing. Your shelter is a paper house in a hurricane, George Orleans. We will take you, and your brother, and everyone you hold dear. We will take this city for our own, and then we will take this continent. The Houses will fall, all of them."

"When did Marie give that speech? You are a newborn, so you can be forgiven for believing her lies." In two strides he was on her, hand around her neck and teeth ready to tear free the truth. Her chair fell, and he pushed her against the wall. "You will not live another minute unless you turn over the boy."

Her tears ran in red rivulets down her cheeks, and she shook, feeling his power and wrath. "She will kill me."

"I will kill you first."

"I don't know where he is. They took him. I swear, George, it is the truth."

He saw it was. She was limp in his hands now, had given up everything. "Who took him?"

"Two men. That is all I know!"

"Why? Because they know the child means something to me? To my beloved?"

She looked puzzled. "What? No. It is not your child. Jacques is part of the…"

"The what?"

"The experiment of the men. One was a doctor. Jacques has been gone a few months. I cannot tell you more. I truly know nothing else. He was raised here but never allowed to be present on adoption days."

"Schneider. Was that the name of the doctor?"

"I don't know!"

"Was there a lawyer, a Pemberton?"

A flash of recognition crossed the woman's face. She wiped the blood from her cheeks, and George loosened his grip.

"Perhaps—I cannot be sure. I wasn't privy to the conversations. I simply watched the boy."

Oh, Lil, she does have your child. "Did they say anything that would indicate where they were taking him?"

"No! As I said…" The woman paused.

"What?"

"Someone mentioned a castle once. I know of no castle." She wept again and covered her face. "I swear, that is all I know. She just left me here to keep prying mortals away. The children are mostly gone; we've taken no one new in ages. Take me now and be done with it, before she does."

George sighed and clenched his fist. "Is the boy still mortal?"

"He was when he left here."

A wave of relief calmed his tension, and he released Marie's minion. "Kill yourself or let her do it."

She leapt at him as he turned, clawing his neck and scalp, trying to force him to end it. He shrugged her off. Killing this pitiful creature, as Bess would call her, would be kind, but he didn't feel kind. The only revenge that would satisfy him would be to destroy the destroyer.

CHAPTER NINETEEN

An unusual love.

Sullivan sat while Phoebe tied his cravat. He knew how to do it, but she simply loved to fuss over him. He would deny her nothing. Except the truth.

"When can we go home, love? I'm tired of these hitey-titey vampires. Shoulda never come here. I can feel your anger at them brothers coming outta your pores. Let's quit this town, Chauncey."

She sat in his lap and pressed a pleading kiss on his lips. He shouldn't have brought her. Another selfish move, another sin added to an endless list.

"I can't quit it yet, Phoebe. Soon, though. Very soon." *God, I hope,* he didn't add. The vial of Elder blood kept him awake during the day, made him restless all night. He wandered the city when Phoebe slept, hoping for a glimpse of Vasil, terrified also that the Elder would reappear.

He'd tried to find his maker on his own, as these bickering Orleans fools seemed to have no plan at all except to bring him into the battle. Now they had started talk of a child when they didn't think he was around, and he was certain there was more to this story than they said. He could easily wring the truth from them, but he just wanted to finish the task and ensure Phoebe's safety.

"Where you going now? Take me. Why do you go without me? Tell me, Chauncey."

The fear in her eyes made him nauseated, but it was better that she suspected him of infidelity than know the truth. And it felt like infidelity. Would Vasil come tonight? Demand to know why Marie still lived?

He quickly pressed a kiss on Phoebe's forehead and left. Clutching the vial under his coat, he now relished its burn on his palm. One drop would kill Marie, Vasil had said. So why did Chauncey so badly crave one drop for himself? The Elders were demons, for sure. Tricksters.

After walking only a few yards down the street, the burn on his hand grew stronger and he released it. *Here I am,* he heard, and he looked up. Vasil held out his arms in mock greeting, his long cape flapping in the night breeze, his hair swirling into a confusing halo of gold around him.

Chauncey leapt up on to the roof and rested his back against the water cistern several yards away from Vasil. "I am trying, Elder. I will find her soon."

"She righta under your nose, ya no see it?"

Chauncey winced at his imitation of Phoebe, a reminder of what was at risk. "Tell me where she is, then, to make this better for us both."

"The Frenchmen are close." Vasil shrugged. "A day or so and you'll see her. That is not why I'm here."

"Why, then?" Chauncey could barely speak, and he couldn't take his eyes off Vasil. *Is this what it is to worship a God, to feel the love that Phoebe feels for her Jesus?*

"You keep calling me. It's annoying, profoundly annoying. I hear it day and night. Your voice is strong, Mr. Sullivan. Your devotion is adorable."

Chauncey looked away, ashamed. "I'll try to do better. I…it is the blood, I think. It's muddled my mind."

Vasil chuckled and motioned with one finger for him to draw near. Chauncey tried to avoid eye contact as he walked to within a few feet, and Vasil's icy breath smelled of warm sunlight on pine branches, of freesia, of cloves and oranges. All of Chauncey's favorite smells, one after another.

"You mock me," he accused. "You cast this terrible spell on me and now you mock me. I don't think Phoebe's God would do that to her."

"Spell? I'm no warlock. You're very confused." Vasil sighed and pulled Chauncey in closer, one scalding hand on each of his shoulders. His eyes shone silver and blue. To his horror, Chauncey felt hot tears fall down his cheeks.

"*Ogottogott!* My good friend, attend to me." Vasil put a finger under Chauncey's chin to collect his gaze. "You have had a bad romance, yes? One in which you are shunned, one that can never be, that breaks the heart and spirit?"

"I am not a lover of men," Chauncey said.

"I am no longer a man, Herr Sullivan. I am everything you hate and love about yourself. You are very, very strong, to even be able to endure my touch. But it is your own true nature you long for, the terrible beautiful power you see in me."

Chauncey cried and listened, hating everything he said, hating him, his beauty, his power. "I hate you! Leave me be. I'll kill Marie, just lift this spell!"

Vasil shook his head and smirked. "There is no spell. You crave my blood."

"You told me it was poison! You are poison!"

The Elder shrugged. "It all depends on who drinks it."

Chauncey's head spun at the words and smells and urges pouring through him. Vasil's touch no longer felt gentle. When he opened his eyes, his knees buckled at the gleaming fangs and black pupils only inches away. Vasil's nails dug into Chauncey's neck as the Elder lifted him off the ground. Gone was the pale icy beauty. This was a demon.

"I am not your God and I am not your Satan. I will make your life *more* of a living hell or reward you well, yes? Kill Marie, and stop calling for me!" Vasil dropped Chauncey to the ground, where Chauncey hugged his knees to his chest and cried. "One more thing, my friend. If there is a child, and if he is special in any way, kill him. If he is not...I think I would like him. Call to me then, and I will come."

Chauncey watched the Elder drift noiselessly into the night.

CHAPTER TWENTY

Some doubts erased.

Between caring for the boys—a task akin to herding snakes—trying to be a good and soothing friend to Bess, and fretting constantly over Marie and her own missing child, Lillian was exhausted and longed for some escape that her medicine didn't provide. At least the guest vampires didn't need to be fed, and she could have food delivered for the boys from Eisner's grocery. She didn't have a clue how to prepare meals, nor did she have time or interest. Perhaps she could hire a cook?

"What would Uncle do?" she repeated to herself again and again. In the old days thoughts of her Uncle Sherlock brought her respite. "He would not have gotten himself into such a mess. I would have Mr. Doyle write a different story for me."

The boys needed clothes, though, and more time outside. And to be enrolled in school. Aileen and Johnnie had never managed to teach them properly on their own, nor had they found a public institution. Bess and Kitty had agreed to take them to buy new shoes and clothes the next day, and that would have to be enough for one week. School could come later.

How had it come to this? Constant fretting over meals for humans, clothes, household chores? All the evil in the world seemed to be crashing down on her, and yet the needs of her charges and friends couldn't be ignored. The boys still grieved for Aileen, each in their own way. Darby had asked the night before if he could see his sister again, and Lillian hadn't known what to say. She'd brushed his hair aside and kissed his freckled cheek.

Is this what being a mother is like?

Everyone in her house had known nothing but loss. Was life that way for everyone? Was happiness a foolish wish?

She walked back and forth in her parlor, alone with the unsociable Sullivans. Phillip and Kitty had gone to their home, the boys were asleep, and George late. He had promised to be back before sundown, after making sure Bess made it home safely. Lillian had been left "for her own protection." But she did not want to be protected. She wanted to find Jane or destroy Madame Lucifer.

She had not yet chased down the members of Mr. Doyle's Society, but she was sure that Doyle himself had more to tell. How could he help, and mightn't he, if approached in the right way? There was something there, something left untold. Lil would visit him again tomorrow morning, she'd decided. Otherwise he might leave Baltimore before she got the chance to try. And she had never explained how he'd changed her life. Perhaps that would make a difference.

Opening her journal, she reread her notation of meeting the Leaping Man. How childish those writings now seemed, her desire to solve a mystery, to make Uncle proud. It had only been a few months ago but seemed a lifetime. Perhaps one day she would have the chance to do *real* good, to right the wrongs of the city, to solve crimes and come home to a wonderful man and a wonderful daughter. Perhaps—

She snapped both the book and the fantasy closed when George came through the door. He rushed over and pulled her in for a long embrace. "Bess is home, and is fine."

Her nerves deadened. So, that was all he had to report. They were no further.

"Come, Lil, let us go to your room."

His voice didn't bear the provocative tone that usually accompanied the request for privacy, and Lillian was glad of it, as she could think of no physical pleasure to be had at the moment. She nodded and said, "Quiet, as the boys are finally asleep."

They crept up the stairs and into her room, sat on the bed and held hands.

"Do you realize," George said with a bit of a smirk, "that right here, only a few months ago, you shot me? Twice."

"Tell me," Lillian demanded. "It is not good news. But I would have the truth."

"It is not the worst news. As far as we know, your child lives. But not at the orphanage."

"We already know she isn't at the orphanage," Lillian snapped. "Why did you go there?"

"The director of the asylum confirmed that was where he was sent."

Lillian pulled back to see more clearly the expression on George's face. He was concerned, yes, but also interested in her reaction. Extremely interested.

"Did you hear me, Lil?"

"Of course I heard you." She paused. "What did you say?"

"According to Spring Grove's records, you had a son. I've learned they named him Jacques."

"Son?"

"Indeed."

"It's not possible. I saw her. I…"

"Did you hold her?"

"No, they would not let me."

"How do you know it was a girl?"

I hate you, Herr Doctor. I will hate you until the day I die, and then I will hunt you down in the next life. I hope you are in Hell so that I may torture you there.

"Lil? Did they *tell* you it was a girl?"

She nodded. "Schneider did. It never occurred to me that he would lie about that. Of course, it makes perfect sense now. They never wanted me to go looking for a boy. It worked."

"No, it didn't. You didn't give up, and now we have the truth. You are victorious over the man."

"But you don't know where he is, or you would have brought him home to me. Isn't that right?"

"Mostly. I have clues, but they are sketchy and we will have to work hard to unravel them."

"Then we will. I will."

"We will."

"Are you disappointed that you do not have a daughter?"

Am I?

"No," she realized. "I believe I will make the adjustment in time. No, I will love him dearly. I already do. But if he is as wild as my Musketeers, I may end up back in the asylum. Boys are exhausting creatures, George."

"I was rather pleased, somehow, to hear it was a boy. I would have loved your child no matter what, but I would know what to *do* with a boy better, I think."

George turned away, reaching for his pipe, and Lillian suddenly knew he hadn't meant to share that thought. Why, it hadn't really occurred to her that George would truly want a child, to be a father to hers.

"Where do you think he is?" she asked.

"I don't know. But I'll tell you all I heard, for you have a good head on those lovely shoulders. Lie back with me and shed some of those heavy clothes, and let's talk through the night. I am tired of running about, and I want to hold you as we talk and plan."

She glanced over at him, surprised. "I am sure you do not just want to hold me."

"For once, that is exactly what I would like."

Lillian let her gown fall to the floor and took George by the hand. He undressed, picked her up, and laid her on the bed.

"As I saw you that night," he murmured. "Nude and beautiful, extraordinary and compelling. I've never encountered anyone like you, Lil, and I've met a lot of people in my days."

"I know."

"You never ask how many women. You are the first not to ask. Perhaps you are the first not to care?"

"You are saying I'm not a normal woman," Lillian replied. "I suppose I am not."

"It is not a criticism. You are above any woman I've known." George blew out a deep breath and brushed a kiss along her jawbone. He pulled her against his body, nuzzled his face against her neck. "Do not look at me for a moment. Your eyes distract me, arouse me. I must speak my mind."

His tone was serious, and Lillian wondered what new transgression she'd committed, what commandment she'd flirted with breaking. Was this George her maker, or George her lover? Or were they the same? It didn't feel so.

"I want to talk about us, Lil."

"I know," she said.

"We are beyond you trying to shoot me, and I believe you've given up trying to understand me, which is splendid, as I don't understand myself. You are adjusting to your new life."

"Am I?" She shook her head. "I seem to falter constantly."

"Time, it takes so much time. You are impatient, Lil. We enjoy one another's company. At least I for one do not feel the need to be away from you at all. Quite the opposite. It's humbling, embarrassing. And new. I've never needed—no, *wanted*—this closeness."

"Are you asking me to marry you, George?" she blurted. She rolled over and stared at him, at his dark eyes that swallowed her whole, at his lips that took her breath away whenever they met hers. Would he have this pull on her if he weren't her maker? She would never know. Did it matter?

Somehow, it did.

"No! I do not think so. Am I? It's been bothering me a great deal, Lil."

"Yes, it has bothered me as well. A most unwelcome distraction in a time of great stress and chaos. Even Bess nags me about it." Lillian sighed and gave him an annoyed frown. "Please work it out and speak to me on the topic when you decide, will you?"

"Could I have your feelings on it?"

She snorted. "Have you ever read the romantic novels of Jane Austen, George? No, I didn't think so. One of her heroes gets it quite wrong, you see. He tells his beloved of all the reasons they really should not get married, and then he proposes. You are reminding me a good deal of him right now."

"I am?"

"As little as I know about love, romance, and marriage, I do believe that one should only make a lifelong promise because to not do so would be unthinkable. It is a grave commitment, don't you think? Especially for one who might live for centuries or more."

"You don't want to marry me," George said. "That is becoming clear."

"That is a convenient excuse you are making. I have said no such thing. I can barely imagine tomorrow." She paused. "Do makers marry their newborns often?"

"Why, I suppose not. I don't know. What has that to do with anything, Lil? I'm talking about us."

"I cannot separate the two, George. I cannot imagine being without you, but..." She saw the hurt in his eyes. How could she make him understand without hurting him?

"You can be difficult, even annoying. Why won't you simply tell me what you want?"

"And you can be arrogant and infuriating."

George looked aggrieved. "Of course I know that. Phillip reminds me daily of it."

Phillip. Your brother, your other child. I would like to speak of these things with him. And perhaps at some point she would. But for now she said, "Then I will not bother. Now, kiss me everywhere and exhaust me until I can stay awake no more, and I will sleep in your arms, safe from everything outside these walls for one night."

CHAPTER TWENTY-ONE

Where is the castle?

"What the blazes is wrong with you, Georgy? It's unnerving."

Lillian watched Phillip half-sip at a cup of tea. George and she were doing the same, while Kitty ate her breakfast of sausages and eggs. They were gathered at the Orleans house to plan their next move, although Lillian knew they weren't much further than the day Annaluisa was killed.

"There's a hell of a lot going wrong right now, Phillip. What do you think is wrong with me?"

Kitty waved her fork at George. "You're not your typical annoying self. More annoying, in fact. You're brooding again. You only brood when your ego has been damaged."

George growled at Kitty, who growled back. He laughed and said, "Kitty, really, have I been that bad a future brother-in-law?"

She frowned. "You brought the wrath of the devil down on us, delayed my wedding, and I'm sure before I'm finished eating my meal will do something else disastrous."

"There must be an Irish saying about this, eh, Kitty? 'Marrying the whole family'?"

"Aye, and it's true. Now show me that ring you're hiding under the table, Lillian. It nearly blinded me when you came through the door."

Lillian clenched her hands together and cast a quick glance at George, who rubbed at his temples. Kitty would make it all worse, she was sure. The woman lived to taunt George, protected as she was by his brother. And he seemed to quite enjoy their verbal sparring matches. "Show me, Lil," Phillip's fiancée pushed. "I'll be seeing if George knows how to do anything properly."

"I'm not sure what you mean, Kitty."

The woman blew out an improper noise that sounded like a horse. "I heard you say your hero Mr. Doyle was a bad actor. He could not be worse than you. Or *you*," she said to George. "Show me the engagement ring. I'd like to bring you down off that high horse of yours if possible. I'm sure you mucked this up."

"It's a gift, Kitty. Not an engagement ring." But Lillian did as requested.

Kitty whistled through her teeth and pulled at Lillian's hand to get a better look. "Unusual, but that is our George." She looked at George and nodded. "That will do."

He bowed his head and swept out his hand dramatically. "So glad you approve."

Phillip looked up from a newspaper article that had caught his attention. "Wait, did someone say something about marriage? *Our* marriage?"

"Really, Phillip," said George. "Try to keep up, won't you?"

Kitty moved her chair next to Lillian's and gave her a peck on the cheek. "When is the wedding?"

"It's not an engagement ring, Kitty," Lillian hissed. "Please, let it be."

"Och! Are all you *dreách foula* so ignorant of normal things? You, at least, were mortal recently."

"But I really don't understand such matters. Bess mostly taught me what I do know. And Aileen."

Kitty crossed herself. "Then Bess and I will have to teach you the rest."

"Thank you," Lillian said. There seemed little else to say.

George groaned and pushed back in his chair. "May we change the subject?"

Phillip put down his paper. "Of course. Now, what was the urgent matter you needed to discuss with us, George? I assume it involves Marie. What did you learn last night that has you in such uproar?"

"I met a vampire at the orphanage. Pathetic woman, slave to Marie. She's likely taken her own life by now, as she revealed too much. Marie will be...vengeful."

"Anyone we know?" Phillip asked. "I thought we were alone in Baltimore."

"It seems she's been here for a while. How long I don't know. Her story was simple: Lillian's *son* was in fact raised here, but he was taken by two men—to Marie, we surmise. She seemed to recognize the name Pemberton, 'the Jackal' who was Lillian's solicitor. We know also that the Jackal is the father"—George squeezed Lillian's hand in apology for his frankness, sensing her discomfort—"so it's a fair working assumption that Pemberton and Dr. Schneider were the two men who took the boy from the orphanage."

"To Marie?" Kitty repeated.

"This is where things become less clear. The woman mentioned that the boy—she called him Jacques—was part of some experiment of the men."

Lillian shuddered. Seeing the concern on the others' faces she admitted, "I believe that I was also part of an experiment. I do not know what, or why."

"The woman believes that Jacques is still mortal, or he was when she last saw him." George turned and looked at Lillian. "Although, of course Lil and I would love him no matter his state, and we intend to bring him home."

"Of course," Phillip concurred, but his voice was filled with doubt.

Lillian pulled out her Journal of Important Observations, which she felt she finally needed in earnest. How silly she had been before, how delusional. Now faced with a real mystery, the life and death of a loved one, every penned word leapt out at her. She examined her notations, her list of clues. Mustering the facts would help draw the larger picture.

"The Learned Order of Psychic Scholars. The Jackal and Dr. Schneider were members," she began.

"Why, I believe my patroness Miss Etta was recently accepted as a member of that society," Kitty remarked.

"And that is why it is critical that you never speak to her about us again."

Kitty frowned and nodded. "Of course, Lil. In the early days, when I first met Phillip, my talk of vampires—"

"Was understandable." Hadn't she done the same with Mr. Doyle? "We must move forward and not waste time worrying about what has already transpired. But we must not make further mistakes."

"The other members of the Society are Baltimore notables," she continued, "who claim to be interested in matters of life beyond human mortality and any and all matters of spiritism. Their newest member—well, in fact he's only a guest—is the writer Arthur Conan Doyle."

Phillip rubbed at his chin, hanging on her every word. "Your great...mentor."

"Indeed. We visited him, and he held something back from us. More curious, he knew Annaluisa Pelosi, although he certainly didn't know her true nature. He showed interest in the murders of Annaluisa and Aileen and understandably linked the two deaths. Johnnie Moran has done the same. The two men have met, somehow."

"How is Johnnie?" Kitty asked.

"Deep in grief. He comes around infrequently to check on his brothers and leaves quickly when he sees they are being cared for. The house is full of memories of his beloved, and, well, I don't think he much likes our guests."

Kitty shook her head. "You mean your guard dogs. They are exceptionally odd, even for vampires."

"What a snob you are, Kitty!" George said.

"I do not refer to their skin color. That man, especially…" Kitty shuddered.

Lillian ran her finger down her list, anxious to change the topic. "'The castle,'" she said after a moment.

"The castle," George repeated. "The vampire in the orphanage mentioned that she'd heard talk of a castle. Jacques may have been taken to one, and we might assume that Marie is there as well. She would likely desire a grand base of operations."

"A *castle?*" Kitty snorted. "I've seen castles, but not since setting foot in America."

Oh, of course, you idiot! "Holmes! How could you be so stupid!" Lillian said suddenly to herself. She turned to George. "The castle. The Society's headquarters. Did you not see the battlements on that mansion?"

"I would hardly call that monstrosity a castle."

"Because you have seen real ones. A poor imitation, I'll agree, but it makes sense, doesn't it, George? The Society, the Jackal and Schneider, the woman you met at the orphanage… They are all related. We know that much."

"Where is this place?" Phillip asked.

"Just on the outskirts of the city, near Loch Raven."

"I know that home," Phillip said. "Doesn't it belong to Congressman Coyle? I met with him during the longshoremen's strike. He wanted to discuss our shipyard."

Lillian turned. "That makes sense. What doesn't is the idea of Marie holding court at a congressman's home and hosting meetings for members of that society. Surely she would be more circumspect."

"Marie, circumspect? What does she have to fear, a monster who feasts on her own kind? She has never been circumspect." George shrugged. "Perhaps she is not there, but it is a good starting place to seek Jacques, don't you think?"

"They did speak of vampires when we visited," Lillian recalled. "Between my letters to Doyle and Kitty's talk to Etta, they seemed rather intrigued. At least, Doyle did."

"Why don't you confront Doyle?" Kitty asked. "Threaten him, torture the information out of him if you must. I would if it were my child."

The three others stared at her in surprise.

"Torture Arthur Conan Doyle?" Lillian sat back, recalling her own desire to do the same but also her humanity. "I think not. Of course, if he had any part in keeping my son captive, he will die by my hand. But I suspect he knows nothing of most of this."

George concurred. "Although, my guess is that he is following some of the same threads we are. He may be a help, if we can find a way to use him. He's also linked up with a journalist. We must remember him and tie up that loose end if it comes to it."

"Loose end?" Kitty snorted. "Some poor innocent becomes a loose end just by crossing your path?"

George growled again. "Aren't you the one who suggested we torture Mr. Doyle?"

"Stop it, you two," Phillip snapped. "Now, *what?* We are to storm the castle, so to speak? Sullivan, Phoebe, and we three? I wonder now if even Chauncey is strong enough to be of help, although he is chomping at the bit to get his hands on her."

"Five of you cannot fight one?" Kitty asked.

"I don't know," George said. "A stretch of her hand could send one of us sprawling, groveling for breath and life."

Lillian shook her head. "It matters not, at least to me. I will not sit by another day. At any moment her heinous experiment on my son could end and she might do the unthinkable."

George stared out the window. "I do wonder if she would accept a bargain. It's all about me. Surely we all know that."

Lillian sighed. "It will not end until she destroys all of us, George. Don't you see? She doesn't want to kill you. She wants to *hurt* you."

"I would have abandoned you all. Still could. Or I could go to her and offer myself—"

"Not a bad idea," Kitty joked, but her face was grim.

Phillip stood and pulled George upright by the arm. "Lillian is right. Self-sacrifice will serve nothing except to make those who love you miserable, George. Don't try to be a hero. We must be free of her, and we never will be if you make a bargain. You will be gone, and the rest of us will be that much weaker without you. What will happen when she determines you are gone and she needs new targets to torture?"

"You knew her best, Phillip," George admitted. "She was your wife. So, what was her greatest weakness?"

"I'm afraid that you were, brother. I imagine it's this simple: She loved a man who cared not a bit about her, who turned her husband into a monster and then did the same to her. She wasn't a very reasonable mortal; there's no cause to expect logic from her now."

Lillian snapped her notebook closed, rose and paced. "She is weak by day, so that is the time to approach the castle."

"We must have cover of darkness," Phillip argued. "We cannot go knocking on the front door with the others in tow. Not unless we want this to end a bloodbath."

"Then we will go tonight and see if Jacques is there," Lillian vowed.

George shook his head. "No. Or at least, maybe not. We have so few cards to play. Let us first find out, once and for all, what Doyle knows. Perhaps there is something we've overlooked that can help. Surely he would side with us against Marie if he came to know the entire story."

"Do you intend to reveal yourself to him?" Phillip asked, shocked. "We cannot afford many more humans knowing about us, George! We have been indiscreet far too long with no retribution. With Kitty and Bess knowing but remaining mortal…"

George looked at Lillian but answered his brother. "We are all agreed on that point. Whether the Elders are watching or not, there are good reasons to stay hidden. Lil's friend and your fiancée know of us. We will not add to that number. I intend for Lil to simply appeal to the man for information."

"You will send *her?*" Kitty asked.

"He cannot harm her, and she will seem less a threat," George replied. "And I doubt she could be kept from him."

Lillian nodded when he looked over at her for acceptance.

"I will brief Chauncey, and we will assemble here tonight," George announced. "After. Then we will make further plans."

"What of Bess and me? Is there nothing we can do to help?" Kitty asked.

"You will take care of the boys—no matter what," Lillian instructed. "There are to be no more orphans."

CHAPTER TWENTY-TWO

Lillian and Arthur.

Arthur drained his cup of tea and threw on his overcoat, intent on learning more about the mysterious Lillian Holmes and the strange occurrences surrounding her. He'd passed the last two days alone, fretting, wishing young Mencken was around, as he wasn't quite sure what he'd gotten himself into and wished for a compatriot or a partner in crime. But Mencken had gone off to try to interview the police and see what more he could pry from the tight-lipped Lieutenant. He'd hadn't yet reported back, and Arthur wondered if the young man had moved on to other matters or was in some sort of trouble. He thought of going to see Officer Moran to find out.

Should I have gone to Boston, left this city and its mysteries, its dangers? Will this be the death of me?

Arthur stood outside his hotel, weighing his options, when the woman in question walked up the street toward him.

For better or for worse, he realized, *I am going to learn what is going on.*

He waited for her, and she stopped a few feet away.

"I was coming to see you again."

"I'm pleased, Miss Holmes."

"May we speak in private? Perhaps on that park bench?"

He offered his arm, and they crossed the street and sat. It was a fine day, Arthur saw, but this lady could not enjoy it. She had the weight of the world on her shoulders and looked like she hadn't slept in a fortnight.

"Miss Holmes, what is amiss? Can I help in some way?" Aside from her beauty, he found her compelling in some way he couldn't describe. She was intelligent, certainly, but she also seemed…at once both strong and fragile. And mysterious. He realized now that he would do a great deal to help her if he could. And he hadn't minded her beau, either, another clever chap. Although, the man had come very close to hinting that Arthur himself was involved in the murders somehow. But they'd left on good terms, Arthur allowed as he studied Lillian.

"Perhaps you can," she answered. Then, after a moment: "You may think what I am about to reveal scandalous, but I cannot change the facts. What did your Sherlock often say about strange facts?"

"Your memory for the man's ways is better than mine."

She shook away his smile and attempt at lightening the mood. "I bore a child when I was sixteen." Then she held her hand over her mouth, as if that were not at all what she'd meant to disclose. Clearly she waited for a response, but Arthur did not trust she would continue to speak if he interjected platitudes. He stayed silent, curious as to why she would even share such a shame.

Lillian turned away slightly. "He would now be seven, or perhaps just turned eight, as I do not have the date marked properly. I believe him to be alive. Two men, a Mr. Pemberton, my former lawyer, and a Dr. Schneider, had control over my life at the time. Until very recently, they ruled it completely."

Arthur tried to keep his expression calm, but her open mention of the two murder victims astounded him, and he knew she saw it on his face.

"They were members of the Learned Order to which you now belong."

Arthur blanched. *So, she does she think me complicit in this affair? Good God, is that fellow George about?*

"I am merely a guest, of course," he said, "and have not been long in the Society's company."

"Yes, I understand that. You heard me speak of Pemberton at the train station. I called him the Jackal, as he is the father of my child...but not by my wishes."

"My girl!" Arthur said. "I cannot believe—"

"No, no one would."

"I do not mean that I think you are lying, but it's very difficult to take in."

"Indeed," she agreed.

"I am sorry." And he truly was. He'd seen enough horrors in his medical practice to make him nearly give up on mankind. Bruised and broken children and women, patients overwhelmed by nervous fits after mistreatment by family members....

"Thank you," she said. "My goal, however, is to find my son. I believe you may hold some key for me, some knowledge of his whereabouts."

"What makes you say that?" And yet, he did want to help. At least, he thought he did. *What had they said exactly, the members of the Society? That Pemberton and Schneider had bungled the business with the child?*

"A look of recognition, a feeling, perhaps."

"Your instincts are correct," Arthur decided to admit. "That is the hallmark of a truly great detective."

"Sir, I have never begged for anything in my life. But I am begging you to tell me what you know. I believe you to be a good man, judging from your writings and your interest in the afterlife."

"I don't imagine myself to be an evil man, but I am no saint," Arthur said. He felt the urge to run from Lillian Holmes. How had he gotten pulled into this befuddling mess? Hadn't she said her man killed the Jackal? Hadn't she indeed said as much at the train depot?

Wouldn't that be George, then? Of course George would want to murder Lillian's rapist!

"Miss Holmes," he began. He scanned the park for threats, at the same time thinking, *You fool!* Could not Lillian Holmes and her beau also be the killers of Annaluisa and Aileen and God knew who else?

He continued, "Between the piling up of bloodless victims in this city, the accusations you level on acquaintances of mine, and some odd notions I've heard about you and your companions, it is difficult for me to know whom to trust, whom to believe. I have urgent business in Boston and am afraid—"

"Where are your instincts, Mr. Doyle? If I were to explain those murders, explain those odd notions about me and mine, would you then trust me?"

Arthur paused and considered. "I would be more inclined to, certainly." Was she insane? Perhaps. Did she know something momentous that he would find interesting? Yes, he thought it likely. So he sat back and stared into her eyes. "Please go on."

"You will remember that I asked about your friendship with Mr. Bram Stoker, and whether you believed in his creatures. In vampires."

"Yes," Arthur said. His skin crawled, his heart raced, and his nerves sizzled as they had only a few times in his life: the first time he saw a spirit, and the first time he heard his dead mother's voice at a séance. "You denied it when we last met."

A child's ball bounced toward their bench, and a boy approached shyly to retrieve it. Arthur couldn't move to help him, frozen as he was in his seat. Lillian gave the ball a solid kick, and they were left in a timeless silence.

"I do remember, Miss Holmes," he said at last.

"Please, call me Lillian." She laughed to herself and looked out at the field where the boy giggled as he chased his ball, which had soared impossibly far. "If you only knew the part you played in my life these last several years."

"I presume you read a great deal? Of my work?"

"My pastime went far beyond that. I was asleep, in a way, fantasizing that I was a great detective myself."

"That is not so unusual," Arthur said, wondering where this was headed. "And a great compliment to me. For it means I created stories you could enter and make your own. The best ones have that character, don't you agree?"

"Indeed. But that is not what I mean. For a while, I had a very strong notion—one that still has a grip on me at moments of great stress—that I am the niece of Sherlock Holmes. Tell me *that* is not unusual!"

"Fantasies can overtake our realities if our realities are too difficult to bear," Arthur found himself saying. *My God, poor thing. Even if she is involved in these murders, it is perhaps because of a mental disorder.* "You may not know that I am also a physician, Miss...Lillian. I have seen a great many ills of the mind. Some drink away their troubles, others isolate themselves. At least your fantasy proved rather harmless, and you speak of it largely as in the past."

"Have you ever had a patient who heard voices? At my worst, I hear the city speaking to me, telling me to do strange things."

"To others?"

"To myself. They have abated...somewhat."

"I see," Arthur said. Clearing his throat he admitted, "There are a few reasons, none of them very pleasant, that a person might hear voices. Certain drugs, extreme stress, and a more serious condition that seems to run in families. But I am not your physician and am not able to make a proper diagnosis. If you would like a recommendation...?"

"I would like to steer clear of such learned men." She turned to face him, and he saw anew her exhaustion of body and spirit. "No offense to you. I am sorry that I must finish this conversation quickly, and we have not gotten to the crux." She closed her eyes and fretted with her bag. "George will hate me, but I know no other way. I must find him."

Arthur's heart began to pound. "Why would George hate you, my dear? It seems quite impossible to me."

"There are rules, strict rules. We are to bring no more mortals into the mix."

So, quite insane. She mumbled more words, but he could not pick them out. He felt the urge to run, but another urge was stronger even than his desire for self-preservation. He could not turn his back on such a lost, injured soul. Did he know another physician in town? This woman needed treatment, desperately.

"You have heard talk of vampires from your society members," she announced.

So, they were back here. It was not a question, and the hair on his neck stood on end. "Dear Miss Holmes—"

"Vampires exist. They are not only the stuff of folklore. I do not have all the answers you will surely want, as I am new to this life..."

She trailed off, and Arthur said, "You truly believe yourself to be...immortal? One who feeds on others?"

"Immortal, no. I can be killed. But I will not age outwardly. I swear to you that I am not evil, not in the way you might think. I take pride in supping only on murderers, criminals of the most awful kind, the dying... An occasional squirrel or rat." She sniffed out a laugh. "One does what one must."

"My dear, I am so sorry you are suffering. Will you allow me to take you to a place that—?"

"No! No one will take me there again!" She wiped at her eye with her handkerchief, and he noticed blood on the white linen. She looked up at him, eyes rimmed in scarlet, pupils black, skin as pale as snow.

He leapt back a few feet, hands and legs shaking.

"I am sorry," she said. "I am simply hungry. It's been a trying time."

Arthur rubbed at his brow, feeling incredibly stupid. *I am in real danger,* he thought, *if anything this woman says is true. I would taste better to her than a squirrel.* Her bloody handkerchief caught his eye, and he tried to remember any of Stoker's work or their conversations about how to kill one of these abominations. With no holy water, crucifixes, garlic, or wooden stakes on his person, he felt as good as naked.

But it is daylight! She cannot harm anyone in the daylight, isn't that true? Mustn't she turn into a bat first, or was that after?

Run, Arthur, run!

But he couldn't. It seemed Miss Lillian Holmes held answers to so many questions about spiritism and the afterlife. He could not leave, so he found himself saying, "You see we are out in the open, and that police patrol this park. And I am armed."

She nodded. "I would never harm you, though, or anyone good."

"You are the judge of who is good and who is bad? Was my friend Annaluisa Pelosi so bad? Or the young maid, Aileen O'Shaunessy? Hardly a hardened criminal, I would think!"

"No! They were both my dear friends, especially Aileen. I am heartbroken over the loss. I am caring for her brothers in my home."

"Your beau, then?" Arthur accused. "Mr. Orleans? Is he like you?"

"Please do not ask about him, or about the others. Mr. Doyle, do not put yourself at risk. I would never hurt you, but—"

"George would?" He glanced around for her handkerchief, but she had put it away. With it gone, gone too was his conviction. "This is ridiculous! I believe none of it!"

"You misunderstand. George is not to blame for those deaths. Don't you see? This is why I need your help. There is one very strong person, completely evil, who is wreaking havoc on this city, on innocents, on my friends. And I believe that she has my son. I also believe you know something about it. I would have your assistance. In return—"

"You will not harm me?"

"Of course I could not harm you! You are innocent. And you are incredibly important to me, Mr. Doyle. I cannot separate you from my hero, so you are my hero as well. But I beg for your discretion." She glanced around and was clearly terrified. "Oh God, I see this has not worked! What have I done? He'll never forgive me."

Her fear only made him more concerned. "What is to stop me from going to the authorities? My God, is Johnnie also—"

"No, Johnnie is not involved with us," she interrupted. "Aileen was not. Annaluisa, however, was as old as this city. You may go to the authorities, Mr. Doyle, but they will laugh at you. And they have no way to stop us. We cannot even stop one another, it seems."

Arthur shook his head, trying to bring some clarity to his brain and remove himself from the spell of this strange woman's words. He longed so badly for answers that he'd begun to believe her. Now he saw that she attempted some sort of sham, and he thought it best he extricate himself from the situation as quickly as possible. "I'm sorry I cannot help you, Miss Holmes. I do hope you find a physician who can." *And I pray you are not truly involved with the murders.*

She put her hand on his arm. "Please, you must believe me. Wait one moment!"

Reaching into her leather messenger bag, she extracted a pistol, which she placed on the bench next to her as if it were nothing more than a handkerchief, and next pulled out a small knife. Arthur backed up another foot, ready to call for help, but she looked up, anguish on her face.

"Please," she said, "block the view of any onlookers." Then, to his horror, she drew the knife across her forearm.

The deepest scarlet dripped from the wound. She pressed her lips to it and he grimaced in disgust. "Lillian! You mustn't harm yourself this way! I will help you, I give you my word."

She did not answer, at least not verbally. A moment later she held up her arm for his examination. The bleeding had stopped. The wound had healed and not left a scar. In only seconds.

Shocked, Arthur lurched forward. He knelt before her and rubbed his thumb along the place where she had sliced her flesh. Although her skin was ghastly pale, there wasn't a mark. A most extraordinary woman, Lillian Holmes. He could not have created her. And yet, as the saying went, truth was stranger than fiction.

He sat back and gazed at her. "What trick is this?"

She smiled, tired lines rimming her lovely dark eyes. "How often have you said to me, in your books, that 'When you have eliminated the impossible, whatever remains, *however improbable*, must be the truth'?"

Arthur rose and paced in front of the bench, searching for his own inner voice to tell him what to do. At last he heard, *Here is proof of something, Arthur. Here is the other world you've sought. Will you turn your back on it?*

He turned and nodded. "I…I will tell you what I know. On one condition."

"Yes?"

"Officer Moran is present for all we do, listens to all we say. If your story is accurate, he has a stake in this story."

"That is most inconvenient," Lillian said. "You are drawing another mortal into a rather precarious arena, and for no purpose. He would be ridiculed if he chose to divulge it later. After Aileen, he is already a ruined man."

Arthur shrugged. "I believe he is already part of this story, Miss Holmes, and nothing will change that."

"There are limits, Mr. Doyle, to what George will forgive." Lillian glanced one way and then another. "For love? I don't know... He is my maker, you see. You and Johnnie... He won't like this."

"Then you will search for your child without my help. It is my one condition."

CHAPTER TWENTY-THREE

The reluctant hero and his friend.

George tapped out his pipe. Just before popping it into his jacket, he flung it as far as he could. It landed somewhere in Loch Raven, a hundred yards away from a rooftop of a house near the congressional mansion.

Sullivan glanced at him. "Why did you do that?"

"I don't know. I'll be damned if I know. I'll be damned if I know anything."

The dark-skinned vampire regarded him. "You've changed, George. Perhaps it's the daylight addling my brain, but you're almost likeable. You never would have admitted to knowing nothing fifty years ago."

George laughed. "Guilty as charged, my good man." He leaned back and regarded Chauncey seriously.

"You're having second thoughts about doing this alone with me, aren't you? I honestly didn't expect for you to believe me, but I thought I'd give you the chance. I will wait no longer."

George shrugged. "I suppose I always believed the Elders existed. I did of course wonder why they ignored Marie—and you, to be honest—if the commandments were real."

"I never promised him that I would kill you and yours, despite his order. He'll find me and that will be that, but perhaps Phoebe will have a chance."

"Vasil—"

"Don't say that name again! You can still go home, George. Take your brother and lover and anyone you care about with you. I don't know why you're here."

"Lillian's child. I must give it a try. If I do not, she will."

Sullivan arched a brow and blew out a deep breath. "I don't hold out much hope for a child left in Marie's care."

"Still, Lillian would die trying to rescue him, and I cannot have that."

Chauncey squinted left and right behind his tinted spectacles. "I say, this is getting intolerable. Much more time out here and Madam Lucifer won't have to do a thing. I'll be a shriveled raisin on this roof."

George laughed. "At least she'll also be weak."

"She's never weak."

"How do you know? When was the last time you saw her?"

"Eons ago. But she holds my bond, and I feel no less shackled by it. She certainly has not weakened." The giant pulled his jacket over his head to shield himself further from the long late rays of sun now stretching shadows over the countryside. "I'm tired. Maybe this is a good way to end it. Maybe God will forgive me if I try to do this one last right thing. Maybe not."

"Maybe not," George agreed. He was not hoping for such forgiveness. Nor was he hoping to end his existence, however likely that outcome seemed.

"She shouldn't have taken the child. I never touched children. I did everything else, but I left children alone. Did you?"

George winced and wanted his pipe back. "My record is not so pure."

"You didn't eat your own kind. You didn't break the commandments." Sullivan reached inside his shirt and clutched at something, a necklace of some sort. George had seen him do so repeatedly in the last few days.

"What is that, Sullivan?" he asked. "A religious talisman? It makes my skin crawl every time you touch it."

"That is the nature of talismans—to make bad men uncomfortable. It makes *me* uncomfortable. But I wear it to give me strength against Marie. More I cannot say."

"You're a queer fellow, always were."

"Yes, Grandpapa."

"Well, sorry about that," George snapped. "How could I have known what I would create? That *is* why you've loathed me for so long. I ruined your life by turning Marie. Well, I don't blame you. At times I loathe myself for the same reason."

Sullivan turned and regarded him again then sighed. His voice was molten regret. "Blame you for what I am? No. Who knows what I would have become. I wasn't the nicest mortal, to be honest. I wanted money. I craved it more than life. When Marie took me…"

George had never seen someone loathe himself more. It was shocking, and for that reason he said, "I simply don't believe you're evil, Chauncey. No more than the next man, mortal or vampire. I believe you are here to protect others, especially Phoebe. That has to count for something. Won't your God care about that?"

"Phoebe's God," the giant corrected. "You're here for Miss Holmes. And your brother and his woman. You're not doing it to redeem yourself."

No?

"I turned Phillip. My own brother. You knew that, didn't you?"

Sullivan shrugged. "Act in haste, repent at leisure." When George stared at him, he added, "Do you honestly hope to save him?"

"Yes, I do, assuming certain outcomes. If I just give Lillian her son and Phillip and Kitty some peace, then everyone is better off. And you did promise not to…not to carry out *his* orders?"

The giant nodded. "Why would I have told you about our meetings? I'm sick of death and having a hand in it. Well, except Marie's case. So may we please go now? I really am boiling in my own perspiration up here."

George glanced at his pocket watch. "Ah, here they come now. The society's meeting has broken up."

A handful of fashionable men and one woman filed from the Loch Raven "castle" and stood chatting for a moment before driving away in cabs. Doyle was not among them.

"It seems Doyle did not come. I have no idea what Lillian told him, as she did not return when I expected earlier today. She's been…unreliable." George steeled himself, realizing it did not matter. Not really. "All right, to that roof."

It would be tricky, he admitted, as no one would mistake them for birds, but they managed to leap to the castle without being seen or creating a disturbance. George wondered if Marie were here, was expecting him, had already sensed his nearness. Hopefully she slept, and all of her lackeys slept as well.

Sullivan grabbed him by the shoulders, his massive hands making George feel like a boy himself. "Look at me, Georgy. You could flee, be halfway around the world within days. You will likely die here. Your Lillian may still not get her boy, and she will have lost her love as well. Are you really willing to let that happen?"

"No, I'm not. That is why you will help find the boy after killing Marie, even if I do not survive this. Promise me."

"You're still a bit bossy, do you know that?"

"I know quite well that you could kill me easily, Chauncey. I'm not the boss of much anymore."

Chauncey nearly smiled. "I'll do my best to find the boy if there's time, George."

"I'm growing on you, aren't I?"

"Don't push it."

They climbed down the back of the house and stopped at a second-story window. The room beyond was empty, and they slipped inside without raising an alarm.

The pistol George carried had started to burn against his back. He'd loaded it beforehand with silver, knowing that the casing would offer some protection, but it grew more uncomfortable by the moment. He only needed one good, clean shot—to kill himself should his attempt to kill Marie fail. It might be worth a try to use it on her if she were sleeping, although he'd also brought a silver dagger. He shifted the pistol, thinking he'd much prefer to shoot himself than stab himself.

He and Sullivan moved to the door, and George opened it quietly and peered around the arch to a long empty hallway. The boy could be anywhere in here, and if still mortal he would not emit a particularly strong scent. Or, what if Jacques and Marie were not here at all? Was he simply about to disturb the family of an innocent congressman? Anyone would get quite a scare when they saw the massive Sullivan bearing down their staircase.

He exchanged glances with the other vampire, and his heart slammed into his chest at the decision he'd made, at what he was about to do.

"Which way?" he mouthed.

Sullivan shrugged. George indicated they should start in the cellar.

"There's a lot of house to cover here, George. She probably knows we're here. Just call out if you find her before I do."

"I'll be screaming for you if I do," George mumbled.

Sullivan nodded and moved to the next doorway to begin his hunt for Marie. George took the side staircase to make his way to the basement. A power so strong as Marie's needed constant feeding and long periods of darkness. And then there was Marie's personal dramatic flair. Perhaps she even slept in a makeshift grave.

CHAPTER TWENTY-FOUR

A goodbye.

Upon return to her house Lillian immediately noticed that Sullivan was gone, and that Phoebe moved uncharacteristically about the parlor. She introduced the woman to Mr. Doyle as "a servant," and Phoebe thankfully played the game, but still Doyle's face paled and beads of sweat broke out on his forehead. Well, she'd introduced him to more terror and murder than he'd penned in all his books taken together. She wondered if she hadn't been exposed to more chaos in her shorter lifetime than he. He'd written about murder and betrayals galore, but those were fiction. Hopefully he thought her the only nearby vampire.

"Where is George?" she asked. "Is he with Phillip and Kitty?"

Bess came running down the stairs, chased by the Musketeers, and dodged behind Lillian's skirts. "I cannot keep this up, Lil!"

"You are doing splendidly. Boys, we have a new cook, and I believe she has made some lovely cookies! You will help her clean up, taking great care to follow her instructions, and then you may play in the yard."

She wasn't sure they had heard a word except for the mention of cookies.

Bess sighed and straightened her dress at the sight of Mr. Doyle. He approached rather meekly, examining her from head to toe as if to determine what nature of woman she was.

"Miss Elizabeth Wheeler," Lillian said, "I have the great honor of presenting Mr. Arthur Conan Doyle."

Bess allowed him to take her hand and then let out a loud squeal. He jumped back a full foot.

"Oh! Excuse me, but are you…?" She looked back and forth between Lillian and Mr. Doyle.

"Yes, he is, Bess. I told you that I knew him."

"I am honored. And a bit perturbed, to tell you the truth." Her tone said she spoke in jest, but Lillian knew that she took the meeting quite seriously. "Because you completely entranced my dearest friend, I was forced into some very awkward situations, Mr. Doyle!"

"Bess!" Lillian protested.

"Do tell." Doyle's smile was nervous as he kept running his gaze about the parlor. Phoebe had noiselessly slipped out.

"Let us sit," Lillian suggested. They surrounded the card table.

"About a year ago, wasn't it, Lil? I was forced to follow an innocent Chinaman all over town, as Lil thought he was a criminal in disguise. I've had to pretend to be at least five different women, have snuck out of my house at all hours, given up on having a normal social life with my friend here, and I have you to blame. I mean, *thank.*"

"Ah-ha! A veritable Watson, I see." He'd relaxed a bit in Bess's company, as most everyone did. "I hope it wasn't all odious work?"

"Mostly. But I also think that Lillian has taught me a great deal of what she knows, and that is far more valuable than what I could offer her."

Lillian shook her head. "Nonsense. Miss Wheeler underestimates herself in every respect. Bess, Mr. Doyle knows about me, about the Orleans brothers. He has agreed to help us."

Bess shook her foot under Doyle's scrutiny, as if her deformation proved her mortality. "I am not a 'creature,' if that is what you are trying to ascertain."

The author blanched. "Oh! I'm very sorry. I...I'm not often made speechless, but I am new to this entire idea of... Well, of course you are not. I can see that clearly."

"Because of my foot?"

"I don't understand."

"If I were a creature, my foot would heal properly. Lillian and George will not admit it, but that is to spare me from attempting anything foolhardy."

Doyle looked aghast. "That would be quite a poor bargain, Miss Wheeler. Given everything I've heard, I must agree with your friends. Frankly, I'm not sure what I think about any of this." He ran his fingers along his mustache and let out a great sigh. "Our bargain, Miss Holmes?"

"Yes, I will locate Johnnie, I promise."

The author gathered himself and patted Bess's hand. "Might I see your foot?"

"See it? Everyone can see it. I walk on my toes." She lifted her worn, deformed shoe slightly.

"I am a physician, my dear. Very little upsets me, and very little disinterests me. Now, you do not have the worst kind of affliction. There is a man in Germany who has had some mild success, although usually with children, in lengthening this tendon, called the Achilles..." He manipulated her ankle and pushed against the ball of her foot. "Tsk. If caught earlier, this would not have been a very bad case at all."

"We lived in a small town near the border of Delaware when I was born. My parents...they did not know, you see. We were not in a big city."

"Oh, well, times are different now. But I do not think this a hopeless case." He sat up and patted Bess's hand again as a few tears of hope escaped down her cheek. "There, there, I offer no guarantees, but I will correspond with my friend and see what might be done. Now, don't cry, this is nothing. I am a physician, it's my sworn duty to help."

"I do not think…I do not think I can go to *Germany.*"

"Nonsense," Lil said. This had to end. What had all her money brought her? No happiness, no sense of peace or pride. Here was a way to change that. "When things have calmed down, I will accompany you to Germany, pay for our trip and any charges for your treatment, and take care of you while you recover. I have been learning German in any case, so I will be a great help, indeed!"

Doyle nearly smiled. "Most admirable, Miss Holmes."

"Now," Lillian said to Bess, "give up this ridiculous notion you have of becoming a 'creature,' as you would say. Mr. Doyle, if you would excuse me for a moment, I must find George and tell him of your presence and what you have told me so far. And I will send someone off to fetch Officer Moran."

She left Bess and Mr. Doyle in the parlor and climbed the stairs to her room, each step feeling higher than the next. Her head pounded from hunger and exhaustion, and she prayed George had fed and brought her back a vial or two from his victim, which was his habit if he was worried about her sustenance. She would chase down a few pills with that or have to venture out again.

What would he say, though? She'd brought Mr. Doyle home. Did makers ever punish their children for being wayward? She was sorely testing George's devotion.

He was not in her room. Perhaps he hadn't returned from his meeting with Phillip. She sat on her bed and took off her hat and jacket, untied her street boots. As she went to her desk to find her bottle of Mrs. Winslow's, she saw an envelope addressed to her in a strange ornate hand next to a velvet jeweler's box.

She froze. Not again! What tidings did Madam Lucifer have for her this time?

She sat and opened the envelope, and smelled the peculiar woody smell that George's blood had, that his clothes carried, that she loved so much. Realizing this, her hand shook. He had changed his mind. He had fled, was saying goodbye. She had pushed him too far by bringing mortals into the mix and had gone off alone. He had run off to save himself. He—

Her heart slamming against her chest, she unfolded the single sheet.

My love,

You will never forgive me, so I will not ask forgiveness. I have not done a single good thing in my life, and it has been a long life, as you know. I now have one last chance to redeem myself, at least in the eyes of my brother, if not yours.

Sullivan has told me of some remarkable, nearly unbelievable visits from one of our Elders. It seems that Marie has been targeted, and he is the intended weapon of her destruction. More disturbing is that our Elder would like all of Marie's family killed, and of course that includes me, her maker, and anyone I love. You and Phillip are thus in grave danger—but not from Sullivan. I believe him. He sacrifices himself for Phoebe, and I can do no less.

My goal is to return to you with Jacques. If not me, Sullivan. He had no real interest in rescuing a child but has agreed to help if he can. He believes he goes to his death, but I like to believe at least one of us will survive. He is the stronger.

I could not face you with my plan, for one look, one word from you and I would have weakened. It is imperative that you and Phillip, Kitty and Bess, perhaps even Johnnie Moran, leave the city quickly with the boys in tow. Sullivan would be grateful if you took Phoebe with you. Perhaps Mr.

Doyle, if you were able to come to an arrangement, can act as some counsel, as I know how you admire his intellect. But do pay close attention to whatever Phillip advises over all others. Please share this with him, as he must know about the threat from our Elder.

I pray that Jacques will become your fourth Musketeer.

You are a wonder, a miracle.

I would taste your lips again, Lil.

Yours,

G.

PS, The money is for Bess. It is one small thing I would like to do for such a brave woman. Please tell her how I admire her.

Lillian's tears mixed with the red stains on the parchment. She opened the smaller envelope numbly and thumbed the small fortune in notes. Bess's family would have their respite from financial ruin. George had thought of everything.

CHAPTER TWENTY-FIVE

Old lovers reunited.

"You haven't changed in the least, George."

He stood at the bottom of the stairs. The voice came from the far end of what seemed, in the darkness, to be a full suite of rooms. How long had she lived here? Annaluisa had said she was in Europe; gossip had put her in New Orleans.

"*Au contraire,* Marie. I am a shadow of the man you knew. Old enough now to have a pale reflection, to have done everything there is to do. No wonder, no surprises."

"And just as full of self-pity. You never felt a bit of pity for me, did you? Or for my husband?"

"Phillip does not need my pity. He is superior to any man I know, despite the misfortune of being my brother and child. For you, no, I will give you that."

A rustling of skirts and scuff of shoes sent chills through his veins. She walked toward him. He'd hoped to battle wits with her for a bit longer, to stall and give Sullivan time to find Jacques. Was Marie the sole vampire in the house besides them? Were there others to fight Sullivan? George couldn't tell. Her power overwhelmed his senses.

Candles flared to life as if by her mental force alone. At first he couldn't find her amidst the brocade and velvet couches, pillows, and chairs. The room looked like an ancient Eastern marketplace. The woman's taste had always been excessive.

Then she moved.

George suppressed a gasp. Madame Lucifer indeed. So, this was what came of a life of cannibalism, of building blood power, of fully embracing one's darkest nature. Sullivan must be a newborn among cannibals compared to Marie. He showed no such signs of deterioration.

A glimmer of a pretty woman still resonated somewhere beneath the black veins, red-pupiled eyes, decayed-looking fangs, and nest of coarse hair. She'd done what she could with women's pastes and potions, he supposed, but the result was frightening. Marie's dress revealed much of her copious figure, but her bosom was also scarred with rivulet-like black veins that covered her in a cloak of spider webs.

Marie brushed her long fingers along her white gown in a practiced provocative fashion, but George knew it to be a sarcastic gesture. She laughed at his expression and seemed not at all insulted or surprised.

I created this horror.

"You don't like what you see, *mon chéri*? At one time you could not keep your hands off of me. Tsk tsk."

George itched to shoot her, reminded of the chance by the burning of the pistol at his back. But she was on guard, alert, expecting him to act. She could move faster than the blink of an eye, much faster than himself. How to throw her off her game?

He spread his arms out. "I am here, surrendering. It is what you wanted, no? I truly didn't understand the depth of your feelings for me, Marie, but Phillip reminds me that my self-absorption blinds me to such things."

Her laughter echoed off the stone walls and made the lamps flicker, made ghostly shadows dance on the floor. "You are nothing to me, George. You never were, and never shall be. Is that really what you thought? That I pined away for three hundred years over our brief liaisons? Your ego almost equals mine! Perhaps I inherited the trait from my maker?"

"I think not. Phillip does not share the trait, and he was my firstborn." *But, Philip was wrong and I was correct. Her resentment for her maker made me a target, not unrequited love.*

"And I your second-born. What a proud papa you must be!"

Do not mention the boy. Give Sullivan as much time as possible. "What is going on, Marie? Why this revenge on my friends? What is this place, and how are these mortals involved?"

The vampiress eyed him before speaking. "I'm a bit disappointed, Georgy. I envisioned this meeting differently, expected a bit of a fight from you. So, that makes me believe all is not as it appears. Your surrender is disingenuous."

"I am sincere. I offer myself to you, for whatever satisfaction it might bring. Take me and be done with this city. I don't for a moment believe you are happy here."

Marie took one stride that moved her many feet, noiselessly. In all his years, George had never seen a vampire capable of such a feat.

"Happy?" She was more hideous up close and smelled of rotted flesh. Would that he didn't need to stall and she could put him out of his misery immediately. The sight of her was nauseating. "What happiness have I found since you took me? What happiness have you found since your mother took you? No, I am not happy in this wretched place and will be gone from it soon. I am, however, intrigued."

"By what?"

"Why didn't you run?"

He shrugged. "I'm tired."

But the statement was a lie. While he'd always told himself and others how tired of this life he was, it no longer rang true. He had been tired enough to turn his back on everything before he became

Lillian's Leaping Man, but now he wanted to live, wanted to live with Lillian and Jacques. Life seemed different now, a chance to experience emotions he'd never before imagined. He wouldn't mention it, of course, not to Marie, but he was no longer a self-loathing vampire seeking a convenient way to die.

Could Marie be taken down somehow? Perhaps he'd miscalculated badly. Should he have tried to conquer her with Sullivan, not let them split up? He'd wanted one of them to find the boy, though. Maybe he should have found the boy and then fled Baltimore. But it was too late now. And having watched her cross the room in a blink made it clear that she was more dangerous than anything he'd ever seen.

"I can believe that. Have a seat, Georgy. It doesn't need to be like this. Father and child should have a nice little chat before I dispose of you."

Where is the insanity I expected? he wondered. *She is calm and studied in her words.* The pistol burned, the dagger burned, and still he worked for more time before the final confrontation. How long had it been? Moments, only.

"What do you gain from this revenge, then, Marie? If it is because I turned you, you could have done this eons ago. Why now?"

"Can't you see with your own eyes? I'm dying."

"I don't understand."

"Look at me. Smell my flesh. I am like the *dreach foula* of old." She smiled, and her ghastly face became more horrible. "You drink only mortals, and that sustenance refreshes you, body and soul. When you drink from our kind, I have found there is no renewal. Only a very slow decline. And the process appears irreversible, though I have tried to gain strength in recent months from mortals."

She smiled again and stared into his eyes. George fought hard not to look away but could not stand the sickness emanating from her. He shut his eyes, and her voice became a hissing whisper.

"I have finally found a way to die, much as a mortal would. Quite naturally. Doesn't that sound appealing?"

George shook his head. "At one time it would have. No longer. And I have no interest in feasting on vampires." He shrugged. "So you want to destroy me before you die. I see."

She laughed again. He expected her to say something, but she didn't.

Fury bubbled up in his chest. "Couldn't you have simply taken me without murdering Annaluisa and Aileen?"

"Annaluisa was a talker. She rather annoyed me. Who is Aileen? Oh, the chit who was maid to your lover." Marie shrugged, as if she could barely remember. "It seemed like the thing to do at the time. I get bored, Georgy."

"And this group of silly men and their secret society. What role do they play?"

Marie ran a finger along her grotesque cheek, coy. "They have served a purpose. Never underestimate what a man will do for money or power, Georgy. A political post...a profitable company...the promise of immortality at the perfect age. It is funny what they consider to be their best age: men wait about ten years too long, women stop about ten years early. You killed the best of my mortal followers, of course."

"The best? A rapist and a demented physician?" George cursed himself, for he had led them to the topic of Lillian, which he'd wanted desperately to avoid. But he was so angry for Lil he could barely hold his tongue; it seemed she had been Marie's pawn for ages. He could just hope that Mr. Doyle had nothing to do with the other scoundrels.

"Someone had to watch over her," Marie said. "At least I provided for her. Give me that much."

Her horrible grin made his stomach turn. She was talking about his Lil. But, how had Marie provided for Lil? How long had she truly known her?

God, no.

"You orchestrated the rape of a woman? You are more abhorrent than I could ever imagine!"

"Of course I did not." Marie looked affronted. "I would have eventually destroyed Pemberton for that, but I had other uses for him first. He was to simply abscond with any child of hers, not to create one. That is the difficulty with mortals, is it not? Completely unreliable."

"What is Lillian to you? Why such an interest in an orphan?" But an awful possibility appeared, crept closer and squeezed the breath from him. Was it fact?

"When was the last time you heard of a vampire giving birth to a mortal?"

George didn't trust himself to speak.

"Or giving birth at all?"

Now the pistol burned his back, but he had to know, had to understand the Truth of Lillian Holmes.

"I waited, watching, wondering when one of the Elders would come. I've broken each of their commandments, and still they left me alone."

George nodded but thought, *Ah, there you are wrong. Your days are numbered far fewer than you think.*

Marie inspected her rotted nails, as if they were discussing the weather. "She was an accident, of course," she volunteered. "A mistake. Who would have expected my union to be fruitful? I thought there must be something special about her, but it seems I was wrong. I have watched, though, and wondered. At times I've spoken to her, and I almost believe she heard me. The effect seemed detrimental; I saw her deteriorate.

"My endearments to her—and yes, you may not believe it, but I did care about her in my own way—they seemed to…torture her. You'll never understand my feelings, and I barely understand them myself. But I found her rather charming the few times I saw her. Enchanting. She looks a great deal more like her father. A pity, that."

"Her father was mortal, then?" George wanted to scream, to tear the grey flesh from Marie, to torture her into saying this was a false story. This horror in the flesh could not be Lillian's mother.

"Another rather charming mortal. As it turns out he was quite insane, but that doesn't matter. They hanged him a few years ago."

"Hanged him?"

"He liked to murder. Fine parentage, your beloved, don't you think?" Marie sighed, and for a moment George thought he saw regret in her eyes, a longing for a different outcome. "He was rather famous, and although the couple that Pemberton hired to raise Lillian thought her father to have perished on a ship, I always thought it a little dull of them not to investigate matters further. Henry Holmes was in all the papers. Mind you, I did not choose him because he was an insane killer. I simply thought he was handsome. See, that is what I mean about mortals. Unpredictable, unreliable."

"It sounds as if he was very predictable." God help Lillian, was she truly the child of this abyssal monster and a heinous murderer? Which horrible traits could be passed down? Why was she so good, so noble?

But so confused, George. So vulnerable.

Marie hissed. "Well, it hardly matters now. She was mortal until Pemberton mucked things up and you interfered further. Her child is mortal, although we have waited a good while to see if he would remain so. In fact, the entire exercise proved incredibly unproductive. He shows no signs of being remarkable in any way. I find him rather tedious, in fact."

"She has a child?" George prevaricated. *Please, Sullivan, please.*

"Oh, my dear Georgy. That is beneath you. Now, put this silliness aside and tell me how things have gone for you these last few hundred years. We have a bit of catching up to do, do we not?"

CHAPTER TWENTY-SIX

The wrong brother.

Mr. Doyle took off his spectacles and handed George's letter back to Phillip, who clutched it tightly and stared out the window. Lillian wanted someone to tell her everything would work out, that George hadn't actually gone to Marie. That she didn't have a child that needed rescuing. That her life, to this point, was one long dream. But these people and their reactions were too detailed, too laced with frustration and emotion for her to be fantasizing. Life had actually become unbearable.

What good would it do to find her son now? What use could she be to him, broken, heartbroken, tired, and unable to change any circumstance around her? *I am like a puppet,* she mused. And it seemed anyone in the world could take over the strings at any time without her leave.

If she could somehow make everything as it once was, though, would she? She sat in the chair she'd typically used when chatting with Addie. She closed her eyes and imagined Addie there, humming an old tune and knitting or doing embroidery, depending upon the season. Thomas would be close by, always close by. Her two servants, the closest she had to family. He would usher visitors, although few and far between, in and out of the parlor, but he seemed always happier once they were gone. His nerves, he said, since the war…and his leg. He'd sneak off to sip a dram of whiskey.

Aileen would be bustling around upstairs, folding the washing or polishing some piece of jewelry. She sang too, but her songs were in

Gaelic and always seemed melancholy. Once Lillian had asked her what she sang about, and she shook her head. "A place I don't know, a place I'll never see." Lillian had made a note in her Journal to find a proper way to take Aileen on a journey to Ireland. Another promise she'd broken.

Lillian would sip a bit of her own medicine, read for hours, and then wait for the sun to set so she could sneak out set out on grand adventures. She'd only had one: the Leaping Man. So, which was the dream? Her life before George, or her life after?

The house was bigger then, wasn't it? How could that be? She watched Phillip, who seemed larger to her now that he wasn't in George's shadow.

Phillip will act. He cannot resist any more than I. We are both slaves to our maker.

Mr. Doyle eyed Phillip nervously then turned to her. "This is grave, indeed. I cannot claim to fully understand any of it, except to say that Mr. Orleans is a man besotted. If what you tell me about this Madam Lucifer is true, then despite his argument to the contrary he is indeed a hero to attempt what he does. Miss Holmes, I am sincerely sorry for whatever has transpired but feel I am out of place here now. I will leave you to your business."

The author's pronouncement shook Lillian out of her numbness, sheer panic taking over. She saw his hands shake as he put his glasses into his jacket pocket. "No! I beg you, Mr. Doyle. I would have your counsel now more than ever. I promise I will find Johnnie Moran so you feel more at ease!"

She clung to his arm and he stared at her incredulously. *You are nothing to him, Lil. Why couldn't this man be my father, be the one to tell me what to do, to guard me and stand by me at all costs?*

"But even Mr. Orleans instructed you to defer to Phillip," Mr. Doyle said. "What could I possibly know about defeating a deadly vampire? I didn't even know they exist until you opened my eyes."

He is simply afraid. He should be. And he is right; Bess, Kitty, and he must leave immediately. And they must take the boys.

"May I ask a favor of you, although I've done nothing to earn it?"

"Your tone is so reproachful, Miss Holmes. I am sorry to have failed you. You seem to have given me powers akin to my fictional heroes. I assure you, I am a very average man."

"You are not. But you are mortal," she allowed. "And the other mortals I care about are numerous. Might you assist them in escaping this city?"

"Escaping?" Bess shook both her foot and her head. "I am not leaving my home."

"Oh, Bess, I nearly forgot. This is for you." Lil handed the tear-stained envelope to Bess, who opened it with trepidation.

"I don't understand." Bess lifted the stack of bills and gaped at them.

"George. He wants your wellbeing."

"I wasn't serious! Oh, Lil, I wasn't serious! Damnation! This is unbearable. Is there no way to rescue him?"

Kitty linked her arm through Phillip's, and the two whispered to one another. Lillian knew Kitty wanted assurances that he would do nothing to save his brother, that they would have a chance at peace. She also knew as well as Kitty that no such assurances would come.

"Mr. Doyle," she said, "I beg you again. Would you take the Musketeers with you, north, wherever your next stop takes you? I will try to convince Bess and Kitty to accompany you, to help. They are good children who have had nothing but heartache. They are not safe here. I have adequate funds to hire additional help if you think it necessary."

"Musketeers?"

"My Irregulars. The boys. Two are brothers of Aileen O'Shaunessy, one is Johnnie Moran's brother."

"Isn't that a role better taken by Johnnie? I cannot simply abscond with his little brothers!" Doyle's eyes reflected open fear now. He would flee, and she wouldn't blame him. If only he would take the children.

Bess stomped her foot. "I'm not going anywhere! I will take the boys to my house. You don't get to orchestrate everyone's lives, Lillian, whether you feel it is for their own good or not."

Lillian was ready to explode from the grief pulling at her heart, the clock ticking away precious moments she didn't have, and a house full of people who needed her care but did not want it or know it. "I don't get to orchestrate my own!"

Kitty placed a kiss on Phillip's cheek and stood near Bess. "I will go with you to your house, if you'll have me. We can take care of the children together. I, too, am not leaving."

"No!" Lillian said. "You must listen to me. There are matters beyond your comprehension, Kitty!"

"And I will take my leave now." Mr. Doyle approached and pressed a kiss to Lillian's hand. "I pray we cross paths again, Miss Holmes."

It sounded very much like he prayed for the exact opposite, and without giving her time to utter a word of protest he donned his hat and rushed to the hallway. The sound of the door slamming behind him felt like her fate was sealed.

Bess followed his departure with a look of deep regret, but Lillian had no time to comfort her about her cure. Her friend straightened herself up and linked arms with Kitty.

Lillian looked to Phillip, who was staring at her. The two held one another's gaze.

"Ah." Bess came over and gave her a quick hug, whispering in her ear, "Get your wonderful George and your child and bring them back."

Kitty wiped away a few tears before going with Bess to collect the boys from the yard, leaving Lil alone except for Phillip.

She shuddered. Everyone would be gone, but they would not be safe. No one had listened to her, no one wanted her direction. Lillian bristled that she was left with the man George told her to listen to, bristled that once again she was being ordered around. She choked back tears and reached into her pocket for her pill box.

"Don't."

"What?"

"Don't take anything."

"Don't tell me what to do! You are not my maker! You are not…anything to me."

Phillip strode across the room and pulled her in tight, pressed a tender kiss on her hair. She hated him for not being George, hated him for being part of the reason George sacrificed himself.

"Has he made amends enough for you, Phillip?" she hissed.

"Oh, Lillian, I'm so sorry."

She grimaced. *It's simply not his fault. It's no one's fault. No one's except George.* And yet, "Phillip, did I bring ruin on him, or did he bring it on me?"

"Stop it! George has done this for us both, and for himself. If we were sensible we'd honor his wish and go far away, save ourselves."

Lillian nodded. "Yes. He could be already dead." *Dead.* The word sounded so hollow.

"No. Our maker is not gone. I would feel it."

Our maker. "We are as brother and sister in a way. Phillip…?"

She'd called his name, but now Lillian pressed her hand to her mouth, unsure of what she wanted to ask. Phillip took her hand and led her to a settee. He stared at her earnestly, waiting to help. George had described him accurately many times: noble and generous. That gave her strength to continue.

"Does he love me? Or does he feel responsible for me?"

She could tell Phillip held back a chuckle, which was almost answer enough. Almost.

"That is not really the question, is it?"

"I rather think it is!" Lillian huffed.

"Lil, I was his first newborn. I can still remember the awful struggle defying rational thought or description. I hated him. I loved him. I couldn't stand to be with him, I couldn't stand to be without him." Phillip shook his head. "I've hidden from him, put continents between us, put him in harm's way, killed to free him from harm. Multiply these last few months by a hundred. And still, I cannot answer the real question for you."

"Which is?"

"Is it love that you feel, or is it that he holds your bond?"

"Which is it for you? Why does he still hold your bond after all this time? You have become friends. I see it. Have you asked him to free you?"

"That is between us," Phillip said in an uncharacteristically sharp tone. "But if you want to be able to answer these questions for yourself, we'll likely have to rescue the idiot."

"He is an idiot, isn't he?" Lillian wiped a tear away and cursed. "What a stupid thing to do. I am far more intelligent than he, I believe, and could have assisted greatly in this mission. And, after all, *it is my son at risk.* How dare he! What was he thinking, Phillip?"

Lillian shot to her feet and paced to wear down some of her nervous energy, and Phillip said, "God only knows, my dear. But this is the deadliest of his stunts."

"So…you think him still alive?"

"Indeed I do. And I suggest that we cannot adequately chastise him for his stupidity until we rescue him."

"He said that I was attend to your instructions."

George's brother scoffed, and Lillian looked into his blue eyes and saw a love like her own buried under anxiety and great pain. And mild amusement. "That is quite ridiculous. Are you likely to take my instruction? No. Nor should you. As you said, you are far more intelligent than George. So, what would you like to do?"

"I won't run away."

"I suspect George knew that. He also knew I wouldn't run. He is so much greater a man than he believes himself, than even you believe him to be. He doesn't want to die, hasn't since he met you."

Lillian shook her head, confused.

"After a few hundred years you will understand him better. George wants to do what is right, but his notion of heroics seems somewhat stuck in the days of our upbringing. I think we'd better show him how it's done."

"I don't understand."

"Why, there is something between surrender and running."

"Fighting back?"

"Yes. I want my brother, and so do you."

"Yes. And I want my son. But we are fewer now, weaker. How can we succeed if George will not? And I'm sure Kitty does not want you to go."

"Please do not assume my love for her is meager, or that she values peace over justice. She does not want me to *die*. But how could she love a man who would abandon his brother? Even if he is an idiot."

They turned as they noticed Phoebe framed in the hallway arch, anger pouring from her. "You brought him to this pit of Hell and yet don't mention his name. You both deserve to die at Madam Lucifer's hand, along with your child and George!"

Phillip approached the woman, but she held up her hand and grimaced. "Don't give me your excuses! You may have convinced Chauncey that he could redeem his soul by killing the *diab*, but I am not so gullible. I pleaded with him to quit this place, and to go away with me." She made a quick spitting noise and crossed herself.

"We haven't forgotten him!" But Phillip's lie didn't roll off his tongue convincingly, and the woman moved closer and beat on his chest. He trapped her hands as she screamed at him.

"You stole my love! What did you say to him in the cathedral? What did you promise him? Lies, all lies! You brought him here as sacrifice to the demon woman. Your George took him today and now he's gone off to his death." Phoebe fell to her knees and pounded her fists on her legs, sobbing and shaking. "You are the *diab!*"

"We will get him back," Lillian said, wondering if they could, ashamed that what Phoebe said was true. She'd forgotten Sullivan ever existed.

Phillip shook the woman and yelled back. "Stop it, Phoebe. This won't help him! Of course we'll try to save Sullivan."

"Selfish bastards!"

Phillip traded looks with Lillian. "It's just us."

Lillian nodded. "Do we have a plan at all?"

"Stupid bastards!" Phoebe hissed. "You never had a plan to kill her. Chauncey said you had a plan, promised you had a plan! Oh, God, he will die. But, no. Dear Mother Mary, have mercy on us. I will get my husband back from her. You can rot with her in Hell for all I care. I am going to find my husband—"

Phillip tried to hold her but she pushed him away violently. "Phoebe, you are not strong, not old. Marie could kill you with a flick of her wrist. You must stay here."

The woman pointed to Lillian. "This devil is a newborn. What use is she? I go to save my husband; she goes to save her lover and child. Women do what women must do. Who are you, monsieur, to deny me?"

"I take it you're coming with us, then?"

Phoebe's eyes burned black, and veins stood out scarlet against her dark skin. "I must get my bones and chalk, my cauldron. Then we go."

The woman flew up the stairs, and Lillian called after her, "We don't have time for this!" Then, to Phillip: "Her bones and cauldron?"

George's brother whispered, "She is an ally, but she could prove...unstable. I suggest we leave without her. Besides, all Sullivan seemed to want is her safety, according to George's letter. We can at least do this much for him. Let's go now."

"Right," Lillian said.

Phillip sighed. "Lead the way to the castle."

CHAPTER TWENTY-SEVEN

Brave mortals.

"God help me!"

Arthur ran as quickly as he could, his breathing labored from his chest cold, trying to put as much distance as he could between himself and the insanity of Lillian Holmes's mansion. He stopped at the monument, where George Washington—at least he supposed it was George Washington—stood atop an enormous column. There was such a monument in every city in America, it seemed.

Taking a seat on an iron bench, he wiped at his brow and tried to calm his breathing. A few couples were out for a stroll, although the night was brisk and a young shoeblack sat forlornly on a step without a customer. How could life go on so normally? Would his life ever be normal again?

Arthur pulled his watch from his pocket and opened it to the inscription that brought bittersweet grief, unfailingly. *All my devotion, Louisa.* Louisa didn't even know he was abroad, but neither would she know his face. Tuberculosis ravaged her body while dementia ravaged her brain. Oh, for once to have her tell him that he was a good and noble man worthy of the blessings life had given him. But no, that was impossible—and untrue.

"You have not the bravery of the lowliest soldier, the inquisitiveness of the poorest scientist, or the imagination to pen a single new story," he accused himself. Faced with the seemingly impossible truth that he'd met and even liked several vampires, he'd run.

"Well, who wouldn't?" he almost shouted. The shoeblack turned and held up his brush.

Arthur ignored him and rested his head in his hands. Lillian had begged him to help. The astonishment and hurt on her face when he curtly abandoned her... Well, those were sentiments he understood too well. Louisa had looked at him that way before, as had his children. He would tend battlefield wounds but would not fight a battle.

A few seagulls circled overhead, and Arthur watched them settle on George Washington. He sniffed out a laugh. What would *that* great man do, faced with a nest of vampires? What would Sherlock do? Why, John Watson would understand, wouldn't he?

No. Terrible men had done something to pry a child away from Lillian Holmes. He believed that. A good man would try to help. Dr. John Watson was a good man, whereas his creator was not. But was there *any* way to assist without ending up dead in the process? He didn't truly owe anything to Lillian Holmes, and yet, he felt that he'd inadvertently had some hand in a part of her misery. Where the blazes was Johnnie Moran, and what did he know of all this?

A trolley clanged somewhere. A cab for hire turned the corner and Arthur ran to catch up. He called out, and the driver finally stopped.

"It's Mr. Doyle again, ain't that right, sir?" It was the driver who had ushered him back and forth to the police station, and the man grinned and tipped his hat.

"Aye," Arthur said. "I wonder if you know a certain officer of the law that frequents Light Street? He's of average height and thin build, fair-haired."

"That's every other copper in the city, sir."

"Irish."

The man rolled his eyes.

"His name is John Moran, very serious fellow."

"You'd mean poor Johnnie, one who just lost his girl?"

"That is the very man! Where can I find him this time of evening?"

"Hard to say, sir. If he's on duty, he'd be far down toward the harbor. Used to spend his time up the street with his lady. Now?" The driver shrugged. "Don't know where he lives."

"Then we'll try the harbor!" Arthur decided. "As fast as you can go, and a bit faster if you please. If we don't find him right away, we'll be coming all the way back and past here to Congressman Coyle's mansion. It's near the lake." *God help me,* he thought, though. *Don't let it come to that. I cannot do this alone.*

"Know where it is, sir!"

The driver seemed legitimately happy that he might have a fare for the entire evening, while Doyle sat back in the coach, trying to take in everything he'd seen and heard in the last few days. If only Mencken were around; perhaps he'd learned something about the murders as well. Right now there were signs that Arthur's associates in the Learned Order were up to very foul crimes, indeed. Could he have a hand in bringing them to justice? Could he, for once, be an actor in his own story?

His stomach churned at the thought of this Madam Lucifer of theirs. *If* she existed, he reminded himself; he vacillated back and forth in his belief every second. He coughed into his handkerchief as the cab bounced over uneven cobbles and trolley tracks at a speed that was likely dangerous and surely illegal. But most of the traffic of the day had subsided, and more swiftly than Arthur thought possible the cab pulled up to a sidewalk.

The driver yelled down to a man pulling his wares back into his shop for the night, "Seen Constable Moran today?"

"Just walked by. Should be near Patrick's Pub by now if he's going his usual route."

They took off again, and Arthur leaned his head out to scout for Johnnie.

He spotted him peering into the window of closed shop, presumably to assure himself all was quiet.

"Officer Moran!"

Johnnie turned and walked up to the cab. "Mr. Doyle! Are you well? Is something wrong?"

"Aye, indeed something is wrong. Might I convince you to join me?"

"I cannot do it, sir. I am on duty." The policeman spread his hands wide in apology.

"I think I know who killed your lady friend, Johnnie," Arthur announced, hating himself for being so blunt. "At least, it's very likely that it will be sorted out soon. Ach, this is not something I want to yell out for all of the city to hear."

The constable's expression of mixed fury and anguish clutched at Arthur's tight chest. Had he ever felt that way about Louisa? Was Louisa still alive, or was a telegram winding its way to him now? A flush of guilt swept through him. He shouldn't have left her side. These good people, whether devils or no, seemed fiercely loyal to one another.

Moran jumped into the cab and shook Arthur's hand. "Tell me everything, Mr. Doyle."

He gave the driver directions and then said, "I don't know where to start, Johnnie. Did you ever notice anything odd about Miss Holmes or the Orleans brothers? Did Aileen ever mention anything of a...let's say superhuman trait among any of them?"

Johnnie furrowed his brow and rubbed at his chin. "George Orleans? Him, sir. He's not right, is he? I haven't been able to figure it out, but he gives me the chills and I try to steer clear of him. I feel awful that my brother is near him so often, but Miss Holmes has given them so much more than I could. It's a blessing right now. I've not been good company since Aileen's death, you see. I've tried, but I have trouble keeping my sadness from them. I've failed them in every way, and Aileen's little brothers…" The constable caught himself and stared, wide-eyed. "What's this, Mr. Doyle? Are you telling me that they killed my Aileen?"

"No, calm down," said Arthur. "Quite the contrary. They claim to be on the hunt for person who did kill her, though. The same woman who killed my friend Annaluisa Pelosi."

"Woman?" Johnnie repeated. "What kind of *woman* might that be? They both looked to be torn to shreds by wolves and drained of blood! But that does not matter. I will kill her tonight!"

"From what I hear, she is difficult to kill. The Orleans brothers have been fighting her for a long time, they say." Arthur polished his spectacles on his handkerchief and kept his gaze away from Johnnie's, realizing he was about to cross a line into madness. He'd been on the receiving end of many incredulous looks during his spiritism lectures, but this was another level completely. "She's a vampire who eats vampires."

"Come again?"

"She is a vampire," Arthur repeated.

"Like in the stories Miss Holmes reads? She drinks blood? I beg your pardon, but that is really daft. A vampire, Mr. Doyle?" The policeman looked torn between laughter and anger.

"Indeed. And the worst kind of vampire. I saw some evidence of the creatures' existence. Unless it was sleight of hand, and I think not." Arthur sighed and looked up at Johnnie. "Your sixth sense is accurate, George Orleans is different. He is a vampire. So is his brother. And, hard enough to believe, so is Miss Holmes."

"Is this a joke, Mr. Doyle? I'm not in the mood for pranks and—"

"No, of course not. I value our friendship, my good man. I know you are sorely grieving, and I would not jest about something this serious. You saw both…victims. You must have realized something truly unusual transpired. You said as much when you described the murder at the Rennard the first day I met you."

Johnnie nodded reluctantly. "Just hard to take in, you know?"

The two rode in silence for a few minutes, not looking at one another, but as they approached Loch Raven Arthur wondered what the pair of them could do against such creatures. Had he acted in haste? He was fairly certain that Donnelly and Coyle, and certainly Poe and that talkative Langhan woman were very normal, if complicit in terrible crimes. But what about Holt and Frederick?

"Your pistol is loaded, is it not?"

"Of course," Johnnie said.

"I am not sure what we will find here. You must be careful, for even the Orleans brothers are terribly frightened of this woman. My primary goal is to rescue a boy who may be captive here."

"A boy?" said Johnnie.

"Yes, Lillian Holmes's son."

"What? Lillian has a son? I don't understand! Is he a vampire as well?"

"I think not. Please do not hurt him."

"Miss Holmes's son?" Johnnie repeated, looking more and more confused. "Are you certain about all of this?"

"Not at all."

The young man shook his head, clearly having doubts. "This seems a job for the entire police department, Arthur. If what you say is true—"

"Johnnie, I've met your Worthington. Do you think he'd believe a word of this?"

"No," Johnnie said, "but I'm not sure I do, either."

"Well, I must try to do something. I stayed in this dreary city for a reason, and I believe that somehow God may have orchestrated it to be just so. If you don't want to join me, I understand. Not everyone can take such information as I just gave you on faith. Likely not everyone should."

The young policeman took a moment to think. Finally he said, "If there is a chance of meeting the monster who killed Aileen, I will not leave."

"You are twice the man I am."

CHAPTER TWENTY-EIGHT

Lillian learns her Truth.

George prayed that this secret of Lillian's would go to the grave with him. As Marie chatted on about her horrific accomplishments, hints of her insanity surfaced. She claimed a hand in every political overthrow, every catastrophic scourge on mankind that had occurred in the last three centuries. And if she were this delusional, couldn't it be that she wasn't Lil's mother, he wondered. How to know for sure? And did it matter, for if Lil never learned of her parentage, would it still affect her?

He thought he heard a noise in the house above and wondered if it was Sullivan. There was no way to be sure, though. No way to be certain if the other vampire had found Lillian's boy and escaped.

As Marie chatted on, she edged closer to George, insisting they sit together on a couch that smelled as old as it looked. The more he saw of the room, the more it seemed to have rotted along with its mistress. Phillip had often joked how fastidious George was about order and cleanliness, but these cloying smells, unsightly décor and air of death would turn any stomach.

"Do discard the silver you're carrying, George. It won't work on me, but the tang of the metal is annoying, distracting."

"I'll keep it just the same. You never know who might turn up." He smiled, searching frantically for some alternate path to her destruction.

Marie cackled, her fetid breath making George inch away.

"What will it take for you to let the boy go, Marie?" he asked. "Am I enough of a bargain?"

"Let him go? Why not?" She shrugged. "I have no further interest in my dear, dear grandson. Let her have him. He's dull and untalented. What a supreme waste of my time. I'd make a meal of him, but it seems somehow a trifle distasteful."

"A trifle distasteful. To eat your grandchild? Yes, that would be."

She stood and waved a dismissive hand. "They are evidently both dull, Lillian and her son. She carries about like an...ordinary lady of society."

"That hardly describes her."

Marie ignored that. "Why should she want him, in any case? The product of Pemberton's rape... I should think she would not want to have anything to do with him."

George grimaced. "I used to think there could be no worse fate than Lillian's, to not know if anyone ever cared for a single moment about her, about her existence. Now I understand how wrong I was. It could be worse: She could hear your callous words. She has been in such pain, she would do anything to not have a child of hers feel that anguish. Turn over the boy to her in exchange for whatever you would do to me."

Marie's eyes bored holes through his chest. She hated him so much.

"You are really very attached to your newborn."

George knew he could not pull off a lie. "Yes."

"Why?"

"I have no idea. It is like breathing. I cannot help it. I should not have to explain such a thing to her mother—you should feel it as well. And it doesn't matter now." *But it really is a good question, George.*

Marie nodded, looking amused. "So, the worst I could do to you would be to kill her. I was considering it, you know, but you had the temerity to visit me first. And it seems a bit unmotherly, don't you think? I never thought you the type to go into battle for love."

"You knew me for a very short time a very long time ago. I am not that boy."

"No, but you look the same." She sighed and cast a lurid glance at him that made his stomach turn again. That he had made love to this abomination, that he had turned her into this abomination… This end was small price to pay for unleashing her on the world. And yet, there was Phillip. He had killed, many times. But he had helped, and loved, and was loyal and brave. And the others? Too many to number. What had become of them? Were they like Marie or like Phillip?

"The boy for me," he offered again. "But not just my death. I will do your bidding willingly. Kill me, torture me, whatever suits you."

"Sullivan, my love!" Her call carried the force of her will; George felt the pull and nearly succumbed to it himself. Of course, Sullivan was her child, his grandchild. She'd felt him, probably from the moment he'd set foot in the city. Now would be a moment of truth.

Sullivan moved from behind a heavy drape and cast a quick glance at George, who ground his teeth together to stop from speaking. Where was Jacques? Had Chauncey even searched him out? Had the vampire been here all along? Was he friend or foe?

"Isn't this a lovely reunion? Three generations, together finally."

Sullivan remained stone-faced. George saw hatred in his eyes— hatred for Marie, thankfully.

The giant's silence drew a hard smack from his maker. It drew blood where her nails scratched him, and she licked drops off his cheek. His hands shook, and he shoved them in his coat pockets.

George prayed that Marie would anger Chauncey more, make his rage boil into a firestorm. But why? What could they do against her even enraged?

"Do you feel foolish, now, George? I still hold the bond on your secret ally. He's no help. It's done."

And it seemed to be. Then, worse, the faintest hint of a familiar fragrance broke through the stench of the suite.

CHAPTER TWENTY-NINE

An unnatural death.

Phillip pulled Lillian's arm and coaxed her away from the top of the cellar stairs, into the hallway and to the foyer. "It cannot be true," she whispered to herself as he did. That they had arrived in time for her to hear as much as she had…

Phillip wrapped a protective arm around her but bolted to the doorway as a cab approached outside. That approach was noisy and reckless. "God Almighty. It's Doyle and Moran. What the blazes are they doing here?"

Lillian grabbed his arm, thrilled to see the pair approaching the congressman's castle though she was not certain what two mortals might do. Pushing aside all thoughts aside except finding her son and freeing George, she ran out onto the porch to greet the newcomers as their cab drove away.

"Miss—"

"Don't speak, Johnnie. Listen, both of you. I believe, I hope, that my son is in this house. We have heard no one about, so I hope also that he is unguarded. Find him. His name is Jacques. Take him as far away from here as you can." She grabbed Mr. Doyle's hand and pressed her lips to it. "Thank you so much for coming, sir! I'm begging you. I know I have no reason to ask you for anything, but I cannot help it. Please, sir!"

"But Miss Holmes!" Johnnie wanted answers, but there was no time.

"No, Moran, come with me," Doyle ordered in a tone that would make anyone attend. The others all looked in amazement at a man who seemed to have never raised his voice in his lifetime. Then the moment passed. The pair rushed off, and Lillian cursed as they burst through the front door into the house.

"I should have warned them to be quiet!"

Phillip took her hand. "Go with them. You should be looking for the boy. I can try…" He cursed and shrugged, then, and Lillian's hopes faded further into the dark night. Phillip had no idea what to do.

"No," she decided. "I have a great deal of unfinished business with Madam Lucifer. I would have my George back."

"You did understand what she said, Lillian? You know who she is?"

"I'm not deaf, Phillip! Please, I cannot think about it. If I do, I will not be able to act."

"Listen to me, Lillian. I mean it!" Phillip forced her to face him and held her by the shoulders. "My mother turned George. She was not herself but a newborn in a frenzy. She has not been able to face either of us since, despite our many attempts to reach out to her. George turned me, and you know how that act has haunted him day and night for three centuries. My father was a murderer—he killed his brother to capture a throne. Our subjects eventually murdered him for killing a beloved regent."

"What?" Lillian snapped. "What does this matter at the moment? We must do something!"

"You are too smart to not take my meaning. Crimes against your family members, against your *mother*—be she the Devil or an angel—will haunt you forever."

"I am not sure I believe anything that devil claims, but I assure you, I would not hesitate for a moment to end her reign of terror on me and mine."

"You may not hesitate now, but you cannot know what you will feel in months, in years… Let me take care of her, if I can."

Lillian pushed Phillip away. "You are quite right. How could I imagine? What a family have I had! You heard her. I was a waste of her time, a total waste, as was my son. I was a mistake." She shook her head. "That is not my mother. I have no mother! I never did, and I never will. That creature let me be raped by one of her servants. Then she stole my child. I have no father! He was hanged, an insane murderer. What would you have me do, Phillip? Leave my George to rot here? This city, this world has not seen the likes of that monster called Madame Lucifer, and you would have me walk away?"

"Quiet!"

"I…I will not be quiet. I will never be quiet again." Lillian loaded her pistol. "Tell me if my silver bullets will kill her. Tell me how to do this. I shall do it with or without your help."

Phillip took in a deep breath and pushed the gun away. "No, they will not stop her. And I know of nothing short of a miracle that will."

Lillian shook her head and pushed past him. She reentered the house and made her way down the hallway to the stairs leading to the cellar.

"After you, Miss Holmes," Phillip muttered as she passed.

George rose and stood statue-still when he saw her reach the bottom of the landing. She stopped for a moment and focused on him alone. He glanced behind her at Phillip then met her gaze again. A half smile passed across his face as a noise of amusement sounded from the other side of the room.

Lillian wouldn't look at Marie, not just yet. "Didn't you know, George?"

"Know what, my love?"

"That neither of us could let you go. I know now that it is not because you are our maker. Is it, Phillip? It is because we love you. I love you. Truly. The maker's bond did not trump my desire to find my child, but I chose you anyway. I will save you, and then I will save him."

"What a lovely speech." Marie's sarcasm was overdone, like everything else about the woman. "I am the one who gave you life."

"No." Lillian turned and faced her. "You didn't."

Despite her words, the horrible truth of her parentage tore through her at the sight of Marie. But Lillian took care to stand as tall as she could, and Marie seemed to become frailer in comparison. It gave her hope.

"What do you know of it? I am your mother!"

"No, you are not my mother. I deny you that title. I reject it, I reject you. I will be an orphan always, although I do have a maker, who has loved me as well as anyone could. That will do nicely."

Marie scoffed. "You cannot reject the facts, my dear. Did you know that George and I were lovers? How does that sit with you, the thought of his lips against mine, his insatiable passion for me, the hours—*days*—spent in one another's arms? The sharing of our blood. That is a particular favorite of his, isn't it, Georgy? Or has he given that up? Would you still have him?"

Phillip put himself between them. "Marie, stop it. What do you want from her? What sin of yours is she paying for?"

"Ah, he finds his voice. My timid husband, cuckolded by his own brother, hiding in corners of the world for centuries. You, Phillip, were truly a waste of everyone's time."

"Ugly, body and soul. You always were, and you are still the most hideous creature. I was pleased when George took you off my hands for a while. You never imagined that I loved you, did you?"

A slight movement of her hand sent Phillip to the floor clutching at his throat, and for the first time Lillian saw Chauncey Sullivan. The dark-skinned giant stared on, as if he watched a play he had no part in.

"That's enough!" Lillian strode to within a few feet of her mother, horrified at the visible signs of her evil life, the stench of her, the insanity in her eyes…and the sadness. All the power in the world hadn't brought her an ounce of happiness.

Marie held her hand out briefly, and Lillian wondered what the gesture meant. Surely she did not expect an embrace.

With a flash of insight, Lillian nearly lost strength in her legs. "You never wanted George. It was never about hurting him."

"Of course it was, stupid girl!"

"I am not stupid. I am quite intelligent. You wanted me—for what purpose, I cannot imagine, as you have deemed me a total waste of your time."

Marie lifted her chin in defiance, but Lillian saw that she bit back a protest and was unsure of herself.

Lillian forced herself to stop shaking. "Why?" She screamed this time. "Why, why, why? How could you do it? How could you abandon me, shame me, lock me away?"

Marie closed her eyes. "Take a look at me. What would you have done?"

Lillian dropped her arm and closed her eyes to spare herself the horrible sight before her, a wretched, evil, tired, bloodied, decaying woman, who should look no older than herself but instead looked as if she carried every disease, every burden she'd inflicted on others, every sin she'd enacted.

"I, madam, would have done my best. I do not know how, but it would have been better than what you managed. I would not have killed innocents such as Annaluisa and Aileen. I would not have ruined a thousand lives. I would not have bargained with corrupt mortals. I would not have abandoned my baby. I am not you."

"Ah, but you are so like me. You just don't understand it yet. I am dying, Lillian. Would you not at least offer me a bit of grace?

Surely I lost my soul long ago. My only salvation could be a bit of your compassion."

"I have nothing to give you. You must rot in Hell knowing you were never loved."

"I left you alone as long as I could bear."

Lillian let the words flow through her, let the truth of them fill her every fiber. She said nothing.

"You were mortal, and lovely. You did not know your mother was a monster. They told you she was dead so you wouldn't look for me. So you would be free. I did something for you."

"But you let a man take me against my will, and then you killed me again by taking my own flesh and blood. I could have loved a vampire. I *do* love a vampire. I could not love a monster."

Marie nodded. "I only wanted…"

Lillian shook her head. "No. There is nothing in the world that will excuse that sin. But I will grant you the thing you gave to me: abandonment. I abandon you. Let George, Phillip, and Sullivan go. Give me my son, whom you find so very uninteresting, and let us carry on with our useless existences as you see them."

Sullivan closed his eyes for a moment. "I am able to sweeten the bargain, Marie."

"You?" Madame Lucifer barely turned. "What use are you?"

The giant pulled a chain from around his neck and let the vial swing free. It was hypnotic. Lillian wanted to sway in time with the vial, and she could have sworn it emitted a high hum. "Let them all go, and you will have your immortality, and health, and beauty. All that is slipping through your fingers."

"Nonsense," Marie whispered, but she moved closer and extended her hand. "What is that? It is old; it is strong. Is this some voodoo magic of that pathetic woman of yours?"

"Ancient, and yet it is liquid still. The fountain of youth, Madam. Elder blood."

Chauncey pulled out the stopper and spilled a drop of scarlet onto his finger. Lillian's pulse quickened, and hunger gnawed at her. She took a step toward the giant, but George ran to her side and held her arm.

"No," he hissed into her ear. The power of his bond crashed through her, and she nearly fell to her knees. He would not let her move. Phillip stood like a statue, too, frozen by George.

"There are no Elders. There is no Elder blood." But Marie stood before Chauncey, body shaking. She grabbed his hand and stared at the drop on his finger, and then at the vial.

"His name is Vasil, and he is my Lord, Heaven help me. He favors me and gifted me this vial."

"Favors you? A lowlife, a cannibal, a *Negro?*"

Chauncey's eyes flashed with the first emotion Lillian had seen on his face. Fury. The gentle giant had awoken. "Fine, Marie. I will keep if for myself and for my love. We will rule together with Vasil's power flowing through our veins."

"Vasil's power? Vasil's poison! If that is powerful Elder blood, take a drop for yourself first, Chauncey." Marie looked on anxiously, barely able to contain herself.

Chauncey dipped his finger in the vial, closed his eyes, and put the finger in his mouth. He sucked on the blood there. No one moved for a minute, until Chauncey blew out a deep breath and opened his eyes.

Marie knocked him to the ground and sucked at his fingertip. He laughed as she grabbed the vial and emptied it in one swift drink, and she stood and lifted her arms in triumph. For a moment she looked young, and healthy, and almost mortal.

Marie turned to Lillian. "Would you still reject me as I am now? I am as an Elder!"

"I only wanted a mother."

"Then die. Die motherless."

Marie extended her hand. Her summons didn't break George's bond at first. Lillian held on to him, crying. All was lost. Intentionally or not, Chauncey Sullivan had betrayed them.

"My baby," she whispered.

Marie suddenly clutched at her stomach and fell to her knees. Youth faded from her body, and the old, foul stench filled the room. She shrieked and struggled, beckoning at last for Lillian to help her. Her black veins ruptured, and in moments all her blood drained from her body onto the floor. She lay motionless, a hideous shell.

George hugged Lillian, who found she could move again. He spoke over her head to Chauncey.

"Why did you not tell us?"

"You felt the pull of Vasil's blood before you knew. I didn't think you wanted Marie's fate."

"No, hardly. Why didn't it have that effect on you?"

"I...I don't know. I took a chance. He said... Well, it is not important. Perhaps I am not so evil as to be killed by it."

"As I told you, my good man. You *are* a good man now, and it is time for you to accept the present."

"How do you know Vasil, Chauncey?" Phillip sounded skeptical, and Lillian wondered again if they could trust their ally. "What exactly did he say to you?"

"He found me for this purpose." Sullivan gestured to the goo and ragged clothing on the floor, all that was left of Marie.

"Tell us about him, please!"

"Phillip," George interrupted, pulling his brother by the arm. "We have time for that later. We must find Jacques. Who knows what allies remain to our foe?"

"Perhaps Doyle and Moran have found the boy," Lillian volunteered.

"Doyle and Moran?" George shook his head. "You brought them here?"

"No, they came on their own."

"I don't know if they are more brave or stupid," Chauncey said, tiredly washing his palms across his face.

"Come, Lil. There's nothing more to see here."

CHAPTER THIRTY

The congressman and his wife.

Despite their victory, Lillian could not stop shaking. She turned away from George to reach for the pills in her bag as they raced down the main hallway of the house, but she couldn't find them. Perhaps even medicine wouldn't cure this case of nerves. They were seeking Jacques. Her *son.*

George reached back and hurried her along.

"Where is Chauncey?" Lillian asked.

They stopped and listened. The house seemed completely deserted. No children or servants stirred, and they heard no noise of Moran or Doyle. It was as a crypt.

"He's fled, I suppose," George said. "I wanted to thank him—"

Phillip held his finger to his mouth, and they were more silent still and heard nothing. "Should we spread out?"

"No!" Lillian said. "There could be any number of traps."

"Darling, traps can't hurt us, remember?" George whispered. "At least not ones meant for mortals."

"I'd prefer all three of us to emerge from this hellish den in one piece, if you please," Lillian commanded. "Follow me."

She scurried up the grand staircase, careful not to make a sound and motioning to the men to do the same. George rolled his eyes and took a great leap to the second-floor balcony, and Phillip followed.

"Well, yes, I'm new at this," she hissed when she arrived next to them.

The first three rooms were empty. George opened the door to the fourth and cursed. Lillian pressed past him, but he put his arm around her waist to hold her back.

"I do believe that is the congressman from the second district."

"Dear God, he's been shot?" Phillip seemed more surprised at the manner of death than the murder itself.

"Quiet! And let me through." Lillian extracted herself from George's embrace and fell to her knees. "I see no footprints or smudges of mud, and it has been wet these last few days."

"Blazes, Lil, what does it matter now? We must find Jacques!"

She looked up at George. "There is an order we must follow. If our murderer took Jacques, it would serve us well to know who he is."

"From a nonexistent shoeprint?"

"It narrows things down, yes!" She crawled toward the body and examined the bullet wound to the temple. "A good shot, indeed. I am not so good. I believe the bullet is still in his head, as I see no second opening." She turned his head to the side and poked through his bloodied hair.

"How do you put up with this, George?" Phillip joked.

"Shut up. Lil, come *on!"*

"Did you hear any shots, George? He was killed before you arrived then, which was over an hour ago?"

"At least."

"Then it was not Mr. Doyle or Johnnie. No, this blood is too dry." Lillian stood and, with logic, fought back her exhaustion and nausea. "So there may be another."

They opened four more doors and found only bedrooms and privies.

"Where are they?" she said. "Where are the servants, other children—doesn't the congressman have children?"

"I'm not sure, but I think not. There are no children's accoutrements in any of these rooms. But where is Mrs. Coyle?"

Phillip opened the last door in the hallway. "I do believe I've found her."

Lillian winced at the unnatural position of the well-dressed lady on the floor, killed in the same manner as her husband, by gunshot. "Do you think she knew the horrors likely taking place in this house? That her husband hosted a monster? Why did she accept a strange child into her home? What explanation—? Oh!" Sad indeed. Lillian knelt by the woman's side and lifted the pistol lying by her side. "She has taken her own life, and I assume only after killing her husband. Is there a note of any kind? Any other clue?"

Phillip held up a leaf of paper in his hand and waved it. "She's good, George."

"It's not such a leap, Phillip," Lillian said. "The gun is next to the body. Perhaps it is only meant to look like a suicide. But I think if you read that note you'll find that Mrs. Coyle was grievously ashamed that her husband brought another woman's child into the home and made the only assumption she could. Would that I could have come here first to claim him for my own. I would have saved her the trouble."

"You think him complicit in the whole plan?" George asked. "Of course, it is his house, and he hosted the men who subverted your life and stole your son. I suppose he waited a bit too long to have Marie turn him. She said mortal men believe themselves in their prime only after they've passed it."

"He is certainly past his prime now," Lillian remarked. "Phillip?"

George's brother nodded. "Yes, it is very much as you predicted. Poor thing."

"Indeed." Lillian ran her hand over the corpse's eyes to close the lids and reverently crossed the arms over the chest. "Another of Marie's victims."

She was wrong, she also told herself. *I do not share anything with her.*

"So where are Doyle and Moran?" George asked.

"Hopefully they are at my home with my son, awaiting our return. Likely fearing the worst."

"Jesus!" said a voice. They turned to find a thin young man, ashen white at the sight of the corpse on the floor.

"Who are you?" Lillian asked. "Ah, wait. A German name I can't quite recall. Arthur told me."

The man nodded and kept staring at Mrs. Coyle. Finally, when he'd had enough of the gruesome sight, he gulped and took out a small notebook and tiny pencil. "The door was wide open. I called— you didn't hear me? I'm looking into... Jesus! I've never seen anything like it."

"Stop swearing, sir." Lillian stared at him in earnest. "What is your name?"

"Mencken. Miss Holmes I presume? I am a reporter for the *Morning Herald*...well, paid by the story, and only part-time right now— Jesus!"

"Yes, well, you have your story. Phillip, give him the letter. I would suggest you not disturb anything, Mr. Mencken. When you are finished taking notes here, go to the fifth room down the hall and visit Mr. Coyle."

"He's dead too? The congressman? Did you kill him?"

"Don't be ridiculous. You're not a good detective, are you?"

"Did I claim to be a good detective?"

"Well, you're not a good journalist, as I would think you need detective skills in that profession."

"Hardly. It's more a literary sleight of hand." Mencken shook his head, snapped out of his argumentative state and turned to George. "The congressman is truly dead as well?"

"Hmnn, very much so. You'll get your story if you solve this one, Mr. Mencken."

"Half the city has a motive for that murder!" The newspaperman looked from George to Phillip and back to Lillian. "May I ask what you three are doing here?"

"I am looking for a boy. I believe the letter will also make that clear."

"About seven or eight years old?" Mencken held out his hand at chest height to indicate the boy's size.

"God, yes! You saw him?"

"Running for all he was worth away from Mr. Doyle and a police officer toward the city. He was crying, and I assumed he stole something from Mr. Doyle. Doyle had sent word for me to meet him here and learn something, but he didn't even give me as much as a hello as they stormed by. I'm fairly used to that treatment but—"

"How long ago was this?" Lillian had to stop herself from grabbing the man by the lapels and shaking him.

"Well, let's see. It took me about forty-five minutes to walk here, so maybe thirty minutes ago? If they didn't catch him, he could be all the way downtown by now."

"Thank you, Mr. Mencken," George said and grabbed Lillian by the arm. "We must fly."

Lillian called over her shoulder, "Don't go into the cellar, Mr. Mencken."

"Good Lord, what is in the cellar?"

"A vicious hungry hound, foaming at the mouth. It would be the death of you."

CHAPTER THIRTY-ONE

Sullivan.

"I cannot do it." Chauncey kept reaching for the vial around his neck, hoping it had magically returned. It had burned him for days, but the loss of it felt worse.

He'd rushed back to Lillian's to remove the temptation of fulfilling Vasil's orders and to ensure Phoebe's safety. He'd told her what he could, that he'd destroyed Marie and never loved her; he'd been faithful all the while. Phoebe had wept in his arms, relieved and ashamed of her doubts at his fidelity.

"Now we can leave this horrible place?"

"I...I have to help Lillian find her boy and then all will be well. We will go far away, Phoebe. Anywhere you like."

He didn't tell her he'd have to turn the boy over to Vasil or kill him. That he was to kill everyone involved in this disaster: Lillian, the Orleans brothers, anyone who knew they were vampires. The plump blonde woman, what was her name? And the writer, Doyle. Had the man fled the city yet? The policeman...

I cannot.

But Vasil would kill Phoebe, would kill both Phoebe and Chauncey without a thought. Of that Chauncey was certain. Could he justify killing everyone to save her, though? No, he could not.

Perhaps Vasil wouldn't know, wouldn't care, now that Marie was out of the way. Would that be enough for him? Vasil seemed to truly care about nothing, Chauncey admitted. Perhaps he'd been right when he said that all men, mortal or not, cared simply for their own skins. But didn't his love for Phoebe count for anything? Or Lillian's love for George or her child? Wasn't there some good, even if it only resided in a few?

What to do?

Run, Chauncey. Run for your life and your sanity.

CHAPTER THIRTY-TWO

A terrible accident.

As the three leapt from building to building, at times flying short distances, George kept a wary eye on Lillian. That she'd dipped into her medicinals he was fearful. No matter, that discussion could come later, once they found the boy. But he wondered and worried that, once again, the facts of her heritage hadn't fully taken hold of her. She would crash, and crumble, and be broken again.

We're all hungry. He felt it, saw it in Phillip's eyes, and knew that Lillian was operating on nervous energy alone. Besides the ordeal they'd all survived, that hunger was making them squabble.

"No, Phillip, *you're* to look to the left."

George didn't care much about who looked which direction. He watched Lillian and held her hand, treasuring the feel of her skin against his, happy also to be in the company of his brother. If their lives could go on like this forever, or for even a mortal lifetime, he would think himself a very lucky man. They had come into the bowels of Hell to rescue him. And he'd known the moment he saw them that they had not come to rescue their maker but to rescue a man they loved.

Or is that merely a fantasy, George? You still hold their bonds. Are you through testing Phillip's fealty and love? It was far past time to release his bond, so George would make it right as soon as they were home.

"You're looking right again, Phillip," Lillian chastised.

"Dear God, woman, let me concentrate! I'm trying to find your blasted son!"

"Don't talk to Lil like that." George settled on a high landing of the First Bank and Loan Association building and motioned for everyone to stop. "The truth is, the boy and those two men could be anywhere. Jacques could have ducked into a building or an alleyway. I cannot imagine they got further downtown on foot than here."

"True," Lillian concurred. "Doyle has that terrible cough. I have trouble imagining that he has been able to keep up with even Johnnie."

"Ah, but he did!" Phillip pointed to the intersection.

George heard Lillian gasp at the first sight of her child. The boy's hair was as dark as hers, and he was also thin and lanky. She looked like he was the most beautiful sight she'd ever encountered, and she clearly loved him as if they'd never been parted.

George wrapped his arm around her and squeezed. "There you go, love."

"Oh, my!" She wiped at tears and buried her face in George's jacket. "It is true. He is real, and mine."

"We'll have to look that Mencken chap up and thank him properly somehow. Do you want to let Johnnie and Doyle take care of this, or go to meet him now?"

She peered down. George knew that she must have fantasized about this moment a million times, but the reality of it was a different matter. "I would have your opinion on that. I am not sure what he will think of me, of being chased by strangers…of anything about his life to date."

"Uh-oh!" George blurted. Jacques had slipped from Doyle's grasp and was now between the two men, running to and fro like a rabbit, confounding them both. "I think they need our help."

He pulled Lillian by the hand, and they dropped down to the north side of the street where Johnnie was scampering this way and that trying to grab the youth. The boy darted here and there, seeming to have no problems avoiding the trolley tracks embedded in the cobbles.

"That's enough, young man!" Doyle called out in choking breaths. "We are not going to hurt you!"

Lillian went to the edge of the street and called out Jacques's name. The boy stopped and stared at her. She took a step forward and held out her hand. He didn't move but kept staring as if he recognized her.

"I won't hurt you. I will never, ever hurt you."

"I have heard that before." He wiped his nose on his cuff and chewed the inside of his cheek.

"I will never leave you."

"Why not? What did I do to you? Please, let me go."

"We are here to help you." Lil held out a shaking hand. Like her own mother had only minutes earlier, George thought.

No, this could not be more different.

"Don't take me back there," the boy said.

"To the home?" she asked.

"No, I liked the home. I want to go there. I don't want to see Madam again."

"I promise you, you will never see her again."

"Cross your heart?" the boy asked.

Lillian laughed and cried at the same time. "Cross my heart."

"Do it, make the sign."

She did.

George had rarely cried in his lifetime but felt that he must turn away lest tears come to him unbidden. Phillip whispered, "He looks just like her, thank God. And somehow, he looks a little like you. That is a lucky stroke."

"She loves him already. It is not like the maker's bond. It is different."

"Of course it's different. I say, George, you really need to relax."

"Hmnn." George let a long moment pass. "Phillip, thank you. For coming."

"You knew I would, you idiot. Don't think you won't hear about running off without us to face Marie for a good long time."

George took a deep breath and visualized the black string of will that bound Phillip to him, the bond of a vampire's "child." He held his end up to a cool night breeze…and let it drift away into the night.

Phillip's knees buckled, but he caught himself on George's arm. "Why? After all this time? I didn't come for this…."

"Let's not talk about it," George said, more embarrassed than he thought he would be, less bereft than he thought he would be.

"See, that is your problem! All bottled up, wondering and worrying constantly…"

And with that familiar chastising tone, Phillip told George what he needed to hear. Nothing had changed. His brother still loved him.

Then: "Jacques, get out of the street! Trollies use this street, see the tracks? You must come to me!" Lillian moved another foot to coax her son to come to her, trying not to scare him, treating him like a frightened animal.

"No!" They turned to see Jacques frozen in front of a trolley that whizzed around the blind corner. Doyle leapt forward and pushed the boy out of the way. Relief swept through George until he saw Doyle catch his footing on a track and fall in the middle of the street. The author lay like an upended turtle before struggling gracelessly to his feet.

George reacted swiftly, but it was not fast enough. The car was already on Doyle, knocking him yards to the gutter. When it passed, George and Phillip ran forward, while Johnnie blew his whistle and chased the trolley, yelling for the driver to stop, but his cries were drowned by the clanking of the cars. Lillian hugged her son and looked on from the sidewalk in horror.

George groaned at the carnage the blow had made of Mr. Doyle.

Johnnie ran up and caught his breath. "This is terrible," he whispered.

George leaned in toward Doyle's bloody head and listened to his chest. He turned to Lil. "He's alive. But not for long." He nodded quickly toward Johnnie.

"Please, Johnnie, go find a doctor," Lillian said.

"Seems a little late for that, Miss Holmes."

"No, it's never too late. Until it is. Now, run, Officer Moran, run!"

Johnnie took off uptown, toward the new Johns Hopkins hospital. George looked at Phillip, who ran his hand through his hair in frustration.

"Really? *I* can't make this choice for the chap. Let Lillian do it. She knows him best."

"Soon we won't have a choice to make. Lil, what do you want to do? He knows too much, far too much. It might be best…"

Lillian hugged Jacques to her, likely so he couldn't see the gore, and kept a tight grasp on his wrist lest he bolt again. George watched her carefully, wondering if her answer would reflect her feelings about the choice she herself had made. Was becoming a vampire worse than death? How could you make such a choice for a man without the ability to express himself?

Well, George reminded himself, he had done so often enough, but not to an innocent friend.

Lillian hugged Jacques and closed her eyes. "Save him."

"I think you are the one to do it, Lil. He'll forgive you much more easily than me or Phillip, don't you think?"

She nodded and motioned for Phillip to take custody of the boy. Running to George, she knelt by Doyle. "I'm not sure precisely what to do."

"Yes, you are. The first time is the hardest. But are you positive of this?"

"No. But I'd dearly love for him to write more stories. He's a wonderful man, isn't he, George? He found Jacques. He rescued him…"

"There's that. And he does have an interest in the eternal."

"Yes, good, we'll tell him that's what we were thinking. Don't mention the stories. I don't want to upset him." Giving a great sigh, Lillian held her wrist to George's mouth so he could open a wound and produce the blood that would heal Doyle. She hissed at the pain and pleasure.

"Oh, yes, *that* will be what upsets him. He won't be upset in the least to wake up finding that he's a vampire." George laughed. "At least it will cure that cough. Sounded like a touch of pneumonia to me. Ho, Lil, give me a sip of you…it's been so long."

She bumped him away with her hip. "Not likely. Now hold his head up for me. You can lap at his wounds if you're that hungry."

George heard Phillip talking to Jacques, distracting him from the scene in the street. What would Lil tell her son? They still had a long road ahead of them. But having him safe in her arms was a good start.

CHAPTER THIRTY-THREE

Bread and jam.

Lillian wondered what Johnnie thought when he returned to the scene of the accident to find them missing. She also wondered what he would do about it. Had Arthur told him all?

She kept a tight grip on Jacques's hand, loving the contact with him, hating how inadequate she felt. It was one thing to want your child in your care, another to know how to provide it. Why, she didn't even have a mother friend to copy, she realized, and wondered how she might remedy that. Aileen had done all right with her brothers, and Johnnie as well. They were good boys, although little rogues. How would Jacques get on with them?

Phillip had taken Arthur to his house and volunteered for the odious task of managing his newborn antics. Lillian would visit soon, she vowed.

"Tomorrow, you must see him tomorrow," George had warned. He would want to see his maker.

"Are you *certain* you want me here now, Lil?" George asked as they arrived at her home. "You are both safe." When he put his hands on Jacques's shoulders, the boy didn't try to wrestle himself free but simply yawned.

Oh, of course, Lillian thought. *He's tired and hungry! Surely there is food in the house?*

She needed Addie and Thomas. Another nervous lurch of her stomach at the thought of how to explain everything to the pair, who now more than ever seemed the only mother and father figure she'd ever have, and that she'd buried Aileen without them even knowing her dead. Perhaps she would forever need to keep them at a distance.

She nodded to George. "I would have you here."

"Where are we?" Jacques asked as he examined the house's exterior. "I thought you were taking me back to the home." His deep brown eyes, so like her own, reflected worry no seven-year-old should have to feel.

She knelt to comfort him. "This is a bit like the home, but better. No Madam, not ever again. She is gone forever. There are three lads to play with, and a lovely yard. We can go to the park every Sunday, where you can sail boats and have all sorts of adventures. Would you like that, Jacques?"

He shrugged. "S'pose. My name isn't Jacques though. Madam called me that, but I hated it. I'm not French. At the home they called me Jack."

"Jack." Lillian smiled. "I like that name. We will never call you anything else." She brushed her hand on his cheek and bit back tears. It wasn't time to tell him the truth, not quite yet. *I'm too tired, and I don't know what to say.*

George touched her back, and she stood. "It will be fine, love," he said. "Take him inside."

He opened the front door, but Lil hesitated, feeling as if entering her home would waken her from the wonderful dream of having her son. A sip of medicine would help right now, but she didn't want for Jack to see that.

"Lil, he's exhausted. So am I." George scooped Jack up in his arms, and the boy rested a head on his shoulder. Lillian stared, wanting to remember the picture accurately for the rest of her life.

George pushed the door fully open with his foot, carried Jack inside and right up the stairs into Lillian's bedroom. He sat Jack on the bed and worked at pulling off his boots. "Tonight," he remarked, "you may sleep in your street clothes."

"I'm hungry."

"As well you should be, boy. Lil, be a dear and go downstairs, get a treat for him, won't you?"

He winked at her, and she gaped. How did he know how to do this? George was the last man on earth to raise a young boy. Still, she ran to the kitchen and scoured the larder for anything that might suit. *Bread and jam, bread and jam. I loved that as a child!*

After cutting off two large hunks of bread and smearing them with jam and butter, and after pouring a jar of milk, she ran back to her room. Jack was sitting up in bed, listening to George.

"Tomorrow you can sleep in the room with the other boys, but we won't wake them now. Does that sound fine?"

The boy nodded. "Quite fine. What is your name, mister? Are you in charge of this home?"

George looked taken aback, but Lillian was too interested in his answer to rescue him. He glanced over and she nodded. It seemed too soon, but if George could help her, she would accept this. *I've never needed so much help.*

A tiny voice inside contradicted her. *You've always needed help. You would never accept it.*

"You can call me George. Do you remember that when you were at the home, sometimes people would come and take away one of the boys?"

Jack nodded. "They got taken. I never got taken. Except by *her*."

"Do you know why?"

The boy shook his head no, but Lillian wondered how many awful reasons he'd created for why no one ever wanted him.

"Because they were saving you for us. We had a hard time finding you, though."

"You were looking for me?"

"Yes. Very hard. Lil, bring over the food."

Lillian sat across from George on the bed and handed the plate to Jack, who devoured the bread and slurped down the milk.

"What's your name?" Lillian's son asked her, with a full mouth and jam smeared across his cheek. She cleaned him off with a handkerchief George offered.

"My name is…"

"It's all right, Lil. Tell him your name."

"My name is Lillian. Lillian Holmes."

"Are the other boys here vampires like you? Vampires I've seen are strong. Wouldn't be easy to play with vampire boys."

"No," Lillian answered. "They are just like you. You will like them. And they have a giant dog named Abraham Lincoln. I think you will like him as well."

Jack closed his eyes. "I like this home better than the other one."

"It's not a home for orphaned boys, Jack," Lil whispered after a time. "It's your home."

His eyes fluttered for a moment, and Lil wasn't sure if he'd heard her or if sleep had won out. No matter, it gave her more time.

Jack whispered something she couldn't hear and then looked at her. "Are you my mother and father? You looked for me…"

"Yes, love, I am your mother. George…"

George looked at Lil for direction. She nodded.

"And I am your father."

Evidently satisfied, Jack rolled onto his side and fell fast asleep.

CHAPTER THIRTY-FOUR

Heroics unmasked.

George spent the rest of the night with Lillian in his arms, curled up in the bedroom formerly occupied by Addie. He slept fitfully, visions of Marie, Sullivan, and the dead Coyles running in a continuous loop through his mind.

Even though they'd found Jack and Marie was dead, he felt a failure, not able to forgive himself for luring Lil and Phillip into the pit of darkness. He'd worried they would come, stubborn as they both were. He should have sent them the letter long after the confrontation, at least if he was being truly noble. *I could have lost them both, lost everything.* He thought of Sullivan, wondered if he'd ever meet the man again. Surely he and Phoebe were on a train, heading quickly away from Baltimore.

"Morning," Lillian whispered, and wiped dark-circled eyes.

"Sleep more, Lil. You'll need a month of sleep to make up for yesterday."

"No, I've much to do. I must see how Jack is and then introduce him to the boys. And you know I must face Arthur. Johnnie will come knocking at my door, no doubt...."

She rose and pulled on her robe. George watched her, leaning on his elbow. She looked over her shoulder at him and sent a glance of apology as she opened her messenger bag and took a sip of medicine.

"We must talk, love."

"I will give it up, George. Just not today. Give me a day or two."

He wondered how soon it could be. The longer he let her habit go, the harder it would be for her to break. But he could give her a few more days, certainly. They'd faced worse.

"I want only to talk about yesterday."

Her shoulders dropped, and he wondered for a moment if her habit of hiding great secrets wasn't more tolerable than this never-ending parade of woes. But the truth was something that had to be faced and he said, "I've never heard you mention your father, of wanting to find him. But learn about him you did."

"As a child, I believed Addie's story of him going down on a ship. At least since adulthood, I wondered if he was more than a cad who either attacked or seduced my mother. I suppose I imagined she might have given up a child much as I did, against her will. That was my hope."

"But to learn he was the famously evil Henry Holmes... Not quite an ordinary cad."

"Did you believe her? I am not certain she spoke the truth. Her flair for the dramatic— Are you afraid for me, George? That I carry his insanity? Or if I was the product of a mortal and a vampire...then I am doubly cursed, am I not?"

"No, I am not afraid. I know you, Lil, you are not insane. I simply wanted to make certain you understood everything Marie—"

"Never use that name again!"

"Everything she said."

Lillian sat on the bed and took his hand. "Would you rob me of this most happy day, George? I have my son. What came before...it is horrific beyond anything I could have dreamt up in my fantasies. Worse than anything Mr. Doyle or Mr. Stoker could have written. But this is my story, and I survived it all. I have two choices, do I not? Be a slave to my parents and risk never living, or something else. Mustn't I put aside the past now that Jack is in my care?"

George nodded, surprised that she was so matter of fact, hoping that he was indeed covering already trodden ground. "I simply do not want these ghosts to haunt you forever. I think it sometimes best to exorcise them, lest they come calling later on."

"But you believe it to be my choice—to carry on or to be ruled by the past." The statement was in some part a question. A hope.

"My dear Lillian," he agreed, "I cannot imagine that I could truly persuade you to do anything you do not want, even if I desired it. It is certainly your choice. And…there is something else."

"My medicine."

"No, please stop worrying about that now. We will come to that in due course. It is the letter I wrote to you. Why didn't you follow my instructions?"

"Did you really expect us to? You knew we would follow you. Or at least hoped. Phillip said that. Is that all? It is not inhuman to want companionship at dark times, George. Perhaps that is a good thing, to maintain some element of your humanity." She gave him a small smile. "And yet, you set out to tackle the problem on your own. You do not control as much as you believe, George. You did not make the choice for Phillip and I, and neither did your maker's bond. So, is that all?"

"But it is a horror! You could have been killed, both of you!"

"But we weren't, and you aren't listening. We chose to come. You did not command us. The very opposite, in fact! You may have hoped, imagined, but you did nothing to force the issue. George, now you are searching for ways to make yourself a devil." She shook her head and patted him on the wrist. "No worries. Phillip and I will not let your heroics go to your head. Certainly Kitty will always cut you down to size. I do wish we could speak to Chauncey. He is a hero as well."

"I would like the same. I imagine he is long gone from our reach."

"Now, will you help me with more important matters? We have a very busy few days ahead of us."

"Might we have a night alone soon?" he asked. Filled with a desperate love for her, he brushed Lil's hair away from her face. She captured his hand and kissed it.

"I rather thought the idea was that they were *all* to be spent in one another's company. I'm not well versed in such things…"

He didn't answer, overcome with a need to make things right for Lil. For himself.

"Lil, you're not a very good vampire. It seems Vasil is real, and you do go about chatting our secrets for all the world to hear."

"I'm sorry."

"You have to do better. I know this has been unthinkably difficult, but you must try—very hard—to do better. Do you understand?"

"Yes, I will try. Goodness, George!"

Is she ready? Am I ready? He wondered in silence for a few moments.

"Because," he continued, "I will no longer be able to stop you from making mistakes. God knows I've not done well so far." George closed his eyes and held his breath. "It is too soon, I'm sure it's too soon. But I must do this. It's a terrible burden. Please don't leave me, Lil."

"What?" She looked confused. "What are you talking about?"

He pulled her close. "I release you."

She lost strength and clung to him. "No, please! What have you done?"

"Did you not want your freedom? It cannot be undone."

"Oh, you stupid man!" She pounded him on the chest. "Why did you do that, George? I am not ready to do this vampiring alone! Are you leaving me?"

He shook his head. "Only if you wish it. In fact, I'd rather marry you. But I needed to know…" He shook his head again.

Lillian sighed. "Oh. I wondered, too. But when I saw you in Marie's clutches, I knew. I didn't come to rescue my maker. I came to rescue my George."

"Then marry me," he said.

"I'll consider it. Oh, look at you! You cannot stand a taste of your own medicine. I will marry you, George." She pressed her lips to his. "I love you so much."

"And I love you."

"It is not so different from mortal love, is it?" she mused. "Not at all."

"Not at all," he agreed. Brushing a strand of hair away from her face he said, "You look as though you are ready to drop. I was going to say that you've had quite a week, but it was not much more demanding than any since I met you, I suppose."

So much, though, since he first met her. The revelations of the Jackal and Dr. Schneider, of the birth of her child, and that kidnapping to the asylum. Her becoming a vampire. Aileen's murder. Her parentage, the destruction of her mother, the rescue of her son, the care of Mr. Doyle and a house full of children… And, he gulped down a bit of worry, there was a matter left undiscussed. It seemed nothing in some ways, and yet knowing Lillian as he did, he wanted nothing unsaid between them.

She had lain back on the bed. He lay beside her and kissed her knuckles. "Love, does it bother you that I… How can I put this?"

"What?"

"That I lay with your mother?" George closed his eyes, wondering if Marie could ruin his happiness from the grave. "It is a very distasteful situation to you, I can imagine, even if it happened centuries ago and I was a different person then. Does it change everything?"

"Did you love her?"

George snorted. "I don't know whether I am happy or ashamed to say that I did not at all love her. I could barely stand to be in her company, except for those brief interludes where... She exaggerated, you know." He could not ever finish that sentence. He had indeed been a different person then. A person who would seduce his brother's wife and revel in the nights they shared, nights bent on physical pleasure alone. He wondered at times that he had not ended up similarly hideous on the outside as Marie. There but for the grace of Lil went he.

Lillian shrugged. "You were a different person then," she repeated. Then she gave a quiet laugh and tried to make light. "And, George, you did not know then what this year would bring. Look at what my letter to a favored author did! Had I known, would I have done things differently? Perhaps. Must I turn my back on everything I have because of it?"

George stared into her eyes. "I dearly hope not."

"Then put all aside and kiss me."

He pressed his lips to hers and ran fingers through her silky hair. "I would lose myself in you, Lil. Every day and night, forever. *Forever.*"

She didn't reply but pulled at his shirt, nibbling every inch of him as she stripped him bare. He shuddered at her caresses and cried out as she punctured his neck and licked the burning flesh there. She grew stronger from his blood and showered him with kisses, running her hands up and down his body.

He pushed her onto her back and pulled the layers of nightclothes from her, frantic to have her soft flesh against his. "Tell me...tell me anything, Lil," he said, desperate to hear her voice. "Talk to me."

"Give me everything, George. I would have another taste of you as you enter me. I am starving."

"Not yet, greedy one," he said with a laugh. He nibbled at her ear and neck, and suckled at her breasts, making her arch and cry out. He covered her mouth then, lest she wake the house, and his excitement grew.

With a strong grip to keep her silent, he worked his mouth down her belly until he heard the loud throb of her pulse at the top of her thigh. He licked the juncture and looked into her eyes, then pierced the skin and sucked at the blood seeping out. He licked at her wound then pulled himself away, reminding himself that too much would send them down a dangerous path, but it took great restraint.

Lillian reached for him and pulled him on top of her, whispering his name and begging for release. He kissed her as he freed his sex and pushed himself inside her body, let her envelop him in tight warmth. He pinned her hands down and told her to be quiet as he pressed deeply in and out. She buried her face in his shoulder, but her low muffled moans brought more flame to his ardor and he slammed into her, harder and harder, wondering if he could somehow claim her body and soul. For she had claimed his.

When he poured into her, he gasped her name. She arched up and dug her nails into his back, calling to God and clenching tightly around him. They fell into an embrace, and he kissed her gently one last time.

"Sweet one, how do you feel?"

"Ah, I would feel this way every hour of every day."

"What a splendid plan."

His beloved was a silent a moment before saying, "I've been thinking, George."

He smirked. "That sounds dangerous. Do tell."

"I'd rather like to be married sooner rather than later. Kitty suggested we should choose a date for our wedding and—"

George sniffed out a laugh. "Yes, I remember. Since when did you rely on Kitty for your direction, though? I thought that was Bess's position."

"Bess would agree." Her face serious, Lillian seemed to steel herself. "Sooner rather than later. Does that frighten you?"

"The prospect of those two women instructing me on wedding plans? That does instill a bit of abject terror, yes."

"I mean it, George! Are you ready? What with Jack and the state of this house..." She shook her head. "I would not blame you for changing your mind."

"Nonsense, of course you would blame me. Your left brow just arched. And of course you would have every right to blame me, as I just proposed!" He shook his head and laughed again. "Lil, last night I wasn't sure we were going to survive to be able to have this conversation. I would marry you today if you were willing to go to the courthouse, but I suspect you desire something slightly more elaborate." He pulled her into a tight embrace to remind her of all she meant to him, but a sudden stray thought had him making a small noise of concern.

"What?"

George sat up and tapped his finger against his chin. "I wonder what Jack will think about his parents getting married. How will we explain that?"

Lillian shook her head. "Darling, he knows we're vampires and doesn't seem to mind. He hasn't had the most normal upbringing. This will only be a good thing in his eyes, I believe. I'd be surprised if it were otherwise."

George watched as she rose, cleaned up and bustled about the room, getting ready to greet her new son and tackle the list of things she must accomplish. He watched her and suddenly realized he hadn't taken his own advice. He hadn't buried any ghosts or forgiven himself for his sins. Not really. But it was time. While he wasn't sure he deserved this happiness, he did know that Lillian and Jack needed him, and it would serve everyone better if he were to say "fuck it all" and get to work.

He jumped out of bed to get dressed, saying, "I'm going to check on Doyle. Come by as soon as you can. And I'm holding you to our night together. *Tonight.*"

"George, one more thing," Lillian said. "The Learned Order…"

"Indeed. You did say you were starving. We must eat tonight before our rendezvous, is that not so?"

Lillian's face showed hunger, anger…and then the emotions lessened. "It would be good to know which of them is culpable first. Perhaps Arthur can enlighten us more on that subject."

"He'll likely be ready for a feast of his own," George said. Then, "Hurry. You really must visit your newborn. It's very bad form to leave them waiting."

CHAPTER THIRTY-FIVE

Johnnie Moran expresses doubts.

Lillian stared at her empty bed and choked back a sob. She should have guarded Jack all night. What kind of mother ignored her child to lie with her lover? Brought home by vampires? Of course he would be scared and have taken the first moment to escape. They'd formed no bond; she couldn't blame him!

She ran down the stairs, hoping to catch George, but was drawn to a racket in the kitchen. Mr. Lincoln was howling and barking. She pushed open the door to see four boys—Jack included—Cook, and Mr. Lincoln all eating a mountain of bacon, biscuits, and eggs.

"Did not!" her son argued with Darby. "You never ran that fast!"

"Did too! All the way to the park and back. I has witnesses."

"*Have* witnesses, Darby." Lillian rubbed at her temples, wondering if she were imagining this. Sally, Sarah— Damnation! What was Cook's name? She was the sister of the Eisner woman who'd helped at Aileen's funeral.

The woman stood and tried to calm the boys but slid on some eggs Mr. Lincoln had drooled onto the floor.

"Miss Holmes, a suggestion?"

"Anything!"

"A maid and a nanny. Don't mean to be overstepping, mind you. Mrs. Eisner said that you seemed a bit... Well, she said you could use help."

"No, please tell me," Lillian said. "I'm not used to such things. Addie and Thomas…they are in Chicago, you see, and I don't know when they'll return."

"I know sisters searching for a post…."

"Yes, right away. Could they share a room? I am running out of rooms."

Cook straightened and grinned widely. "I will speak with them today. When could you meet?"

"If they come with your recommendation they may start the moment they arrive. You know the room that belonged to Mrs. Adencourt? It is now theirs. But they will have to ready it themselves. I think there are linens and such somewhere…"

"There, there, don't be troubled about those things. First things first. We three will make a list of what's needed and present it to you. The boys—especially Jack—could use some new clothes as well. If you like." Cook seemed a bit tentative.

"Yes!" Lillian said. "Thank you, thank you! And Bess and Kitty will help with the clothes. They love such things. Oh, Lord, I must speak with Bess. She will be so worried!"

"And there is the gardening and such," Cook piped up. "You don't have a man to do the garden and heavy work?"

"Can you do that too?"

Sally—yes, it was Sally—rubbed her hands on her apron and laughed. "Let me sit with the Misses Dawson and see what is what. At least the cold weather is here and the weeds will stop growing. Oh, miss, you do have coal coming, don't you? Temperatures will be dropping very soon!"

Lillian groaned and shrugged. "Maybe Thomas arranged for that ahead of time. I'm not sure."

"All right, then. We still have time. I'll see to it all."

"Thank you so very much, Sally. I believe there are accounts at Eisner's Grocers and the general store across the street."

Sally laughed again. "Yes, I believe so, as I am Jacob Eisner's sister, remember?"

"Of course you are." *God, when did I become so unreliable and forgetful? I do need so much help!* And, although a shot of anxiety filled her at the thought, she knew that it would be best to always be clearheaded. Would giving up her medicine be as bad as the last time? Would she need help again? Surely George would help her. But Jack, he must not know, must not see…

Her son swung his feet from the high stool at the table and stared at her. He waved a bit shyly, and Lillian felt her legs grow weak. It was something akin to falling in love, this tug at her heart of maternal joy. How many such moments had she missed? *No, do not go back. There is too much to be done.*

"Boys, I have pennies for you!" she called. The Musketeers lined up in front of her, wiggling in excitement, but Jack just watched. "Do you remember the rules?"

"Don't go far," Darby said and saluted.

"Be careful," Paddy added and saluted.

"Mr. Lincoln is to go outside again?" Billy asked.

Lillian laughed. "I give up. Mr. Lincoln may always come inside, as long as he is not muddy. You also must bathe him in the yard, but he may sleep in your room. Is that all right, Sally?"

"You are the mistress, Miss Holmes. I would suggest that Mr. Lincoln not eat upstairs, though, as he is not tidy at meals."

The boys cheered, and even Jack joined in. "Can I play too?" he asked.

"It's not a game," Darby chided. "We do investigatin' for Miss Holmes. And she pays us. We're her little lieutenants."

"That's right, my lieutenants. I want to know if certain people are still in the city. No hearsay, no gossip of old ladies. I shall write the names down, and you will ask Cook to help you with the pronunciations. Commit them to memory." Lillian pulled her smallest notebook from her bodice and recorded the names of the members of the Learned Order, as well as H.L. Mencken. She glanced up at Sally, wondering if the woman could read, but Sally nodded knowingly and took the list from her. Of course, she also looked at it and offered a questioning look, no doubt wondering why Lillian spied on the city's finest men.

"Jack, you will come with me, as we must call on the very nice man who pushed you to safety last night," Lillian said.

"He chased me forever," Jack complained.

"And I will thank him for that as well."

Lillian led Jack by the hand into the parlor, afraid to speak to him or look at him too long, lest he vanish into thin air.

"We must buy you a new suit of clothes," she said. "Several. And new shoes. Oh, my, it's chilly and you don't have a coat. Well, we'll stop at Hutzler's Palace before going to Mr. Phillip's house, how will that be?"

"'Sall right. I'm not cold."

The rap on the door startled her, and Lillian waited for someone to answer it before realizing how long it had been since Thomas had been about. She muttered, "I can still open my own door, at least. I think."

On the porch stood Johnnie Moran, pale and tired, anxious and furious. Not since Aileen's murder had he worn such a fierce expression.

"Oh, Johnnie, I was going to call on you today."

"Call on me, Miss Holmes? Where? In the street where I left you and the dying Mr. Doyle? At the congressman's mansion where there has been a double murder?"

"A murder-suicide," Lillian corrected, wondering how Mr. Mencken had gotten on with his story.

Johnnie brushed his cap on his trousers and cursed. "Hopefully you'll visit me at Spring Grove, as the doctor at Johns Hopkins must think me insane. I brought them to the spot and found barely a splotch of blood where Mr. Doyle lay dying. At least the congressman and his wife were still in the mansion, or my job would have been taken from me."

"Come in, Johnnie. I have but a moment, but I promise I will get to all of your questions in due time."

"You'll get to them all, Miss Holmes, right now, or we'll be having a chat down at the station. I want to know about what Mr. Doyle told me. But first, where is his body?"

Jack looked bored. He sat on the floor, running his fingers along the carpet and making the noise of cannons and guns while Lillian weighed how much she could safely relay. George was right—she'd been a terrible vampire. She prayed that Vasil would not make a visit to exact some terrible form of Elder justice just because she had to tell Johnnie something believable.

"I see you at least kept your hands on the boy."

"My son."

Johnnie nodded. "If that is so, I'm happy for you, miss. Now, Mr. Doyle?"

"He is…alive. He can't see you now, but…it's quite miraculous, actually." Lillian bit at her lip, thankful at least that Johnnie didn't know to look at her left brow.

"I don't believe in miracles, Miss Holmes. I'm not sure I believe in anything I've been told these last few days, but I can see I won't be getting the truth from you. I'll give you today to produce Mr. Doyle, dead or alive, and then I'll be calling in the paddy wagon."

"Johnnie, don't leave! I promise, we will sit with Mr. Doyle in a few days and he can explain everything to you."

The young man just shook his head and put his cap back on. "I'll see him today or I'll take you to the station. It is your choice."

Jack suddenly stood. Pointing past Johnnie he said, "The lady says to trust Mama."

"Mama?" Lillian murmured the word, letting it roll off her tongue, saying it again. Then, "Wait. What lady, Jack?"

"The lady in the white cap with the red hair. She is trying to talk to you, mister, but you aren't listening to her. She says you do that a lot."

"What new trick is this, Miss Holmes? A cruel one, for sure!"

"Quiet!" Lil squatted and looked into Jack's eyes. "How old is the lady?"

He shrugged. "Maybe like you, or a little younger. She's pretty."

"And can you ask her what name she uses?"

"She says her name is A-leen. She talks like the women down Fell's Point. The Irish women, not the Negro ladies."

"My God." Lillian looked at Johnnie, who stood frozen with his hand over his mouth.

"Did you tell him her name?" the young man accused.

"No, we've barely spoken. Perhaps one of the boys mentioned her?"

Jack spoke again: "And she said that this man will understand about everything if you give him a chance. He's smarter than you think."

"Lord." Johnnie sat in a chair. "That sounds like Aileen."

"Do you see anyone else, Jack?"

"Right now, or ever?"

"Ever. Let's start there."

"You mean the spirit people?"

"Yes, the spirit people."

"I always see them. They're mostly nice to me."

"Well," Lillian said. "Wait until Mr. Doyle meets my son!"

Johnnie pulled her aside by the arm. "Is this another one of your tricks, Miss Holmes? I know you're clever, but you're not too clever for me."

"I swear, Johnnie. I swear on my friendship with Aileen, it is not a trick of mine."

"Well, you don't believe him, do you? Maybe he's...not quite right, if you take my meaning."

"I do believe he is 'quite right,' and I do take your meaning. But I also know the one man who can help tell us if this mystical talent is real or imagined. And as you wish to see Mr. Doyle, we may as well kill two birds with one stone. Come with us, Johnnie."

"Doyle? Where is he?" Johnnie squinted, one eye closed, still doubtful, which was quite understandable.

"At the home of George and Phillip."

"Splendid. Right into the lion's den."

"Oh, now, they aren't as bad as they seem. Just a pair of quarrelsome brothers."

"Mr. Doyle said some fantastical things about them. I would have the truth. Before we go there, will you tell me one thing?"

"Ask away."

"Did one of them kill my Aileen?"

"No!" Lillian said. "You do them a great injustice! They would never harm an innocent. Well, not in a good long while, at least."

"Did *you* kill her?"

Jack looked up at her, and Lillian reminded herself that there was nothing wrong with the boy's hearing. Many a time as a child she'd listened to adults talk as if she weren't there, and she should be circumspect about what came out of her mouth.

"No. The one who did that is destroyed. Gone forever, Johnnie. We will tell you the full story, but not now." She cast a glance at Jack.

Johnnie nodded in understanding. "All right, then. Lead on to Mr. Doyle. But this had best not be a trick." Contrary to his words, he stood still for a moment, staring at Jack. "Could you talk to the lady anytime you like, young man?"

Jack nodded, and Lillian's heart broke. She hoped for Johnnie's sake it was true, and he'd finally be able to tell Aileen all he'd ever wanted to say to her but never had the chance.

"All right then. No tricks. I am armed, Miss Holmes."

"As you should be. As we all should be."

CHAPTER THIRTY-SIX

Casey would waltz with a strawberry blonde…

"It's intolerable!" Phillip complained, pacing the room. "I cannot abide another minute of it! Can't Lillian take him to her home?"

"Whatever is wrong?" Lillian asked as she took off her coat and ushered Jack into the house.

"Hello, Jack!" Phillip bowed and smiled.

"Hello!"

George came out of the kitchen, swept Jack up into a spin then propped him on his shoulders. The pair laughed and ran about the room, dancing to piano music coming from a small chamber off the parlor.

Phillip tapped Lillian on the shoulder. "Who is that, and what has he done with my brother?"

"It's a lovely sight, isn't it, Phillip?"

"Yes, I dare say it is. Ah, Officer Moran, good day to you!"

Johnnie managed a nod but didn't bother changing his scowl. Lillian feared for him. He loathed the Orleans brothers; that much was clear. She knew neither George nor Phillip would harm him out of hand, but they wouldn't tolerate mortal interference either. They'd been through too much to eke out this partly tolerable existence. She must convince Johnnie to accept reality and, somehow, to become their ally. The full truth was key, for he would love whoever killed Aileen's attacker. At least, Lillian dearly hoped so.

Phillip tapped her on the shoulder again. "Lil, please go chat with Arthur. He's driving us all mad with that playing. Bess and Kitty went shopping to escape it."

"Arthur is playing the piano?"

"Nonstop. I've not seen the likes of it. He's not very good. I think we've heard 'The Band Played On' twenty times already today." Phillip tapped his foot as if to correct Arthur into playing the waltz rhythm properly. "Awful."

"Could he play before he became a vampire?" she asked.

"Droll. Go speak with him. I fear he is going off in some odd direction. George seems to think it's fine, being that he is a child of yours and likely to be unusual, but I disagree."

"I will see him now. Please distract Officer Moran for a while."

She turned to find Johnnie mere inches away. "I'm not easily distracted, Miss Holmes."

"No, no, I suppose you aren't. You must listen to me, my friend. Aileen meant a great deal to me, and by extension you became dear to me as well. I love your brother, and her brothers. I would have things go well for them—for all of us." She turned and called out, "Phillip! George! While I visit with Mr. Doyle, please tell Johnnie everything. I mean every single thing. From the day you met me until Mr. Doyle came to be at that piano. Will that suffice, Johnnie? I truly must speak with Arthur alone for a bit."

George shook his head. "Lil, you are playing with fire. I—"

"It is the only way. Please. This once, please trust me. What do you say, Officer?"

Johnnie mulled over her offer. "Only if you let me lay eyes on him for a second. Just to see for myself that the man is not dead."

"Yes, that might be best. Then you will be more likely to understand, as you saw his state last night. My God, was it only last night?"

Lillian peeked into the music room, and indeed, Arthur sat at the piano, a man obsessed, playing the same chorus again and again. She opened the door a bit further, and Johnnie looked in. He let out a gasp, and Lillian quickly shooed him away.

"Will that do?" she said as they returned to the parlor.

Johnnie nodded and scratched at his chin, looking completely baffled.

"I will leave you all to catch up," Lillian promised, "and see what to do with Arthur."

George came to her side and placed a kiss on her forehead. He leaned in and whispered, "No matter what, tell Doyle it will be fine. Even if you don't believe it. He must hear that from you now."

"I remember the things you said to me. Has he eaten yet?"

"No, he won't have a bite. You must convince him. He can fade, Lil. Your hero can still die."

"I will not let that happen. Unless, unless he wants to. That would be his choice, but he's not in his right mind now, so I must choose for him. Oh, and I have something quite important to discuss with you about Jack." She squeezed George's hand and cast a glance at her son, who watched her carefully. "It seems he sees spirits."

"What did you say?"

"Hmnn." She let out a sigh. "Never mind. Let me attend to this serious matter before that serious matter."

She put down her messenger bag on a chair and took off her hat, steeling herself for Arthur's anger. *Dear Mr. Doyle,* she thought. *If I had only known, I never would have written to you. I would have simply read your books and then put them aside and gone on to others. I am so sorry that I was not in my right mind.*

"Well, you cannot undo anything, Lillian," she muttered then. "So do what you can do."

She returned to the music room, approached the writer-turned-newborn-vampire with care and slid onto the piano bench next to him. He hesitated for a moment, and she knew it was the nearness of his maker affecting him, but he played until the tune ended and finished with a flourish even though the notes were not correct.

"You play with great vigor," she said.

"I am terrible."

"Not quite terrible. Perhaps rusty?"

"Terrible."

He turned and stared at her, and she felt tears well up in her eyes. She said, "I made the choice for you. You were a breath away from the end."

"I only remember the boy, and then crushing pain. I awoke to this." He gestured to himself, if not at any part in particular. "Your friend Phillip explained the rest."

"I have no way of thanking you for saving my son from certain death. I presume you would have acted equally heroically to save any child in that predicament."

"I have never acted heroically in my life. Anyone would help a child in danger."

"No, not all of us, Mr. Doyle. I knew you were a kind man from the first letter you wrote to me. My regret is—"

"How great would your regret be if you were shipping my body to Scotland? Greater, or less?"

"I imagine that depends upon what you think of my choice. Perhaps you loathe me now; that would be quite normal. Perhaps you will come to loathe me; that also would be quite normal. I do not know. But I also know that this life is not all horrible."

"I will die shortly in any case, will I not? How can you drain blood from innocent people? I refuse."

"You will not be able to stop yourself," Lillian warned. "I am shocked you have lasted this long. Hunger usually drives one insane in those first hours."

"I…I am ashamed of the hunger. Phillip made me drink. I cannot bear to know what…who it was. That is what I loathe you for most. That I want to drink and kill. I did not truly understand what you were until I became like you. You are a monster, and now I am one."

"There is a way to make it less monstrous. We—George, Phillip, and I—we feast only on those who are dying or who are clearly murderers."

"That is less odious? It's a mere excuse to justify your existence. If you cared about justice you would do yourselves in and take me to Hell with you."

"That is an option, always. But I am in love, Mr. Doyle. And I have a son. In many ways, I am now alive for the first time." She sighed. "Our circumstances are clearly different. You have had a good life, and now it is made less good by me."

"A good life? What do you know of me, of my life? You think I am one of my characters." He choked out a half sob. "I have a dying wife. But I also have children, a home and my studies. All are lost now."

"They would have been lost anyway if you died," Lillian said. Then, "I am sorry." She choked back sudden tears. "I am very, very sorry. I made the best choice I could at the time."

What good would it do to tell him he could blend in, that his wife and children wouldn't know if he played things wisely, that he could go on as if nothing were different? Was it true? Probably not. Her companions were vampires; she was to marry one. He *had* lost everything.

She wept and couldn't stop herself. *I was wrong. So wrong.* Doyle put his head on her shoulder and cried with her. His sobs made him shake, and the two held one another in consolation.

He sat up and wiped at his tears, was clearly shocked that they smeared his hand with blood. "Damnation. Is there no water in my body?"

Lillian sniffed out a laugh. She was no good at this. George had been so much better.

Doyle stared at her. "Did you at least kill the woman who held your son?"

Lillian nodded. "Yes. Thank you. She is gone forever."

Turning back to the piano, Doyle shrugged. "I wonder why God wanted this for me. I worked so hard to solve the great riddle of what lies behind the mortal veil. I thought it was my purpose. Does this not bar me from ever learning the truth? And am I not damned for—?"

Lillian interrupted, not wanting him to spiral down into a new depression. She said, "I still intend to become the greatest female detective in America. That has not changed. Why must you stop your studies? In fact, I have quite a candidate for you to examine."

His eyebrow quirked up, hope appearing on his face. He had not looked so alive since the night before. "Who?"

"My son, the very boy you saved—which must mean something! But we will get to that. Now, you must tell me your decision. I will not stop you from dying again, but if you want to live, you will have to eat. I can give you sustenance for now. That is what George did for me. It will soothe the hunger until you are ready to hunt on your own. To make your own decisions."

"How can I decide such a thing? It is unthinkable!"

"I understand," Lillian said. "Perhaps it will help to remember that you can always change your mind. It will become more difficult as you grow stronger, but in the coming days and weeks, if you decide you would prefer death, you need only to stop eating. I will not force anything on you again."

"It is inconceivable to me that we are having this conversation."

"Yes," Lillian said. "I understand. But it gets better quickly; I can promise that much. George tells me there are very lonely, depressive times in which this life is untenable, but the same is true of mortal life. With purpose, you might weather them well. For now, might I offer you a bit of help?"

"Blood, do you mean?" Doyle asked, seeming to resign himself. "Ah, euphemisms. Yes, just for now. It is not the blood of an innocent person, though, is it?"

"No. It is mine, and I am no innocent, as you've noted. But it will do until you are ready for more."

She drew her teeth across her wrist and he winced, but his disgust turned to lust in seconds and he grabbed her arm. Now he knew it was not legerdemain.

CHAPTER THIRTY-SEVEN

Sullivan.

George sat on Lillian's roof for a moment alone, swinging his feet off the edge, wishing he'd thought to buy a new pipe.

It was evening again, and the house was too full. Two young ladies—new maids—had appeared, but from whence had they come? Why did Lil have to bring in *more* people? Well, vampire maids were few and far between, he admitted, so they would have to make do with mortals. He couldn't imagine her doing all the washing, cooking, cleaning, and so forth.

Oh, and the boys. Lord, what about the boys? Were they all now his as well?

"No, one belongs to Johnnie," he reminded himself with relief. But Johnnie was in a very sorry state indeed. George had chosen to use some dramatic demonstrations on the skeptical if quick-witted man, and Moran had finally succumbed to the obvious. Whether he would allow his brother to live amongst them was questionable.

Johnnie was grateful for Marie's death; that much was certain. And, George thought, the man was a bit frightened, perhaps because of some of the dramatics. He'd lost his fiancée, seen his friend crushed by a carriage and then brought back as a vampire, but he had no one normal to talk to about any of it. Would the constable put aside his fear but not his loathing of vampires and run about, trying to rally mortals to fight them? Or had Marie's death mollified him? Only time would tell.

Phillip, he thought. *He's the one to make this right. He'll know how to soothe Johnnie a bit. And some ready cash wouldn't hurt the man either. Maybe we could buy a nearby house for him?* No doubt the constable lived in one of the cramped guest houses catering to those employed but a step away from destitution. George would fix that, he swore, first thing in the morning. It was an easy enough gesture, whereas making the man believe he and the others were no danger to law-abiding mortals would take more time.

He peered down into the empty street. Nine o'clock, with the quiet that sometimes signaled an imminent snowfall. But no, it wasn't nearly cold enough.

"May I join you?"

Ah. That voice. George stood. "Sullivan! We've been wondering about you. I was certain you'd quit the city already."

"Phoebe would like that."

"Then go. We are grateful beyond words..." George put his hand on Sullivan's shoulder as he saw the giant vampire shake. "Whatever is wrong?"

"Do what you can to avoid angering an Elder, George."

"Your meeting was frightening, I imagine?"

"More than that. I cannot explain."

"Tell me about him."

"No, and do not ever mention his name. He can be...summoned."

George watched Sullivan carefully, regretted any part he may have had in putting anguish on his face. Finally he said, "It seems we socialize on rooftops, Chauncey. An odd choice."

"I'm to kill you. All of you. Especially the boy."

George examined his countenance, saw the sad resignation etched there. And yet, nothing seemed to have changed. "Ah. But you're not going to, or you wouldn't be talking. You'd be acting.

And 'especially the boy'? Why would a lad capture the interest of the Elders?"

"Marie violated the law. She bred. That makes Lillian and her child threatening in some way I don't fully understand."

George's stomach dropped. How foolish of him! He'd forgotten that aspect of Lillian's birth. Even if Sullivan didn't act, they were in grave danger. But Sullivan was the most immediate threat.

"What happens if you don't comply? Ah, Phoebe."

Sullivan shrugged. "Both of us. I do not much want to die anymore, either."

George was silent, thinking. Beside him stood the giant. Both stared down into the street. They shared an odd camaraderie.

"You're done anyway, George. All of you. If I don't kill you, he will."

George glanced at him. "Then why not save yourself?"

Sullivan shoved his hands in his pockets. "Never did kill children, George. Never had the nerve. Still don't. I don't want to die, but I'm also tired of this life. Maybe Phoebe's prayers will earn her a spot in Heaven. I'll no doubt rot with my own Lord in some special hell he's created for me."

"Run, Chauncey. Go as far as you can, as quickly as you can."

Sullivan nodded. "I had already decided as much. It may postpone the end." He glanced at George. "Honestly, *he* seems a bit...lazy, I suppose. Ambivalent? He wanted Marie to die, but I got the sense that he didn't care very much about anything else. Almost as if you all were but an afterthought. But, George, if the boy is unusual in any way, keep it hidden. I cannot promise that *he* won't come himself, or find another slave to do his dirty work."

God, the spirits. How many already knew? George's heart skipped a beat. "Unusual how?"

"Ah," the dark-skinned giant said sadly. "I see it on your face. Don't play cards, George."

George nodded, and there was a brief silence. "We never said it, all of us. Chauncey, thank you. This chance… You cannot know what this means to Lillian, to Phillip and me."

"I did it for myself. I had no choice."

"Ah, well, you sound like me now. There's always a choice. We are all free of her because of you."

"Thank *him*. He gave me the idea and the means." Chauncey chuckled darkly. "Maybe he's not such a bad Elder after all."

Then Sullivan was gone, leaving George to wonder if his beloved was destined to ever have a moment of peace in her life.

The *clip-clop* of cab horses below made his heart leap. Lillian! She had been gone most of the day, tending to Arthur and visiting Bess. What a strange weakling he'd become, slave to the woman he'd created. No, though, he'd not created her odd style, great mind, beautiful body and face. How had the union of two devils created such an angel?

Lillian stepped from the cab, Jack clutching her hand, and George leapt down into the back yard. When he entered the kitchen, a young woman, one of the sisters—God, what had Darby said her name was?—looked up from her sweeping and squealed.

"Please, I am Miss Holmes's fiancé. Do not be alarmed. My name is George."

The woman curtsied, and her black curls bobbled to and fro. "Mr. George. I am Ella, Miss Holmes's new nanny." She bit at her lip. "Although, to be honest, I've not yet met Miss Holmes. But I've met the boys. They left a mess in here, and I don't want to answer to Cook in the morning."

"Carry on, then, Miss Ella. And, welcome to the fold."

George shook his head, wondering how this house, although expansive by Baltimore's standards, could hold a married couple, four boys, a large dog, a maid, a nanny, and a cook. God, if Lillian intended to bring back Addie and Thomas, the pair would have to pitch tents in the back yard. His morning in bed with Lillian seemed like a fleeting dream, and he cursed. He'd thought of nothing else all day but repeating the tryst. Well, hardly anything else, if Arthur and Johnnie had taken a dent out of his time. What now to do about this awful reminder of Sullivan's?

When he entered the parlor, Lillian smiled and he let out a breath. It didn't matter, he realized. Nothing mattered. He had her, and they had Jack, and they would work through the details.

"An interesting day, Miss Holmes, was it not?"

"Indeed," she replied. "Jack, run off to your room and try not to wake the other boys—if they are in fact asleep."

Jack did not go. He tugged on her arm, and she stared at him.

"He'd like a goodnight word or kiss, Lil," George said, surprised he understood.

"Oh!" She knelt and pulled the boy in for a hug. "There, you sleep well and we'll have splendid adventures tomorrow."

The boy ran next to George, who wondered again that such sweet and kind creatures as Lillian and Jack could have come from Marie and Henry and the Jackal. But so it was, and after a hug the boy scampered up the stairs. Lillian put her hand over her mouth and laughed, although George knew she was on the verge of tears again.

"It will take time. I'm so happy for you," he said. He closed the distance between them and pulled her in. "I love you, Lil."

"George," she whispered, and angled her face up for a kiss.

The unmistakable sound of the Musketeers scrambling down the stairs made him groan. Would they not have even a kiss?

"Boys, you should be in bed!" Lillian said.

The quartet giggled at having caught them in an embrace, but they all lined up, ready for duty. Jack pushed in between Darby and Billy. Mr. Lincoln barked a few times but managed to sit rather obediently next to Paddy, who had a grab of his fur.

George sat, knowing that his patience would be sorely tested, only vaguely interested in whatever new mission Lillian had sent the boys on.

"All right," she was saying, "but five minutes and then off to bed with you!"

He only half listened as the boys went on in a circuitous fashion regarding the whereabouts of the remaining members of the Learned Order of Psychic Scholars. Etta Langhan was back in her home, which was of no consequence; the woman was surely innocent. Congressman Coyle and his wife—dead, of course. Mr. Doyle was not to be found, Darby reported. But Messieurs Donnelly, Holt, Poe and Frederick were also not to be found. No doubt laying low, George surmised. For with Coyle's death and Marie de Bourbon missing, the jig was certainly up. They would not get their immortality or riches.

He watched Lillian carefully. Was it worth it, to pursue these men and destroy them? She needed a long break from murder and drama, although he did not blame her for desiring revenge. No, he decided, he would never share what Sullivan told him. If they had only a decade together, even a year, it would be better than running and fighting. In a way, he thought, it would be as if they were human again.

Lillian dispensed pennies for the information and shooed the boys and Mr. Lincoln upstairs.

"I think that does it for tonight, George," she said. "Now, where were we?"

He stood and scooped her into his arms. She kicked and giggled a bit uncharacteristically, and her giggling increased when her hat fell off and he pulled the pins from her chignon.

"Have you eaten, my dear?"

"No, and I'm famished."

"Perhaps we can have a naughty snack of one another tonight."

"Perhaps."

She pressed her teeth to his neck and nibbled as George moved to the stairs, already in discomfort from the constriction of his trousers. Things would be quick at first, and then they would have time to—

"Oh!" The nanny had pushed through the kitchen door into the parlor and frozen, hand over her mouth. "Begging your pardon, Mr. George!"

Hell. To hell with servants and this house full of distractions. Married life would have to be different. It was different in his fantasies. Now he was the one who wanted to set the date for the wedding. *Imagine that, Georgy.*

"That is not your fault...Miss Ella, is it?" he asked, mastering his annoyance. "This is your mistress, Miss Lillian Holmes. Lillian, say hello to the nanny."

"Hello, and welcome." Lillian waved a bit as George carried her to the staircase. "I will speak with you more properly tomorrow. Are you finding everything satisfactory?"

Ella nodded, eyes wide.

"Is your room suitable?"

"Yes, miss."

"Is your sister quite happy as well?"

"Yes, Miss Holmes."

"Very well. Have a good night."

They left the nanny downstairs, speechless, but as George carried Lillian up the staircase he asked her how Doyle was getting on. "What's to be done with him?"

"I was hoping you would help me take him hunting tomorrow night. He's a very hungry man, and I would hang on to some of my blood."

"And then?"

"It is up to him. I've taken one choice away from him, and I won't do so again. I would dearly love him to stay here, to live, but he has obligations. A sick wife, most notably."

"And the Learned Order?"

Lillian sighed. "I think I have neither the time, the energy, nor the taste for revenge right now. Perhaps someday."

"I am glad to hear it," George admitted. "I brought you some nourishment, so we need not be interrupted again." He reached into his coat pocket and revealed the tip of a blood-filled vial.

Lillian nodded. "I'm too tired to ask where you got it." She took the vial and drank it down in a single swig, and then she snuggled into his arms and was sound asleep within moments. George reached her bedroom with the continued discomfort of his arousal, but the peace in his beloved's sleeping face was more important. He dearly loved to see her happy.

And, no matter, they had many such nights ahead.

CHAPTER THIRTY-EIGHT

A shy newborn.

"I do not like this place, George." Lillian linked her arm through his and stared at Arthur, who peered into the night as if he'd never seen darkness before. Of course, Annaluisa had been killed on this roof. Yes, she had known something of Lillian's mother, for sure. And she had paid a terrible price for that knowledge. "Did he choose this spot or did you?"

George pointed to Doyle, indicating the location had been his choice.

Arthur had taken to flight well, and Lillian felt some pride in her newborn. He had been ill during the day, which would come and go and gradually abate. But now he needed real sustenance or the hunger would kill him or drive him insane.

Arthur turned. "She was a friend, Madam Pelosi. I know now that she hid a great secret from me, but still, she was kind to me and we had splendid conversations."

"You understand that you helped destroy her murderer, sir?"

Arthur nodded. "I'm glad for that little role. Johnnie visited me today, and I believe he feels the same vindication for his Aileen. Although, of course, his loss is so much greater."

"We will look after Johnnie," Lillian said, wondering exactly how they would do that.

George approached Doyle and clapped a hand on his shoulder. "Arthur, if I may, we should not delay in the search for someone suitable. You are weak and will grow weaker by the hour."

"I cannot do this." The Scotsman hung his head and dropped his tense shoulders. "I do not have the heart for it."

A racket in the building on the floor below them stopped Lillian from speaking. A man and woman argued violently, and at a scream from the woman she, George and Doyle dropped to the balcony outside that window. Through the lace curtains they could see that the man—large, round, and in his cups—had knocked the woman to the ground. She held her cheek and cried.

"That will not do," Lillian said.

The man pulled the woman roughly to her feet and she cried out again, shaking and sobbing. "I didn't do anything!"

"You do not leave this room without my permission! How you test me!"

"But I only wanted a little meal!"

He hit her so hard that she fell to the floor in a heap, unconscious or dead. Then he started kicking her.

"We must stop this," Lillian whispered. She could not have hoped for a better victim, and she prayed Arthur would act—or she would.

George pushed the window up, and the man stared at him in wonder.

"What? How?" He stepped back a few feet.

"Would you like to try that on me?"

"Stay out of it!"

Arthur stepped in front of George. "Ach, you son of a bitch. *I* will not stay out of it."

"No? Go ahead—"

Before he could finish, Arthur knocked him to the ground and punched him in the nose, which made a nauseating cracking noise.

"He takes after his maker, doesn't he?" George said, turning to Lillian. "You both seem to like fisticuffs."

Lillian looked on in mixed pride and regret as Arthur made a meal of the man and then sat back and cried. He would be fine on his own, she saw now, but her hero would also suffer great remorse each time he ate. She pitied him that.

"I will miss him dearly when he goes," she said to George. "This man will definitely return to his wife."

"I believe I will miss him as well," George said. "But we have some time. He wants to interview young Jack. And my guess is that he will not go back on his promise to help Bess with her foot."

"How can he help her now? He can barely think of facing his family. He will not reach out to colleagues!"

"Ah, my little newborn," George said, "I have seen many meeker souls than this become ruthless killers in my three centuries, find ways to hide their nature. He's getting a taste of two things that feed his personality and his hunger: blood, and the feeling that he is doing something righteous. Our task is to keep him on the path of right. We can do that by giving him a family. Maybe even establishing a House."

CHAPTER THIRTY-NINE

Friends.

George laughed as Bess stomped her little foot in frustration. "No, I will not take it back. I suppose you are forced to spend it."

"I cannot even show it to my family! They will think me a bank robber!"

"Bess, sit down, your cheeks are so red they are emitting a strange glow. We cannot have any more deaths. Now, what do you think a great Watson should earn for putting her own life at risk for a friend? For going to an asylum, and then to an orphanage guarded by a…'creature'? For helping her find a son? What price would you put on that?"

"That, sir, is called friendship. No payment is required." Bess took the stack of notes and threw them up in the air. They fluttered down around her, and she made it quite clear that she was not going to pick them up.

"You are quite frustrating at times," George said with a laugh.

"You sound like my Lil," Bess replied. "Only you both are twenty times more frustrating than I."

Phillip folded his newspaper and yelled at them both to be quiet. "Arthur has finally stopped playing the piano, and now I have to listen to this bickering?" he complained. Then, "Elizabeth, listen to George. Money is not an issue for us. It is his way of thanking you, and you must sometimes allow him his odd ways. He is not a normal man. There is no need for your family to suffer."

"It's charity," Bess said, "and charity—"

"Please, might we have some quiet?" Arthur yelled across the room. "We are conducting a serious investigation!" The author sat with Lillian at a table across from Jack with a small standing mirror between them. Arthur held up various small objects that he kept from Jack's view and asked the boy to identify them.

George watched Lillian, wondering if she remembered that they had sat at that very table with Annaluisa conducting a séance. He had begun to fall in love with her that night, the same night he went to her room to silence her. It had been only two and a half months ago. Now he was to be married in a week, had a son, a rather easy relationship with his brother, and freedom to live as he wished. Of course, their lives could be cut short soon at the hands of Vasil, assuming the Elder's threat was serious. He sounded quite lackadaisical, to hear Chauncey tell it. But the threat gave George the curious feeling that he was human again, not secure that life would go on forever. Oddly, wondering if today could be his last, wanting to accomplish a few things before the end, gave life a sweeter taste than before.

He felt Phillip staring at him. "What is it?"

"Nothing."

"Spit it out now. You'll say it eventually."

Phillip laughed. "That's quite true. I'm simply gratified that you finally understand what I've been trying to tell you these last few years."

"What?"

"That your misery was always a choice."

George threw a cushion at him, and his brother threw it back, laughing. *So right you are, Phillip,* he thought. But he didn't say it. There was no reason for it to go to Phillip's head.

EPILOGUE

Dear Arthur,

Thank you so much for the telegram reporting your safe arrival. I am devastated at the further deterioration of your wife. Would that I could have known her. I am also greatly saddened that I could not be there to support you at this difficult time. I understand some of the torture you might have felt at the decision facing you with regards to her illness. But, as we have discussed in depth, some matters are to be left in God's hands.

You will be happy to know that Jack is thriving and is still speaking of having many adventures within your spirit realm. It is sometimes very disconcerting, but he seems not at all bothered by the ghosts who speak with him. George has made me promise to keep Jack's talents quiet, and again, I entreat you to keep his identity secret. George and I want the boy to have as much normalcy in his life as possible. The Musketeers have taken so well to him. They are a happy if mischievous band of fellows.

We are sorely in need of space, and are buying a house on the same street so that Addie and Thomas Adencourt, my former governess and butler, have a fine place to spend their days. They are newly returned from Chicago. Oh, yes, well, you did see them at the train station that first day! I do not know if they are aware of our "nature," but I am certain they will turn a blind eye toward it if necessary. I would trust those two with my life.

I am pleased to report that Johnnie Moran has agreed to reside in that house with them, along with his brother. In that way, we will all be close.

Johnnie seems better by the day. He asked me to say hello to you should we correspond. I thought of asking him to accompany us on our visit to collect Bess in the spring. I do hope that her presence is not a burden with your wife's illness. Do give her my love, and let us know how her medical treatment progresses.

I know this time must feel very dark indeed. I remember it well. Please know that George and I would give anything to be with you now. We were discussing the wedding just this morning, and what a blessing it was that you agreed to give me away. It shall remain one of my most treasured memories, always.

Dear Mr. Doyle, I miss you so much. I even took to rereading your stories during my recuperation. It was happily successful, and George and I have agreed that it is quite for the best that I do not take medicinals of any kind, ever again. Thank you for your advice before you parted. In any case, I do not feel the need for them.

I am anguished by your talk of aiding the troops now engaged in South Africa. I have heard horrors about this "Boer" war, although I suppose all wars are thusly horrible. You are at a fragile point in your recovery, and the battlefield may not be the wisest choice. Please do write when you have time, and let us know of Bess's progress and when we can visit.

Ever,
Lillian Holmes

Just as she finished writing, George tapped her shoulder and she jumped.

"Johnnie is downstairs, wringing the life out of his cap and talking about a murder on the outskirts of town. I think I saw that Mencken chap outside, no doubt lurking to find a good story."

"Wasn't the murder-suicide at the castle enough to get both of them promotions?"

"Johnnie is so dedicated, and Mencken is so ambitious. They make a fine team."

Lillian smiled. "I feel the need for a good investigation."

George lit his pipe and grinned. "I think you like sparring with Mencken as well." He turned and indicated their son. "Jack and I are building a fort in the back. He has made me promise to sleep outside in it with him tonight."

Lillian laughed. "Wait until Phillip hears."

"Phillip is helping to build it! Thomas is out there telling us how poorly we're doing. I think if I leave them alone, they'll have it done and forget about me. Or maybe I'll try to charm him."

Lillian folded her letter to Arthur and cupped her hand on George's face, taking a moment to admire how her ruby ring gleamed against his pale skin. "You're a handsome devil, George. But those good looks won't work on Thomas, trust me. He'll have you working again before I'm out the door with Johnnie."

George sighed and pressed a kiss to Lillian's head. "No one told me about this part of the bargain."

She laughed and grabbed her messenger bag.

George stood and gave her one last embrace. "Don't forget your pistol. And bring me back a little snack, love. It doesn't seem I'll get out tonight."

ABOUT THE AUTHOR

Ciar Cullen hails from Baltimore. She spent her high school years as a theater geek, attended UMBC and studied archaeology before pursuing an advanced degree at Indiana University. She left Indiana to live in Greece for 8 years, working on the artifacts from a prehistoric cave site. Ciar also sweated out a few summers in Missouri on a First American site. She wound her way to England, where she studied archaeological remains at the British Museum of Natural History for a time. Finally, she inadvertently settled in New Jersey, married, and adopted a number of rescue cats. After several positions in nonfiction publishing, she landed at Princeton University, where she helps run the molecular biology department.

Ciar started writing late in life on a whim, and considers herself a hobbyist. This is her 18th book. Her website is www.ciarcullen.com and she loves to hear from readers. You can also chat with her on social media sites.

Did you enjoy this book? Drop us a line and say so! We love to hear from readers, and so do our authors. To connect, visit www.boroughspublishinggroup.com online, send comments directly to info@boroughspublishinggroup.com, or friend us on Facebook and Twitter. And be sure to check back regularly for contests and new releases in your favorite subgenres of romance!

Are you an aspiring writer? Check out www.boroughspublishinggroup.com/submit and see if we can help you make your dreams come true.

www.ingramcontent.com/pod-product-compliance
Lightning Source LLC
Chambersburg PA
CBHW071124170626
46809CB00002B/490